T0028864

LETHAL LIFESTYLES

A NICHELLE CLARKE CRIME THRILLER

LYNDEE WALKER

Severn River Publishing
www.SevernRiverBooks.com

ISBN: 978-1-64875-516-3 (Paperback)

ALSO BY LYNDEE WALKER

The Nichelle Clarke Series

Front Page Fatality

Buried Leads

Small Town Spin

Devil in the Deadline

Cover Shot

Lethal Lifestyles

Deadly Politics

Hidden Victims

Dangerous Intent

The Faith McClellan Series

Fear No Truth

Leave No Stone

No Sin Unpunished

Nowhere to Hide

No Love Lost

Tell No Lies

To find out more about LynDee Walker and her books, visit

severnriverbooks.com/authors/lyndee-walker

For Kennedy, who makes me thankful every day for wonderful surprises. I love you.

1

A statement is only as true as the source is trustworthy. It's an old reporting adage I'd seen proven more times than I cared to count in nearly nine years covering crime.

So when I needed to know how to pull off the perfect wedding, I went straight to the fountain of bridal wisdom—my mom. She arranges them for a living. And when she told me they're stress-inducing, sleep-stealing monsters that, done right, seem borne of fairy dust and swathed in heart-shaped bubbles, I felt pretty good about having a serious edge over the average Maid of Honor.

For seven months, I bugged Mom long-distance, getting the lowdown on every last nuance, then running local interference for my friends Parker and Melanie. Seamstresses. Florists. The baker Mel wanted, who got downright offended when Parker's mother called her fondant "simply above average." Everything handled. Everyone happy.

Especially the bride and groom. Go me.

By rehearsal weekend—a celebration getaway for the wedding party at the vineyard that would play host to next week's ceremony—I'd switched on event cruise control, confident all my spinning plates would careen happily through the honeymoon sendoff.

I strolled into the log cabin main hall for the Friday-night kickoff dinner hauling a Ralph Lauren tote stuffed with everything I'd need to remedy ruined stockings, makeup mishaps, a bad hair day, or a nervous stomach.

But my magic bag had nothing for the corpse that turned up before the salads were served.

* * *

We couldn't have asked for a more perfect start to the evening: birds serenaded us through the open French doors, a pink-orange sunset lending the photos a romance that can't be manufactured in a studio. Mel's smile could've lit up the entire Shenandoah Valley.

"Hold it." Larry furrowed a brow and set his prize Nikon next to a purple and silver rose centerpiece on the U-shaped banquet table. Perk of working in the news business: free photography. Our photo editor's current mission in life was chronicling every minute of buildup to the happy day.

Larry rounded the end of the table and laid both hands on my shoulders. "You scoot half a step this way." He pulled me toward Parker, ordered our editor-in-chief to fall in next to me, and proceeded to inch everyone else into the spot he deemed just right for the perfect shot. Since Parker knew the vineyard's owner, we had the place to ourselves for the weekend. So he and Mel had invited most of their newsroom family out for a pre-pre-wedding celebration in advance of tomorrow's rehearsal. Melanie's parents would fly in Saturday morning and stay the week, her mom excited to be back home in Virginia to help with last-minute prep. The other out-of-state guests would arrive next Friday and Saturday—flights, hotels, and transfers all arranged, families both happy. Check.

Hustling back to position, Larry lifted the camera. "All eyes on Mel and Parker, and smile, y'all," he said. "Lovebirds, look at each other like you'll never get tired of it."

The grin that threatened to split my face in two came easily. I'd shared a cube wall with Mel for seven years, and Parker had become a good friend once I got over wondering if he was a murderer. With some cupid-playing on my part, our shy but striking city hall reporter had snagged the heart of Richmond's very own Casanova—if Casanova had a Crest-commercial smile and a killer knuckleball. Parker's days of throwing serious heat ended when a torn rotator cuff killed his dreams of being Nolan Ryan, but he was still formidable when he took the mound for charity events.

Larry fired off ten shots in half as many seconds and lowered the camera to chest level. Opening his mouth and raising one hand to direct the next pose, he flinched when a shriek floated through the terrace doors, just louder than the birdsong.

Every eyeball in the room that didn't belong to a stranger rotated my direction.

"What?" I raised my eyebrows. "I just got here. And we don't cover Augusta County."

Mel's eyes stayed a smidgen too wide, and Parker looped an arm over her shoulders, pulling her into his side. "Sounds like someone found a rat in the barn." He flashed his trademark megawatt grin.

Larry shooed Parker and Mel into a doorway, muttering about lousy timing when the filmy white curtains ceased their billowing just as he got his shot lined up.

"Hold that thought, Larry," I called, hurrying to the reception area. I'd spied a fan there on my way in.

I shoved the heavy split-log door open and stepped through—right into a solid wall of man. Who smelled like the wine hadn't agreed with him. Ick.

Stumbling back into the door, I opened my mouth to apologize.

The largest, best-sculpted frame I'd ever seen sped past like my five-foot-eleven self was little more than a mosquito, not even offering a wave with his dismissive Hulk grunt as I called "sorry" at his back. We had a few in our crew who'd had too much fun in the tasting room, too. Probably running for a bathroom before he puked again.

Striding to the outlet, I pulled the plug for the fan, hefted it, and turned back toward my friends. Mid-step, I paused when the dismissal-grunting voice carried from the office off the end of the lobby.

No.

Hulk did not just say "dead body."

Or if he did, it was in the metaphorical sense of the term.

Three steps closer to the dining hall, a less forceful voice filtered into earshot.

Nope. Five-star eavesdropping can be a handy skill for a crime reporter, but I was not at work.

I made it two more steps and froze, my eyes falling shut.

Panic is a distinctive note in the human vocal range. I'd heard it so much, it registered instantly.

Whoever was talking to Hulk on the back side of that wall? Heading straight through panic to freaking the hell out.

I hustled the fan into place, my brain trying desperately to produce a scenario that wasn't a gateway to disaster. No dice. When the curtains were set to "true love cloud" and Larry barked approval, I backed out of the way —and kept on backing until I reached a white door in the corner of the dining room.

There could not be a corpse at Mel's rehearsal.

Except what if there was?

And here I'd thought I had all potential problems covered.

"Excuse me," a voice chirped from behind me.

Speaking of problems—I spun to find Mel's childhood best friend staring daggers from behind her Splenda-coated smile.

Maisy was less than excited about a "new" friend being chosen maid of honor. To the tune of arranging appointments and "accidentally" texting me the wrong time, telling Melanie's (very Baptist) mother I'd been thrown out of a church last summer, and even questioning my shoe recommendations for the bride. But I'd managed to keep her antics from aggravating Mel, so whatever. As long as my friends ended up with the perfect wedding, this chick could shoot me go-to-hell looks from here to doomsday.

"Sorry." I stepped aside.

She pushed the door open to reveal a princess-perfect dressing area with a powder room off to one side.

And another door on the opposite wall.

When Maisy slammed the door to the toilet over a last withering glare, I blew right through the cute wooden "Everyone gets cold feet, turn around!" and "Other way to happily ever after" signs on the second door, finding myself in a narrow peach-pink hallway. Turning left, where the lobby should be, I crept along the wall.

A bit of cajoling the next door I found jarred it enough for me to hear Hulk's uber-bass loud and clear.

"Absolutely sure? You heard the part about the thief, right?" Disgust curled around the words. "I opened it, Mr. Jinkerson."

I closed my eyes and sagged against the wall. Maybe I'd heard him wrong. A wine bandit might still be a snag, but it wasn't a catastrophe.

"What if you panicked and didn't realize what you saw? You said there wasn't a face. How can you be sure it's a person when there's no face? What if it was a...um...a monkey?" Mr. Jinkerson's high pitch took on the breathy edge of grasping at threads.

My head thumped back against the wall as Hulk let out a growl.

"Since when do monkeys wear Tech rings? We have a dead body out there, sir. And that might not even be our biggest problem. Why that barrel?" Hulk's voice boomed, and Jinkerson shushed him, gulping air and stammering for a good minute.

"Bad luck," he finally managed. "We don't know anything about anything. Calm down."

Good advice. We should all take it. I pulled in a deep breath. Think, Nichelle.

One thing at a time.

Obviously, these people had to call the police.

And a police presence was no way to kick off a fairy tale. Not the kind I wanted for Parker and Mel, anyway.

Until I knew more about this situation, the best way I could help everyone here was to get the wedding party off the property for a few hours.

How? Dinner hadn't even started yet.

Wait.

Dinner hadn't started.

What if it couldn't? A kitchen mishap is way less of a downer than a corpse.

So we'd tell Mel the oven malfunctioned or some such, and load everyone up to go to a restaurant. One with a long wait for a party of twenty. With any luck at all, the local cops would find an easy answer. If not, I'd have time to break it to Mel a little softer than sirens screeching up as people dug into their fried chicken.

Perfect.

I raised a fist and tapped on the dark-stained oak.

From the clatter on the other side of it, I might as well have fired a starter pistol. Thirty seconds of rustling papers and clearing throats later, Hulk cracked the door a smidgen wider, one eyeball and half his nose poking through. “Can I help you?”

I wedged one Manolo between the door and the frame, hoping my flash decision to play it straight wasn't the wrong one.

“I wish I hadn't overheard you gentlemen, but I did.” I kept my voice set to library whisper. “I'm the maid of honor for Mr. Parker's wedding. I'm also the cops reporter at the *Richmond Telegraph*. Maybe I can help?”

From the other side of the door, Jinkerson's breath hissed in so quick it sent him into a coughing fit. “Reporter?” he wheezed. “Jesus, no. No press. No comment.”

Hulk moved to shut the door, and I threw myself against it, partly because I had more to say, but mostly because I wanted to keep my right foot.

The impact took him by enough surprise that he let go of the knob, and I stumbled into the room.

Managing to catch myself before I ended up in a heap on the plush merlot and sapphire rug, I smoothed my tangerine sundress and eyed the slight man behind the large carved desk, who looked increasingly in need of a paper sack to breathe into. Mr. Jinkerson, I presumed. I plastered on my most unthreatening smile and softened my tone, nudging the door shut behind me with one foot.

“Augusta County isn't even in the *Telegraph's* coverage area, gentlemen. But I've been around this track a few times, and it sounds like y'all could use some advice. Let me help.”

Hulk relaxed his at-attention stance a half-millimeter. Jinkerson, who appeared to be Hulk's boss, tipped his head to one side and narrowed his eyes.

“How exactly can you do that?” That came from Hulk. A closer look at him revealed lingering tinges of green under his late-spring farmhand tan. His hand went to his midsection and I focused on Jinkerson. He was flushed, sweating, and practically hyperventilating—but he didn't look like he might vomit any moment.

While I had nothing for why anyone would put a body in a wine barrel, I figured chances were decent it hadn't happened recently if said barrel was ready for opening. Which meant getting the wedding party out of the way would help me and the cops both.

"I can get your boss's guests out of here before the police arrive," I said. "We'll tell them there was something wrong in the kitchen. I'll divert dinner while you talk with the police."

Odds were, the local law enforcement folks would sort this out in less time than it takes to pick out the perfect sandals—the vast majority of criminal cases are pretty open and shut. It's just that people only hear about the interesting ones, so folks tend to think a deluge of squad cars always equals intrigue.

They exchanged a glance, and my eyes darted between them.

Jinkerson turned back to me, failing to blink for entirely too long. "I like it," he said finally.

Perfect. I pulled in a deep breath, my tone flipping to brisk and authoritative as I looked at Hulk. "You go back out and stand guard until the sheriff gets here."

He made a face that said he'd rather spend his Friday evening playing hopscotch than guarding a wine barrel full of person, but turned for the front door when Jinkerson nodded.

I laid my hand on the back door to the office. "Give me five minutes, and then call 911."

"Thank you," Jinkerson said, looking a little less gray.

"Try not to worry too much. I've seen my share of these things, and most of them are pretty easy for the cops to handle." I stepped back into the hallway.

Maid of honor to the rescue. Again.

2

Twilight's carpet of indigo settled over the fields and mountainside beyond the wide porch, the last tinge of pink vanishing from the horizon as I slipped back into the dining hall.

"Too dark for more scenery shots," Larry said, lowering his camera.

Someone's stomach let out a snarl and our editor-in-chief laughed. "Maybe we should check on dinner," Bob said.

Before Mel could step away from the table, I cleared my throat and put my forefingers in the corners of my mouth, blowing a wolf whistle followed by my most reassuring smile.

"It seems there's been a little issue in the kitchen," I said.

"What kind of issue?" Mel's brow furrowed and I shrugged.

"Nothing that won't be handled by tomorrow." I hoped. "But for this evening, I'm afraid we need to find other arrangements."

"A place that can seat twenty people as a walk-in on a Friday night?" Parker shook his head. "We'll starve."

"We might if we didn't have you." I grinned. "Since our UVA Hall of Famer here is probably the closest this neck of the woods gets to celebrity, I'm betting there's magic to be worked."

I walked around the table and dug my iPhone out of my bag, searching for upscale dining near me.

The room I was standing in came up, as did two other vineyards and three spots in town.

Second on the town list was a hotel. I touched a few links. Large bar, private dining room, great menu. Done.

Hefting the tote onto my shoulder, I swung my arms, herding my colleagues toward the parking lot. "Y'all load up and follow me," I said. "Local grass-fed steaks and the most extensive wine list in five counties, twenty minutes away." Probably closer to twenty-five, as out in the sticks as we were, but I didn't want anyone balking at the distance.

Lucky for me, news folks are used to jumping in the car and taking off at the drop of a lead.

I held my breath until the last car pulled out of the vineyard's drive anyway, then nodded along to the light discussion about summer vacations coming from the other three seats in my little red SUV, which were occupied by Bob, Parker, and Mel.

We turned off the gravel road that led to Calais Vineyards just as the first strains of sirens floated out of the distance to the only ears listening for them.

Mom was right: This wedding business could keep a girl on her toes.

* * *

Pulling up at the Blue View Inn, I tossed the valet my keys and towed Parker to the hostess, who had a put-on air of snootiness that dissolved when my friend flashed his megawatt grin and I introduced him. She pointed to the bar and said she'd notify the manager and the chef and have a table ready in less than an hour. I couldn't have asked for better—long enough to extend the evening, but not so long that everyone wanted to go back and order takeout.

"It's the smile," I said, winking at Parker as I waved our friends into the bar. "Nine out of ten women are bound to dissolve into a puddle when you break out your superstar grin."

He chuckled. "I'm glad it's still good for something."

I shot a pointed glance at Mel, who was engrossed in one of Bob's many war stories, and poked Parker's ribs with one elbow. "I'd say it's been good for a lot."

He slung an arm around my shoulders. "Have I thanked you today? She is the best thing that's ever happened to me."

My heart stuttered, watching him watch her. So much for Grant Parker's famously notch-ridden bedpost. Our newsroom stud was well and truly in love.

My eyes drifted to Mel, who had turned toward us like she could feel Parker's gaze on her, and my insides went all squishy at the joy on my friend's face.

Whatever was in that barrel notwithstanding, this wedding would be the best any of us had ever seen—surely a maid of honor with my lengthy disaster resume and knowledge of police procedure could see to that.

* * *

Three hours and ten bottles of wine later, the server handed Parker the check and I laughed when Bob snatched it, tossing out his AmEx card before Parker could argue.

Dinner was a rousing success. But it was time to go, and I wasn't a thousand percent sure the vineyard would be clear of squad cars. I knew Parker and Mel would find out about the dead guy eventually, but I wanted more information before I had to break it to them.

The server returned with the black leather folder, and I laid two fingers on his elbow when he spun back for the kitchen. "Where's a good place to go for music and dancing around here? Somewhere not too college-y," I said.

He twisted his lips to one side. "There's a new place just up the road—they have this whole roaring twenties thing going on. Vintage cocktails, jazz music, dark booths. A real-life speakeasy. And classes are out right now."

I nodded and thanked him, turning to smile at Mel. "I have one more surprise up my sleeve tonight," I half-shouted, leaning close to her ear so she could hear me over the bustling dining room as I explained my idea. Her face split into a grin as she nodded, tugging on Parker's sleeve.

We stood, Parker's arm closing around Mel's shoulders as he bent his head to whisper something that made her smile and swat at him. That was happily-ever-after material right there.

Letting my eyes roam the walnut and leather dining room, I counted six couples who were each staring at their respective smartphones and four women watching their husbands watch baseball on one of the four flat-screens in the bar. The woman at the table in the far corner was staring Chinese-star-variety daggers at the room in general, her eyes seeming to follow Parker as he led Mel away from the table—probably to avoid looking at her companion, his perfect salt and pepper hair glinting in the low light as he nodded to whoever was on the other end of his phone call.

My gaze stayed on her for a moment. Closer to Bob's age than mine, she was downright stunning: perfectly coiffed blonde bob, diamond earrings the size of ice cubes, and a Chanel pantsuit that wouldn't have hung any better on a runway model. Poor thing. Cell phones are awesome, but they can kind of suck sometimes too.

Shaking my head, I directed everyone back to the front, pausing to ask the hostess for directions to the speakeasy.

Four doors up and around the corner. Perfect.

Bob fell into step beside me, putting a hand under my elbow as I picked my way over the cobblestone sidewalk. I adored the look of the streets left-over from colonial Virginia, but they did not adore my shoes.

"You okay, kid?" my editor asked, tightening his grip on my elbow as my heel slid into a crack between two stones.

"Just tired, chief."

He nodded. "Not surprising. When do you ever have time to sleep?"

"Here and there. Often behind my sunglasses when some of the more windbag-ish attorneys get on a roll in front of a jury."

He chuckled. "Excellent time management. But I'm serious. You work eighty hours a week, and for the past few months you've been on a mission to throw these two the perfect wedding. I'm wondering where that leaves you on your priority list. There's more to life than work, Nicey."

I snorted. "Look who's talking."

"That's different," he said. "I'm old. Since I lost Grace, the *Telegraph* is all I have. At your age, it shouldn't be."

Smiling as Bob swung the door to the Jazzy Flapper open, I stepped onto the scarred wood floor, breathing in musky pine-laced air that took me back to seventh grade and Friday nights at the roller rink. "I have all I can handle these days keeping Andrews at bay and getting Mel to the altar."

"I just want you to be happy." Bob followed me to a round table near the dance floor and patted my shoulder. "I never thought I'd know what it was like to have a daughter, you know?"

I closed my eyes for a long blink. Yep. I knew. "The feeling is totally mutual, chief. But if you make me cry, I'll take a two-week vacation while Parker and Mel are in Aruba."

He raised both hands. "Truce."

"What are you surrendering, boss?" Parker asked, pulling the third chair at the table out for Mel before taking the fourth one for himself.

"My right to meddle in Nichelle's lack of a social life."

Parker's brow furrowed. "But what about—"

I shot one Manolo into his shin as the corners of Bob's mouth turned up.

"All—all that volunteer work? And her workout classes?" Parker stammered, reaching under the table and tossing me a what-the-hell-is-wrong-with-you look.

"Volunteer work?" Bob asked.

"Reading to a class at my friend Jenna's daughter's school." I waved a hand. "I go on Thursdays when I don't have court." I turned to Parker. "Everyone has their tuxes set for next weekend?"

He nodded. "My mother assures me that my cousins have taken care of that. They're supposed to be here in time for the ceremony run-through tomorrow." Something resembling worry flitted across his face, vanishing before I could question it.

Having all the paternal cousins as groomsmen was a longstanding Parker family tradition. Which meant the altar would be lopsided in the groom's favor—to the tune of seven. Mel worried over it for weeks before she finally let it go with an "I don't have seven friends I could ask, anyhow" and a dreamy smile about her children having a big family to play with.

Another box checked. Each one got us closer to a perfect day.

The band stepped up onto the little stage across the room and took up instruments, an upbeat jazz riff drowning out the need to converse. Parker arched one eyebrow at Mel and pushed his chair back. She giggled and extended a hand.

He led her to the center of the floor, an unconscious grace in his movements that spoke of the almost-professional athlete he once was. Pulling Mel close, Parker said something into her ear and she nodded. Shuffle-stepping backward twice, Mel twisted her hips side to side before Parker pulled her back to him, lifting her off her feet and tucking her lower body under his right arm, then swinging her high before he set her down.

"Thundering tap shoes." I whistled.

"Are they auditioning for a spot at the Savoy?" Bob asked, leaning close.

"Or *Swing Kids* is the next Hollywood remake." My wide eyes never left Parker and Mel, my brain racing through the fantastic photos this would make next weekend. A crowd closed around them, clapping in time to the music as our bride and groom shuffled and shook a perfect Lindy Hop across the middle of the dance floor.

Even the band applauded when the last notes faded.

Parker tugged Mel's hand until she bowed with him before they strolled back to the table, cheeks pink and eyes sparkling.

"Hey there, Fred, Ginger," I said. "Been spending your evenings with Arthur Murray?"

"The instructor took to calling Grant Mr. Charleston at the second lesson." Mel grinned and Parker shook his head.

"I think we've established that his praise is inflated by his opinion of my biceps."

"Someone have a crush?" I asked as a waitress stopped to take drink orders, giving Parker a nearly involuntary onceover.

I stuck with a mojito, but everyone else ordered one of the more exotic-sounding vintage cocktails.

Mel leaned close to my ear as the waitress moved to the next table. "The list of people who don't have a crush is way shorter," she said. "I worry sometimes."

I squeezed the fingers she was resting on my shoulder. "You shouldn't. He doesn't even notice it."

Standing, I pulled Bob out of his chair. "I'm going to be boring after the show they put on, but you want to spin me around the floor anyway?"

"I used to cut a pretty mean rug." He put one hand on the small of my back and steered me toward the floor.

We made it through five bars of the slower song before he caught my eye and arranged his face into his most severe dad-like look. "What's bugging you?"

"Bugging me?" I echoed, pasting on a smile.

He raised one eyebrow and shook his head. "Save the 'I'm tired' line, because I know better. I stumbled into the kitchen looking for a bathroom just before you herded everyone off that vineyard like something was on fire. The ovens were working just fine, and the food smelled heavenly. Plus, you've been distracted since before we left. What gives?"

Damn.

I pulled in a deep breath. "They found a body in one of the wine barrels."

He stumbled and landed one loafer on my toes. "You can't be serious."

I caught him and led us into the next step. "Because this is the kind of thing I find it fun to joke about, chief. I ran everyone off so the cops could do their job and our happy couple didn't have to have their bubble burst. Yet, anyhow."

Bob's feet fumbled around trying to find the right steps, his drawn brow telling me his mind was on more important things than the cha-cha. "You don't really think you can keep a body a secret?"

The music stopped and I pinched my lips together and locked eyes with Bob. "I think I can for tonight. I'll worry about tomorrow later."

He nodded, muttering through a smile as we turned back to the table, "Whatever you say, kiddo."

* * *

Three more rounds of drinks, and I was pretty sure Parker and Mel wouldn't remember any lingering squad cars in the morning regardless. I sipped a second mint iced tea, my thoughts trailing back to the vineyard. The obvious question: Who would dump a corpse in a wine barrel?

Followed by the ickier question: What would be left of said corpse after a while?

Shelby saved me from pondering that by dropping into Parker's chair and raising her glass in the general direction of the happy couple. "I never thought I'd see the day someone dragged Grant Parker to the altar," she said.

"Looks to me like he's racing her, not being dragged." I kept my tone light, because though Shelby and I'd had our share of barbed exchanges back when she was trying every trick in anyone's book to steal my job, she'd become something resembling a friend in the past year, and her face said this stung more than a little.

"Yeah, yeah." Shelby put the glass on the table and shook her head, a wry smile touching her full lips. "Can't say it doesn't smart. I might've spent a few teary Jose Cuervo and Ben and Jerry's nights telling myself Grant Parker wasn't the long-term relationship type when he dumped me. I never would have pegged quiet and brainy for his undoing, but good for her."

The band launched into another song, and Parker and Mel threaded their way through the dancers toward us. Mel sprawled across the empty chair, Parker leaning on the back of it. I signaled the waitress and asked for two waters, which arrived just as Bob returned from the men's room. Parker downed his in three gulps, laying a hand on Mel's back when she folded her arms on the table and flopped her head onto them.

"I think we're ready to sleep this off," he said.

I pulled out my phone and checked the time, ready for a few winks myself. Almost midnight. Hopefully their perfect wedding wasn't on the verge of turning into a pumpkin.

3

All was quiet in the driveway, though I'm pretty sure I didn't take a breath until we rounded the lodge and the guest houses came into view.

Not a squad car in sight.

Phew.

I walked Parker and Mel to the largest cottage and hugged her while he opened the door. "Sleep well, doll," I said as he flipped the light on.

Waving to Bob and Larry as they disappeared into the cabin they were sharing, I glanced around. Because Parker knew the owner, a handful of us had been offered guest houses on the property. Mel and I had booked everyone else into a few nearby bed and breakfasts, holding the last two cottages for the parents.

Convenient under normal circumstances. Downright handy for snooping with a dead guy on the premises. I half-jogged back up to the lodge, hoping to find Jinkerson in his office. Strike one. The building was pitch dark, the doors locked. Turning back toward my cabin, I spied the trio of big barns spaced across the south end of the property. I knew one was for horses and two were for wine, but couldn't remember which was what. I climbed into my car and let it idle down the hill toward them.

Putting the windows down, I listened as I rounded the back corner of the first barn. A hoof stomping followed by a colossal snort said the thoroughbreds didn't care for me disturbing them so late. "Sorry, buddy," I whispered, killing the engine as voices carried through the midnight chill. Bingo.

I reached into my bag and fished out a pinkie-sized flashlight before I hopped out of the car.

Careful to light only a foot or so of the path in front of me, I tiptoed through the dirt and grass, ears pricked for any signs of non-equine activity.

Behind barn number two, I found Jinkerson, Hulk, a Sean Connery lookalike I recognized as the vineyard's owner, and a shorter, rounder man with a shiny badge pinned to his starched beige shirt. Judging by the size of his Stetson, I pegged the latter as the local sheriff.

Non-city law enforcement is kind of like the Catholic Church in that the more important you are, the bigger your hat. The camel-colored ten-gallon that topped off this guy's uniform said he was in charge, or very close to it.

I stayed hidden behind the corner of the building, killing the light and leaning against the cool wood siding.

"Now, Dale, I can't say anything for certain until we have lab results, and even with pressure that's gonna take a few days to get from Richmond—maybe more because of the wine and the condition of the remains. But off the record, the clothes and the ring are pretty clear identifiers." The lilting Virginia accent and booming bass combo had to belong to the cop.

"I don't have the time or the desire for any unpleasantness clinging to my name with the Governor's Cup so close, Jim." This voice was more assured—and held an edge of annoyance. Dale Henry Sammons owned the property my Manolos were sinking into—as well as the Richmond Generals baseball team, the nameplates on a couple of buildings at UVA, and probably a hefty handful of politicians from every level one could find. Not the kind of guy who'd want this publicized—or dragged out. I resisted the urge to peek around the corner again, focusing on his words. "I'm sure you understand when I say I want this taken care of quickly and quietly."

Me too. I held my breath as the sheriff's voice floated to my ears again.

"There are two different types of marks on the barrel lid, both pretty fresh in the wood, which means it was opened twice—recently. We'll need to talk to everyone who had access to this barn this week. Assuming Burke is our victim, I'm going to need to interview your people in Richmond too."

Crap hell. That didn't sound anything like open and shut.

"The less police presence we have here, the better," Sammons said. "Jinkerson, you'll arrange for the staff to go to the sheriff for interviews. And Jim, why don't you come up to Richmond on Monday?"

"Whatever you need, sir." Jinkerson's tenor still held the high squeak of stress.

"When did you say your guests arrived?" Sheriff Jim asked.

"Most of them this afternoon, I believe," Sammons replied. "I had business in DC that prevented me from being here to greet them."

"We may need to talk to them too, then?" The sheriff tried not to sound like he was asking, but his voice went up on the last note anyway.

"I'd really prefer if you'd wait on that until we're sure it's necessary."

"Who'd you say was here?"

"I don't believe I have. What kind of host am I to bring people out for the weekend and then run them through the Virginia inquisition?" Sammons said smoothly. "Let's focus on the big things first. If you need anything else later, we will, of course, be happy to oblige."

Retreating footsteps said they'd started back toward the lodge. I stayed still until they were out of earshot, then scrambled back to my car and dug out a notebook and pen, scribbling as fast as my hand would fly over the paper.

Burke.

People in Richmond. Baseball?

Governor's Cup. Horses, boats?

Thief. The big guy said something about a theft earlier.

And the question of the moment, which got a double star: Why was Dale Sammons keeping us a secret from the sheriff?

* * *

Back in my adorably posh guest cottage, I double-bolted the door and flipped on the crystal-drenched chandelier, too focused on finding some answers to fully appreciate the careful attention to shabby chic detail as I pushed a gel-planted fishbowl of roses to one side of the distress-painted flute-footed round coffee table and opened my laptop.

Laying my notes next to the keyboard, I clicked into my search bar and started with Dale Sammons.

Seventeen-hundred-plus results. I scrolled through the top five, highlighting and copying passages about his education, work, and hobbies into a word-processing document.

Forty-five minutes later, I sank back into the overstuffed pastel loveseat, pulling the computer into my lap and staring at the words I'd just saved. Pretty standard privileged family upbringing, rowdy but nothing serious college mishaps, a falling out with his old man, and a few brushes with the law, followed by a solid career in baseball ownership with the Generals looking for their fifth pennant in seven years. The vineyard, which he'd inherited when his father died, seemed to be his latest fascination. Not famous, but it had a good reputation and steadily increasing name recognition and revenue.

All fine, in the most mundane sense of the word.

Journalism in the Age of the Internet 101: Nothing curious usually means nothing helpful. But not always, so I saved the file to a folder labeled *Calais* and went to the next item on my list: the victim.

The cop hadn't given a first name, but his comment about talking to people in Richmond and a ring made me wonder if the guy was a ballplayer.

Typing *Burke+Richmond Generals* into my search bar, I clicked enter and held my breath.

Almost five hundred hits.

The images showed me snapshots of a good-looking guy with dark hair, blue eyes, and a straight nose—and he was wearing a baseball uniform in many of them. Damn.

He didn't look much older than me, and his smile dripped confidence. I blinked away a pricking in the back of my eyes, focusing on research.

Getting bogged down in the sadness that goes with covering crime is a dangerous road.

Just the facts. I opened a file and started typing what I knew. One—my hopes of keeping Parker and Mel insulated were screwed, because any kind of celebrity plus the location of the body discovery meant the guy's death would be news. Shortly, anyway. The local newspaper had shuttered the summer before, which meant I had until word of Burke's death made it out of the sticks to come up with a way to break it to the bride and groom. And my readers—I might end up with a story out of all this, after all, if the sports desk didn't snatch it up.

My fingers stilled over the keys. The sports desk.

Parker.

Baseball.

What if Parker knew this guy?

Clicking a photo of Burke (his first name was Mitch, said Wikipedia) up to full size, I squinted at his uniform.

Huh. It was an older style, and that wasn't a Generals logo on his shoulder.

I went back to the text results and found a bio.

Pitcher out of Virginia Tech, drafted by the Generals farm program a decade ago. I jotted that down, hoping my slightly manic Tech fan editor might remember him.

Scrolling past the childhood and college info, I clicked expand on his career section.

He played five seasons, never made it out of the minors, and became the assistant PR director for the Richmond Generals.

Crap.

Parker had to know him. Sammons probably hadn't mentioned Parker's name to the sheriff because he wanted to break this news to Parker himself.

I checked the clock: coming up on three. Chances were slim that Sammons would've bothered Parker after the sheriff left, and I couldn't wake my friend in the middle of the night to tell him someone he knew was dead and the guy's murder could throw a monkey wrench in his wedding as a bonus.

Closing the computer and pulling my dress off, I killed the lights and crawled between the zillion thread-count sheets on the canopy bed. Setting the alarm on my phone for four and a half hours in the future, I laid it on the other pillow and flipped onto my stomach.

My eyes fell shut, Mel's happy smile and Mitch Burke's aristocratic features flashing across the backs of the lids. Maybe my subconscious could come up with a way to avoid completely trashing the bride and groom's Saturday.

4

Knock knock.

"Nicey?"

I lifted my head from a cloud of goose down swathed in silk and tried to blink.

"Nicey?"

Knock knock knock. "Anyone home?"

Bob. Why was Bob at my door?

Knuckling sleep and last night's mascara from my lashes, I glanced around the plush little bedroom. Cottage.

Wedding.

Dead guy.

Aw, hell.

I snatched up my iPhone, cursing the alarm before I saw that I'd only been asleep for three hours and change.

My editor is a morning person.

I myself am usually pretty chipper as long as the sun is up, but not on less than four hours of fitful, how-do-I-avert-this-tidal-wave-of-disaster half-sleep.

"Coming," I mumbled, grabbing the dress I'd dropped the night before and tugging it back on.

I flipped the lock and cracked the door open, swinging it wide when I saw the tray he had balanced on his left arm.

"I come bearing coffee." He grinned as he walked in. "Wow. It looks like Barbie's dream house in here."

"Yours doesn't?" I asked.

"Entirely different theme—think Pacific northwest hunting lodge."

"Ah. I prefer my girly girl room."

"They chose wisely all around it seems."

He crossed the perfect pincushion living room and set the tray on the bar, pouring a cup and offering it to me. I rounded the end of the counter and snagged the little bottle of white mocha syrup I'd brought from home, tipping a few drops into the cup and adding milk from a pitcher on Bob's tray.

"How're you this morning?" His brows drew down as his blue eyes swept the living room, coming to rest on my laptop and notebook, still on the table. "Find out anything interesting last night?"

I waved him toward the dusty lilac and pink sofa and took the tufted cream wing chair catty-cornered from it, sipping my coffee. Bob knew everyone (and sometimes it seemed like, everything)—him waking me suddenly seemed like more of a gift from the guardian angel of weddings than an annoyance.

"Nothing good, I'm afraid. Local law enforcement says foul play. And Sammons doesn't seem to want the cops knowing what's going on here this weekend."

Bob tipped his head to one side. "Why not?"

I raked my teeth across my bottom lip. "I think I might know. But I want to think I'm wrong."

"Uh oh. Do I want to hear this?"

I sighed. "I think Sammons doesn't want Parker in this because the guy might be his friend, Bob. I heard the sheriff talking about a ring they found on the body, and he mentioned a last name. Google tells me our likely victim did PR for the Generals, and used to play ball..." I let the words trail off as every drop of color drained from Bob's face.

"Not—" He cleared his throat. "Not Mitch Burke?"

Hell and damnation. I'd rather trade my entire shoe closet for Birkenstocks than have to tell Parker his friend was dead a week before his wedding.

For the first time, my stomach clenched around an even more horrifying thought. "Oh, shit. Was this guy on our guest list? I assumed he was here because he worked for Sammons, but...damn, chief. What are we gonna do?" I covered my face with both hands, resting my elbows on my knees.

"Grant would fling his College World Series ring into the James before he'd invite Mitch Burke to anything." Bob pulled in a deep breath. "We have much bigger problems this morning than the guest list."

The resignation in my editor's voice pulled my head up and sent my heart into my stomach. "Huh?"

"You know better than anyone how a murder investigation works. It's going to take the sheriff a bit of poking around to come up with a list of people who disliked Burke. And our groom will be at the top of it, I promise you."

* * *

My eyelids dropped. Not a tidal wave of disaster. A freaking tsunami.

Think, Nichelle.

I blinked a few times, meeting Bob's gaze. The grim line where his mouth should've been told me he was worried.

Worried Bob was never a good thing.

"I think I need to get caught up here, chief. Tell me the story."

Bob sat back and steepled his fingers under his chin. "It's a long one. I'll try to hit the high notes. Burke and Parker had roughly the same amount of talent on a pitcher's mound."

The road this tale was about to take—potholes and all—sprang to life in my head. Triple mocha with whipped cream damn. I swallowed hard. "Old rivals?"

"In pretty much every sense of the word, the way I've heard it." Bob nodded. "All the way back to the state championships in high school."

"Did they go to the same school?" I sat back in the chair, picking up my coffee and trying to focus. My brain wanted to sprint in sixty different directions.

"Not even the same county. They didn't see each other until the state finals, as a matter of fact."

"No pressure there." I shook my head.

Bob leaned forward and sipped his coffee, his eyes taking on the faraway look that meant he was running through old memories. For all the total recall my own brain could play, I didn't understand how Bob's head wasn't utterly cluttered with all the millions of things he'd done and seen and heard or read about. "Our old sports editor was a baseball nut. Couldn't get that guy to give a whit about football or basketball, but baseball season rolled around and he was in my office demanding more editorial space for the foreseeable future. He pulled in stringers from all the colleges and covered every game in the area. Even the big high schools."

"Wow." A page count that would allow for such things was more foreign to me than wood-soled clogs.

"Things were so different back then. Some ways better, some ways not." Bob smiled. "When I first took over as editor-in-chief, Landon swore we'd see an increase in sales if I gave him the space, so I shuffled pages out of business—they're always light on news in vacation season anyway. And our subs and rack sales did spike. Parents love seeing their kids in the paper. It became an annual thing."

I nodded, willing him to get on with it.

He took the cue. "The first time I laid eyes on Grant Parker, I was approving a sports front. Larry had a hell of a shot of him hurling a fastball that took up a third of the page, and Landon popped 'Superstar Material' in ninety-six point block letters above his head. The story was the high school regional tournament, in which Parker—who was just a junior—pitched two shutouts."

"Damn." I knew he was good, but that good, that young? It was hard to get the Grant Parker I knew to talk about his playing days.

Bob nodded. "On page two was Mitch Burke, the pride of the Shenandoah Valley, leading his school to their first regional title in thirty-seven years."

"So they played each other in the state tournament? Who won?"

"Always racing ahead of the story." Bob chuckled.

"I have a wedding to save here, chief."

"Parker did. But it was ugly. They faced off in the last round, the one for all the marbles, and both games were hard, but the one Parker and Burke started? A pitcher's duel for the ages. Eighteen innings. Four hours in, Burke threw one grapefruit off a tired arm to this kid from Parker's school who could run like the wind. He didn't even hit it over the fence. Inside the park homer. Parker got carried out of the dugout, and Burke walked off the field bawling like a baby. Sleeper sports story of the summer—we sold out every rack in the city the next morning."

"For the wrong kind of guy, a loss like that isn't easy to get over."

Bob touched the end of his nose with his index finger, nodding. "For a lot of people. I've thought often the past few years that I wish Parker had been the loser that afternoon. Things might be whole lot different now."

He pinched his lips together, and I shook my head. "I thought I got it, and now you've lost me."

Bob laughed. "Grant is so confident. So easy. It's one of the things I admire about him. If he'd lost, his day would've mildly sucked, and then he'd have gone right back to being him: happy he got to play and knowing he gave it his all. That's the kind of guy he is. Burke was not that kind of guy."

Uh-oh.

"It ate at him. We heard he got offered a scholarship to UVA the following spring too, and didn't go because they signed Parker first. The coach told Landon that off the record, so we never ran it."

My eyes popped wide. Giving up a scholarship to a division-one school is some pretty serious hatred. The wiki article floated through my thoughts.

"But I read online last night that Burke went to Tech. Maybe they just made him a better offer and the UVA coach was pissed about losing him."

Bob nodded. "I can't say for sure that's not true."

I watched his face when he stopped talking.

"But?"

"Excuse me?"

"There's a 'but' in there you didn't elaborate on. What is it?"

"It just never stopped after that, Nichelle. That College World Series ring Parker never takes off? Who do you think he beat to get it? Not in the finals, but on his way to them."

"And to a guy like Burke, that meant he'd have surely won if it hadn't been for Parker."

"And he might very well have. All loyalty to my alma mater aside, Mitch Burke had a hell of an arm."

"Then why didn't he ever make it out of the minors?" Parker would probably still be throwing fastballs for the Generals if he hadn't gotten hurt.

"Lack of focus. Got a little too into drinking and girls. Messed up one too many times and got cut."

"How was that Parker's fault?"

"In anyone else's mind, it wasn't by a longshot. But Burke convinced himself his downhill slide began when he went out to celebrate the fact that Parker wasn't playing anymore."

I blinked. "Hang on. What?"

"I know it's crazy. I know it's horrible. But trust me, Mitch Burke was not the sanest or nicest guy you've ever met."

Celebrating someone's dream-ending injury was pretty damned far from anything resembling nice. If Bob was right, the victim was a tool. "How do you know this, chief?"

"Burke's father is the President of the Virginia History League. Family goes back to some famous boat from Jamestown, plantation aristocracy that turned a small fortune into a very large one when an ancestor got into iron-work and construction a hundred or so years ago. Richard Burke—that's the victim's father—had a few friends on our board. When Mitch got kicked out of baseball, I got an order to call him for a job interview.

"His clips were good. He needed experience. But I was willing to give him a shot. Since everyone on the sports desk knew why he wasn't playing ball anymore, I asked him in the interview if he'd gotten a handle on those problems. He told me they were all Parker's fault—and why he thought so —and left. Didn't tell me if he wanted the job. Didn't ask me about a salary."

"Wow."

Bob put one hand up. "That's not all. Richard Burke isn't the sort of man who gives up easily. After I talked with Mitch that day, I started getting pressure from upstairs to fire Parker, who was the best damned baseball reporter I'd ever read. It didn't take but two phone calls to find out where it was coming from." Bob nodded at my dropped jaw. "Obviously, I didn't. So Mitch got a job keeping stats for the Generals. Publicly, he said he was thrilled, looking forward to working his way up. Privately, I heard he blamed Parker for being stuck in an entry-level job he hated."

I put a hand to my temple. "That's...Jeez. But, um, Burke is the one who's dead here." I blew out a long breath. "And surely the guy you're describing had a long list of enemies."

"Were any of the rest of them on this property yesterday?"

"Only one way to find out." I set my cup on the table and stood. "Start digging."

"Where?" Bob kept his seat.

"I need a washcloth and a hair tie, and then we gotta go see if we can rouse Parker."

5

There wasn't enough concealer in North America to help the purple circles under my eyes, but a ponytail and some sunglasses later, I opened the cottage door and stepped onto the little porch. The pink pillows in the white wicker rockers looked even more inviting than the night before. Too bad Bob had pretty much ensured I wouldn't have time to sit down for the rest of my stay.

Jogging down the steps, I turned toward Parker and Mel's cabin. "What do you think, chief? Tapping on the window?"

"Why don't I just go to the door and tell Melanie I want to have a word with Grant if she answers?" Bob grinned. "Not everything has to be cloak and dagger, Nicey."

I laughed, which felt so good I kept doing it for a little too long. "Point taken," I said when I caught my breath. "You could be offering marital advice."

"I do have plenty of that." He stopped walking and shook his head. "Damn, I miss her."

"I'm sorry." I put a hand on his back and stood with him for a few blinks until he started walking again.

"I'll hang back and then join y'all in a minute?"

He nodded and started toward the door.

Before he got halfway there, Parker's voice behind me nearly sent me out of my skin. "Pretty here, isn't it? Generous of Dale to let us stay."

I spun on one wedge and forced what I hoped was a calm smile. "I can't think of a better place to begin a life together," I said, turning my head to whistle at Bob. He did a double take when he saw Parker and strode back to us.

"What're you two up to this morning?" Parker asked, wiping his face with a mint green towel so plush it looked like a family of Whos could be living inside.

"Looking for you, as it happens," I said, holding the panic out of my voice only because I'd had an awful lot of practice.

"Here I am." He draped the towel around his neck, the ends falling over his bare shoulders, which hardly registered. Hundreds of women would be more than a little thrilled to have shirtless, sweaty Grant Parker smiling at them.

I just wanted the wedding fairy to conjure a way to avoid ruining his day. In the next two minutes. I moved my eyes from the towel to his face, trying to look interested in what he was saying. "Mel has a million things on the list for today, but I couldn't pass up the chance to run out here before everyone was up. At least, before I thought anyone would be up."

I shot a what-now glance at Bob and he clapped Parker on the back and steered him toward the steps of my cottage. "Come have some coffee with us, son."

Parker fell into step beside me for a few strides, his eyes burning a hole in my profile until he stopped and swung me to face him. "What's wrong, Nichelle? Is it the cake? The flowers? Jesus, tell me the seamstress didn't ruin Mel's gown."

What I wouldn't have given for any one of those problems in place of Mitch Burke in a wine barrel.

I sighed. "No—"

"Inside, kids. Come on." Bob cut me off and waved us to the front door, shaking his head when I raised a brow at him. "You never know who might be listening," he murmured as I walked through the door he was holding open.

Right.

Parker paced the width of the living room, which took him all of four strides each way. "What's going on?" he blurted as soon as Bob shut the door.

Bob and I exchanged a long look. He nodded, and Parker stopped pacing. "You two are scaring me."

"I'm sorry, Parker." I sighed. "I'm not—dammit, there's no easy way to say this."

"Say what? Andrews is canning me? Your ATF agent friend told you Mel is a fugitive? Or she used to be a man? Just tell me."

I crossed the room and laid a hand on his arm. "One of the vineyard employees found a body in a wine barrel last night."

His face went blank. "A what?"

Words tumbled from my lips so fast they practically tripped over each other. "It's terrible all the way around. The victim, their loved ones, your wedding, Mr. Sammons—I have a shorter list of people I'm not worried about or feeling sorry for. I wanted everything to be perfect for y'all, in case you hadn't noticed."

Parker nodded, his eyes fixed on the fireplace across from him. "Perfect," he echoed.

I patted his arm and turned to Bob, telegraphing a "your turn" with my wide eyes.

Bob nodded and cleared his throat. "Why don't you have a seat, Grant?"

Parker's eyes slid from me to our boss and back again as he moved to the loveseat and flopped down. "There's more?"

There always was.

Bob took the chair, his jaw tightening as he leaned in, resting his elbows on his knees and fixing his eyes on Parker's expressionless face. "From what Nichelle overheard, we're pretty sure the body they found was wearing Mitch Burke's college ring."

Parker's breath stopped, his still-sweaty blond head dropping into his hands.

I took half a step toward him, trying to decide if he needed reassurance or comfort, before three raps on the door froze my foot in midair.

* * *

Sammons. The sheriff. Melanie.

I filed through a mental list of possible visitors as I patted Parker's shoulder and moved to the door, trying to come up with a reason I didn't want company that wouldn't sound like I was hiding something.

I suck at lying.

But a hungry black bear on the porch would've surprised me less than Maisy, carrying a bag of bagels and wearing an exceptionally Splenda-riffic smile.

I slipped through a crack and shut the door behind me, pasting my own fake smile in place and keeping my body in the doorway and one hand on the knob.

"Good morning?" I couldn't stop my voice from rising at the end of the simple platitude.

Maisy spoke through the smile—which looked plastic and bizarre. "I thought you might be hungry."

"Since when do you care?" I didn't bother to try to hide my curiosity. She'd been nothing but nasty and backstabbing since she first set eyes on me.

"I want Melanie to be happy." Still with the creepy automaton grin.

"Me too. But I don't think you have to be my BFF to accomplish that. Just try to be nice in front of her."

She nodded, still holding the bagels.

I waited three beats for her to reply. When she didn't, I clapped my hands together and grinned, forcing brightness into my tone. "Fabulous. We're all on the same page then. Enjoy your breakfast, Maisy." I put my hand back on the doorknob.

She started to turn back to the steps and paused, the bag of bagels falling to the soft grey wood-planked floor.

I froze, the knob turned a quarter of the way, and followed her wide-eyed gaze. What now?

Maisy was looking at the window—or, at what was on the other side of it.

Parker. Minus a shirt. In my room at before-respectable-hour in the morning.

* * *

"All on the same page, huh? I guess I have a few chapters to catch up on." Maisy backed down one step, the fake smile twisting into a sneer.

"I promise you, it's not what you're thinking." My fingers curled into a fist, nails biting into my palm. The truth was so far from what Maisy assumed, one couldn't hit the other with a long-range missile. But how the hell was I supposed to stop her from thinking terrible things without blabbing about Burke? I was still holding out hope that we could spare Mel this particular clusterfuck, and I wanted to get Parker and Bob's thoughts on that before anyone else found out what was going on.

But I also didn't want Mel—or anyone else—to think I was sleeping with her fiancé.

Before I could decide what to say, Maisy turned on her cerulean sandal pump and stomped down the steps, striding in the direction of the lodge.

Awesome.

I took a step toward her huffily set shoulders, then paused and backed toward my door. I couldn't leave. And Mel was still asleep. I'd catch up with Maisy after I took care of Parker. If I could take care of Parker.

I pushed the door open and stepped through, falling against the back side when I shut it. "Just one thing. I just want one good thing to happen today." The words came out under my breath, my chin dropping to my chest.

"What was that?" Bob asked, his eyes straying from Parker, who had straightened, his unblinking eyes locked on the little stone fireplace.

I waved my hand. "Unimportant. Has he said anything?"

"Not a word." Bob's brow furrowed as he watched Parker.

I shoved off the door and crossed to the loveseat, perching on the arm and reaching for Parker's shoulder, painfully aware of his lack of proper attire and hoping to God no one was peering in the window.

Poking one finger at his skin, I caught his eye when he turned toward me. "What's going on in your head?" I folded my hands into my lap.

"I'm just—Jesus, Clarke." Parker's voice was hoarse. "What happened? How did they find him?"

"I wish I had an answer for that. I overheard very little. They found him in a wine barrel, and the sheriff thinks he didn't put himself in there. That's all I've got."

Parker shook his head, his eyes drifting back to the fireplace. "I can't believe this." He stood. "I should go find Dale and see if I can help."

I glanced at Bob. "What are the chances we can keep Mel insulated here?"

Parker paused, his hand moving to run through his hair. "Keep Mel safe." He nodded. "I need to take care of her first."

Bob cleared his throat. "Grant, son, I'm more worried about you than anything else. Melanie is strong. She'll be okay, even if we do have to tell her—" He raised one palm when I opened my mouth to object. "I said 'if,' not 'when.' We have bigger things to be concerned about, Nicey."

My eyes wide, I looked past Parker, shaking my head just enough to let Bob know I wanted him to shut up.

It didn't work.

"Mitch Burke is dead, and you were on the premises when the body was found, Grant." Bob's best impartial reporter voice delivered the words, but Parker still looked like he'd been punched in the gut. "Where did you go when you got here yesterday? Who were you with?"

Parker pulled in a deep breath. "You can't believe..." His gaze jumped from one of us to the other before it settled on me. "I mean, I guess you could. You did. Before."

I sat up straight and locked eyes with Parker.

"No. Way." I punctuated the words with head shakes, grabbing his hand in both of mine. "I was wrong then. I know better now. But Bob has a point—the local sheriff doesn't know you like we do, and we need to make sure your alibi is airtight before this gets out of hand."

He held my gaze for five beats before he squeezed my hands. "Thanks, Clarke."

From the corner of my eyes I saw Bob, studying Parker with an odd unreadable look. I squeezed back and smiled to keep my friend's attention on me.

"No worries, Parker. We'll dispel any suspicion and save the wedding too. Have you seen my track record?" I flashed a grin I hoped was more reassuring than maniacal, standing and spreading my arms wide. "I got this. Maid of honor superpowers, activate!"

That got a semblance of a laugh from Parker, who babbled something about needing to wake Mel so she could get her parents from the airport as he stood to leave.

I walked him to the door, wondering if I should try talking to Sammons or the sheriff first. Turning toward the shower, I caught a worried frown creasing Bob's brow and dropped onto the loveseat. "I want to erase that look from your face, but something tells me you're about to blow my attempt at a good mood all over the valley."

"Grant didn't say where he was." He let the words fall one by one, his tone flat.

"You can't possibly—" The rest of that stuck in my throat when Bob's eyes met mine.

Cold. Serious. Suspicious.

"My God, you really do. Bob—how could you?" I croaked.

"I asked him outright, and he went around the question."

"Because he was hurt that you'd even think such a thing! I would've done the same in his place."

"How about when I first told him it was Burke? He didn't even flinch. He knew this guy, for Chrisssakes."

"He was in shock! Not everyone dissolves into a puddle when they hear about a tragedy."

Bob met my eyes and shook his head. "I'm not big on emotional outbursts myself, but you saw me this morning when you said Burke's name. And you saw Grant when I did. Step back and consider that, and then tell me I'm wrong."

I shook my head hard enough to dislodge my hair from its ponytail. "I don't have to consider anything—I know him better than that. Apparently, better than you do. Two years ago, I thought the worst of a man I saw as an egotistical ass, and you told me I was wrong. Now I'm telling you: You are wrong, chief. Grant Parker is my friend. And he might be a lot of things, but he's no murderer."

"Nicey, try for some objectivity. You don't understand. Burke—" Bob sighed and tossed his hands up when I cut him off.

"Hated Parker. I heard you the first time. And I don't want to hear any more of this ridiculousness—not even from you." Especially not from him. I blinked back angry tears, striding toward the bathroom. Pausing in the doorway, I turned back and cleared my throat. "You can either get on board with clearing this mess up and saving their wedding, or you can get out. The door is unlocked."

6

I clawed gouges in my scalp scrubbing my hair, the hot water streaming down my cheeks mingling with tears. Bob, of all people. On both counts. I couldn't believe I'd yelled at my beloved editor any more than I could believe he'd looked so suspicious of Parker. What the hell happened to my fairy-tale rehearsal weekend?

By the time I had some makeup and a pair of gray linen shorts on, I was ready to get it back. Add a peach silk tank top and my favorite nude Tory Burch wedges, and I was downright determined.

My phone buzzed against the marble of the bar top as I strode into the living room. Sliding my finger across the screen, I raised it to my ear. "Hey, Mom."

"How's it going, baby? All those plates still spinning?" Her voice was bright.

Barely. Not that I was telling mom that. "Dinner last night was great, and wait 'til you see the photos Larry got when they arrived. This was a spectacular idea."

"I'm so glad they're having fun," she said. "How about you? Ready for a break yet?"

"More than ready." Every word true. In more than one sense. "I'm headed up to the lodge to talk to someone about lunch right this second." And I would. I just wanted to talk about the murder victim too.

She wished me a good day, and I told her I loved her and clicked off. The phone rattled against my car keys when I slid it into my pocket.

Plopping my sunglasses in place as I jerked the front door open, I decided Sammons or one of his minions were my best bet for information.

I half-jogged toward the lodge and made it a quarter of the way there before I noticed Hulk, coming out of the far end of the field nearest the barns.

Spinning mid-stride, I kept myself from tripping only because I'd had a lot of practice (long legs plus lack of grace equals tumbling experience).

Hurrying his direction, I slowed my steps when he saw me and started my way.

"Good morning," he said, putting out a hand. "I was kind of hoping I'd run into you. Wanted to say thanks for helping us keep our heads last night. I grew up on a farm, but that was a sight different than a hog slaughter."

I shaded my eyes with one hand, dropping my head back to look up at him. This was a mountain of man—he had to be six foot seven at least, and his shoulders probably had a couple inches on my entire arm span. And from what I'd seen last night, he knew this place inside out. First on my list of questions: Cause of death.

"Believe me, I sympathize," I said. "My work tends to involve corpses fairly often, and the scenes still aren't easy to stomach. I'm sorry you had to see that."

I paused, keeping an interested smile in place. Old reporter trick: Most people don't like silence. If you keep quiet long enough, they'll start talking to avoid it.

His massive shoulders lifted with a sigh. "I wish I could've been more help to the sheriff. I was surveying crops all afternoon until I went into the barn to check those barrels. The next few weeks are important for last summer's vintage, and timing is everything."

I nodded, keeping my lips tight together. Keep talking.

He looked around, throwing his hands up and letting them slap down against his dusty jeans. "Nothing gets murdered out here but a few deer during hunting season. Who would do something like this? I mean, sure, Burke was a dick, but come on. Nobody deserves that."

My eyebrows floated up. The way Bob told it, Parker had good reason to dislike Burke. General unpopularity could be helpful to my friend if Bob was right about him being a suspect. "The victim wasn't everyone's favorite guy?"

Hulk snorted. "If that tool was his own momma's favorite guy, I'll eat my socks."

Yikes. But...yay. In a weird way.

"Anyone in particular that really hated him?" I kept my tone light, my eyes wide, and my smile in place.

He shrugged. "You could start with probably half the women in the commonwealth."

Womanizer. Not surprising. Though a quarter of the population of Virginia was a mighty large suspect pool. I studied Hulk's face, wondering how far I wanted to push with the questions. I might want to talk to him again, and I didn't want him to get wary.

Before I could decide, a Ford King Ranch pulled up and Dale Sammons kicked the door open. "Morning, Franklin," he called, settling his Ostrich boots on the grass. "Morning...?" He let the word trail and lifted his eyebrows at me, his eyes darting back to Franklin.

"Nichelle," I blurted, stepping forward and putting a hand out. "I'm the maid of honor in Grant and Melanie's wedding."

"That's right." Sammons nodded, flipping my hand and brushing his lips across my knuckles. "You came down with them to look the place over at Thanksgiving. Enchanted. Again."

I smiled, letting my hand drop back to my side and resisting the urge to wipe it on my shorts. "Nice to see you again, sir." I hit the last word a bit hard, keeping the smile pasted in place. "Thank you again for everything you're doing for Grant and Mel. This is a beautiful place you have."

Sammons glanced around, a smirk replacing the grin. "Wasn't much to look at when I inherited it, and look what I've created. What good is there in doing something if you're not going to do it all the way?" His tone stayed pleasant, but the razor edge just beneath the chipper would've sliced through one of the hundred-foot oaks lining the drive. I slid my eyes to Hulk and caught a flash of a scowl so brief I might've imagined it.

Huh.

I didn't get my mouth open to reply before Sammons tipped his head back to address Hulk. "You're out early for a Saturday. Everything still moving on schedule? We can't allow this unfortunate mishap to derail anything."

Franklin nodded. "I was concerned about the south fields, so I left the drips on overnight and came back to check them."

"And?" Every trace of chipper vanished from Sammons' face and tone. I mimed a statue, afraid to breathe and remind him I was there. Eavesdropping in plain sight is a handy skill for a reporter, and I'd spent years perfecting blending into the background when necessary.

"Perking back up," Franklin said. "We'll keep an eye on them through the week, but I think we're in the clear."

"What about the other barrels?"

"I haven't checked them yet," Franklin said. "I was kind of afraid to."

Sammons blinked, his face falling as he nodded. "Of course. This tragedy has taken a toll on us all. Poor Mitch."

Everyone's eyes dropped to their shoes, and Franklin scuffed the dusty toe of one kayak-sized boot back and forth across the dewy grass until it shone like a new penny.

After ten beats, I cleared my throat. "I'm so sorry for your loss, Mr. Sammons."

"I appreciate that. Mitch was a good boy."

Franklin coughed over a snort and I fought to keep my eyebrows where they belonged.

Sammons shot Franklin a shut-the-hell-up look and offered me a melancholy half-smile, shoving his hands into the pockets of starched designer jeans that had never seen the business end of a farm day. "It's sad for the whole Generals family. I thought we'd had our share of tragedy when we lost Nate."

His mention of the pitcher whose death in a fiery boating crash had exposed Richmond's sinister side brought back memories that hit me like a swift roundhouse to the gut, even two years later. I blinked as I nodded. "That you did."

"It's such a shame this had to happen in the middle of Grant's wedding," Sammons continued, his eyes on the field behind me. "Though I suppose if we were going to lose someone, at least there was never any love lost between him and Mitch. We won't have a groom who's in mourning."

Franklin's head tipped again, and I narrowed my eyes at Sammons, not caring for his syrupy tone or his insinuation.

"I'm afraid you might be mistaken there, sir." I let a blast of frost coat the words. "Parker isn't the type to be unmoved by a young man losing his life, no matter how poorly they got along."

What was with everyone? First Bob, then Sammons. I wanted to build a wall around Parker before these men he'd respected for years hurt him with their lack of faith.

Sammons nodded, but didn't speak again, motioning for Hulk to follow him and walking back toward the barns.

Wow. I'd never been quite so unceremoniously dismissed.

And I covered cops.

Shaking my head and muttering a colorful descriptor I'd picked up from said cops, I whirled for my car, fishing a notebook out of the console and jotting a few lines:

Women: Did Burke have a girlfriend? Or five? Any with access to barn?

Hulk/Franklin: Could know more than he thinks. Might be a good source. Avoid spooking him.

Sammons: slime ball extraordinaire. Where was he yesterday? Verify DC alibi he tossed out last night?

Across the bottom of the page, I scrawled in all caps: *WHAT DOESN'T HE WANT "DERAILED?"*

Wondering if the sheriff might talk to me, I tossed the notebook and pen into the passenger seat and set my GPS for his office.

* * *

The building's exterior was straight out of *The Brady Bunch*, deco architecture with a cream and chocolate rock facade and dark wood trim. I pulled the smoked glass front door open to find a dispatcher sitting behind a wall of Plexiglas and faux-wood paneling. She pursed her rose pink lips when she looked up, scanning me from head to knees before she raised her pencil-thin brows and offered a drawling "Can I help you?"

Not fazed by the unwelcoming attitude, I smiled and pulled my driver's license from my bag. "I'm wondering if the sheriff might have a moment to talk this morning."

Her scarlet acrylic claws clicked against the little plastic card, her blue eyes narrowing as she stared at it long enough to read every line five times.

"This is a Richmond address," she said when she finally looked up. "What do you want out here?"

Deep breath, bright smile. "I just came from talking to Dale Sammons," every word true, "and I think I might have some information that could be of use to y'all."

Her eyes went so soft and shiny at Sammons's name I wasn't sure she heard the rest of what I said. "Mitch," she whispered.

I studied her a little closer. Late twenties, big blonde hair, a touch too much makeup. The kind of beer-commercial pretty I used to think Parker would go for before I knew him better. And she knew the victim. From the quaver in her voice, she might've known him well.

There was my way past the front desk.

"I'm so sorry for your loss." I dropped my voice three octaves. "What a terrible shock, and then for you to have to come to work today."

A tear hovered on her mascara-thickened lashes for three breaths before it splattered onto the paperwork in front of her, followed by a small shower of friends.

She nodded, hiccuping twice and blowing her nose before she took a deep breath and looked up at me. "We don't get too many murders out here."

"So I've heard."

Her bottom lip disappeared between her teeth as she looked over her shoulder. "He said he wasn't to be bothered this morning, but..."

"I'd sure like to help if I can." I fixed a soft smile on my face and held her gaze.

Nodding slowly, she buzzed me through the heavy double doors, pointing down the hallway that stretched beyond them. "Next to last door on the left," she said. "His name's Jim. Jim Rutledge."

The phone let out a string of sharp bleeps.

"Thank you," I mouthed as she reached for the handset.

I strode down the wide hallway, squaring my shoulders before I rapped on the burnished mahogany with Rutledge's name affixed to it via brass plate.

"What, Ella Jane? I told you twice, leave me the hell alone today. I'm not up for listening to you cry over Burke anymore until I figure out what happened to him."

Hulk's comment about women rang in my ears. Was Ella Jane really distraught, or could she be putting on a good show? I filed that for later as I turned the knob and poked my head into his office. "Good morning, sir," I said in my most earnest voice.

Rutledge was considerably shorter without his hat, the still-tight upper body evidence of a fit form that had softened around the middle with age. From the lines framing his eyes and the snowy hair at his temples, I'd put the sheriff in his mid-fifties. He held a sheaf of papers, photos spread on the desk before him, wire-rimmed glasses perched on the bridge of his wide nose.

He raised his blue eyes to my face for a full thirty seconds before the nose wrinkled as his eyes narrowed. "Who in God's name are you, and how'd you get in here? Ella Jane!"

Before I could open my mouth to explain, a crash that sounded an awful lot like a rolling desk chair colliding with a filing cabinet rang down the hallway, a panicked scream rattling the framed photos on the walls: "Daddy!"

Rutledge jumped to his feet, charging straight at me. I leapt backward, narrowly missing a sprinting Ella Jane. She stopped short when the sheriff appeared in the doorway, her matching blue eyes wide as she reached for his shoulders.

"What now?" Rutledge's voice was tight with frustration, but he didn't yell.

I flattened myself against the wall and stayed quiet.

"Where are your keys?" She gulped a deep breath. "Leroy Fulton just called hollering about thieves again, and when I tried to talk him down like usual, he said he's got a Winchester auto and he doesn't need your help."

Rutledge's eyes fell shut. "Dammit, Leroy."

He pulled the keys from his pocket and whirled for the back of the building, hollering for a deputy as Ella Jane trailed behind him.

Forgotten in the melee, I tapped one foot and pulled out a notebook, scribbling as fast as my hand would fly. Names. Relationships. Gun manufacturer.

Big ol' question mark.

Sigh.

I'd come here to earn the sheriff's trust—and the glare he shot me before everything went batshit told me that might not be easy. But while I wasn't walking out with exactly what I'd hoped for, priority one was keeping Rutledge off Parker's tail for a while longer.

It sounded like Mr. Fulton was handling that for the immediate future.

Which gave me a bit more time to check off priority two: proving Bob wrong.

7

I'd just started the car when my phone went to buzzing in my bag. I checked the caller ID as I frowned at the clock—how in God's name was it only eight thirty in the morning? It felt like it should be at least noon.

"Hey there." I put the car in reverse, pinching the phone between my shoulder and my ear.

"Good morning, beautiful." Joey's low, sexy voice made my insides go mushy. "I didn't wake you, did I? I was trying to let you sleep."

I snorted. "Bob woke me. Three hours ago."

"What? Why?"

"Dead guy in a wine barrel that's a very long story I'd rather not rehash right now."

The pause was so long I pulled the phone away from my head to see if the signal had dropped. "Joey?"

"You—there's a corpse? Are you kidding?"

"Boy, how I wish I was. Just left the local sheriff's office. Trying to keep this wedding from imploding at the last minute."

"Can't you ever have boring days?"

"I'll be plenty bored next Saturday night, dancing all by myself." There was no bite to the words, but they hit the air before I could stop them.

The biggest here-we-go-again sigh I'd ever heard rushed out of the phone speaker. "Baby, it's a bad idea for me to show up at a big social event with a room full of nosy news people. I wish like hell..." He trailed off.

"Don't." I choked on the word. "Please don't say things you don't mean."

"Where in the name of all that is holy would you get the idea that I don't mean that with everything in me?" His tone softened and my defenses crumbled into a pile of rubble I was terrified my heart would join soon.

Why did everything have to be so damned complicated?

I was falling for this man. After months of something resembling a real relationship—the very best months I'd ever spent with anyone—I was sure of that. And as hard as I tried to keep my heart insulated, the falling part wasn't even the problem.

Joey was...amazing. Sweet and thoughtful and protective. Not to mention sexy as hell.

Nope. He wasn't any problem at all.

The problem was his "business," which had ties to organized crime.

Which meant everything about our relationship had to be a secret. I knew he was right. That's why I hadn't said anything to Bob the night before. But it meant dancing with my guy at Mel's wedding was off limits. As was talking to anyone but my BFF about him, and I'd about given up on that lately because Jenna didn't love me being with Joey. Even my mom was dropping not-so-subtle get-serious-or-move-on hints, though they came mostly from an increasing fear that she'd never have a grandchild.

All that well and truly sucked.

I let out a wistful sigh. "Maybe we're overthinking this. Nobody I work with knows you." Parker did, judging by his half-comment the night before, but he'd be so wrapped up in Mel he wouldn't notice if Amy Adams streaked his reception.

"And you don't think they're all going to be clamoring for a background check the moment I lay a finger on you?" Joey's voice was soft. "You don't just want me to be there, you want me to be there with you. I won't make it to the second dance before we'll be swamped with questions we can't answer."

"Why can't you be a random guy I just met? I'll tell them I joined eHarmony."

"Because your friend the groom saw me at the hospital last fall, and you can't be sure he won't remember. If you get caught in a lie about who I am, they'll really start digging."

"Parker will be so busy he won't have time to look at us."

"At his good friend, who's the maid of honor, and the mystery man she deemed important enough to bring to his wedding?"

And there was the mic drop. I couldn't argue with that, because the stakes were too high if I turned out to be wrong.

Daydreams of swaying close to Joey in my frothy silver gown, my hands on the shoulders of his tuxedo jacket (God. Joey in a tux. My stomach flipped clean over. Twice.) faded, pragmatism taking their place.

"I'm being difficult," I said softly. "Again."

"You're cute when you're difficult. And I love that you want me there. I just don't think it's a great idea."

"I know."

"Does this mean I'm out of the doghouse? Darcy's getting tired of me."

"Darcy wouldn't know a doghouse if one fell on her." My little toy Pomeranian was possibly the most pampered dog on the planet, and she made no apologies for it.

"I really am sorry," he said. "Though I'm sorrier you're not enjoying your weekend—what the hell is going on out there?"

I didn't realize until I finished talking how much I'd needed to unload everything. My chest suddenly less tight, I took a deep breath. "It's only their wedding, and possibly Parker's whole life, on the line here. No pressure."

Joey was quiet for a minute before he cleared his throat. "You're absolutely sure your friend isn't capable...?" He didn't actually say it, which saved me from biting his head off.

"I'm sure. Surer than some other people he thinks he trusts, which is pissing me off." Bob flashed through my head as I turned into the vineyard's half-mile, winding gravel drive.

"Far be it from me to argue with your people instincts, but just keep this in mind: I've seen plenty of humans at their worst. Anyone can surprise you with the right motivation."

Parking the car, I flipped the mirror on the back of the sun visor open. Ick. Both of us could pack for a week at the beach in the hollows under my eyes. I plopped my sunglasses back into place. "Thank you," I said. "But assuming I'm right, I need to move on to who it could actually be before this whole thing blows up in my face. The local sheriff will probably suspect Parker too, when he gets wind of their history, so we're playing beat the clock."

"Coroner's report?"

"Not ready until next week. If we're lucky. They use the state lab. The only thing working in my favor so far is the vineyard's slimy-as-snails owner. He seems to want this taken care of quickly and quietly, but I get a seriously creepy vibe from him."

"Do I know this guy? I don't remember you offering a name."

"I'm not sure I would've. Dale Sammons—"

Joey's sharp intake of breath stopped me before I could get the "he also owns the Generals" out of my mouth. My eyes fell shut behind the glasses. That sound was never a good one outside the bedroom.

"What?" I forced the word out. Things that worried Joey tended to be to the Sharknado end of the oh-shit-stay-out-of-this scale.

A string of curse words came out under his breath, followed by, "Listen to me, Princess. If there's a law Dale Sammons hasn't broken, it's only because it hasn't suited him to. If your victim was part of his inner circle, there's a good chance you're right about your friend not being responsible, and a better one that you're about to get in way over your head." He sighed, his voice taking on a pleading note that sounded alien coming from him. "You cannot get involved in this. Talk your friends into moving their wedding, and let the cops do their job."

8

Five minutes of pressing got me nothing but a repeated loop of "You can't think I'm that stupid. Anything I tell you will only make you get yourself in more trouble. Please, for once, can you just trust me?"

I hung up with a promise to watch myself, climbing out of the car cursing the whole stinky mess under my breath. Trust him. What about trusting me? Surely he knew I'd learned a thing or two in the past few years about being careful and avoiding poking hornet's nests. Or maybe he didn't.

Silver lining: He'd confirmed the excessively creepy vibe I'd gotten from Sammons. And honestly, Joey's fear that I wouldn't let this go was well-founded. How could I?

Relocating the ceremony a week in advance? Impossible. Everything was set. Any place nearly as beautiful as the vineyard had been booked for a year or better. If we didn't have the wedding here, it was the courthouse or postpone, neither of which I considered an option—yet, anyway.

I paused halfway to the door of the lodge, wanting desperately to talk to Bob, but still too annoyed with him to go find him. I dropped my head back and studied the wide, impossibly blue sky. Two wispy clouds floated across it like this was still the picture-perfect day I'd imagined.

Pulling out my phone, I checked the clock. A questionably respectable phone hour for a Saturday, but questionable is better than nothing. I tapped my favorites list.

"'Lo?" Kyle sounded like I'd woken him. Oops.

"Morning." I tried to keep my voice level. Didn't work—even I could hear the stress-induced elevation.

"Nichelle?" Now he was awake. "What's wrong?" The words were slightly muffled, and I pictured him scrambling to a sitting position, rubbing his electric blue eyes as he pinched the phone between his cheek and shoulder.

Kyle and I were high school sweethearts who'd lost touch for a decade —until my ex showed up in my city as the federal government's new Super-Cop. We'd had our share of fits and starts to the whole "just friends" thing (mainly thanks to Joey, in one way or another), but had finally settled into a solid "don't ask don't tell" groove that kept us from driving each other nuts.

Days like this, it was especially nice to have him in my corner.

"Everything." My voice cracked, and I swiped at my eyes. Deep breath. Clear throat. No tears, just facts.

"One thing at a time." His voice was low and soothing, belying his years of ATF Agent practice talking to hysterical people.

I moved to a shady spot on the far end of the building where there wasn't a person in sight. Starting with Mitch Burke and the wine barrel, I finished with Sammons and the wedding that was about to be a catastrophe, careful to leave Joey out of it.

"How?" he asked after a pause. I heard cabinets shutting and his coffeemaker burbling in the background. "How do you find this shit, Nichelle?"

"I think it found me this time."

He sighed. "And you don't like the guy who owns the place?"

"I get a bad vibe from him." Every word true. "You don't recognize the name?"

"Not from work. Just from the news."

A guy who made Joey nervous, managing to fly under the feds' radar? This day just kept getting worse.

What was Sammons up to? A million possibilities flew through my head. And the owner of Richmond's baseball franchise into any one of them was a headline worth chasing. I wanted to dig until Sammons was looking at a federal indictment, but I had a wedding to rescue. If the guy was dirty, he'd still need a shower once Parker and Mel were off on their honeymoon.

First things first.

"I can't let their wedding fall apart, Kyle," I said, the desperation in my voice surprising me.

"Agreed. I like Parker a lot. He took me to a couple of ballgames after the Okerson thing last year, and we keep up online. I'm looking forward to next weekend. And I'm a hundred percent with you on suspects—if Grant Parker murdered anyone, I'll hand over my badge today and go teach science somewhere. Let me see what I can find on your victim—it sounds like there's a chance I could turn up a few more enemies that will pull heat off Grant."

Score. Having Kyle on my side gave me a much stronger argument for Bob, which I fully intended to exploit. And it made me feel better about trusting my instincts too.

"Thank you, Kyle."

"Anytime. Call me if you need me."

I clicked off the call, pushing everything out of my head but the task at hand. Sammons. If Joey was that freaked by him, there was something on the internet I'd missed. I was halfway back to my laptop when my phone buzzed. Text from Melanie. I slid my finger across the screen, holding my breath. Surely nothing else could go wrong.

FML. My folks had a flight delay, but I can't turn around and come back now or I'll be driving all day. Can you and Grant hold down the fort?

Hot damn. Her being stuck at the airport would actually be helpful, in the grand scheme. Thank you, Delta. I smiled as I tapped a reply.

Got you covered, doll. See if they have a chair massage thing and pamper yourself. Will you make it back for lunch?

I stared at the bubble with the dots that meant she was typing.

Shit. It'll be close. Can you stall?

Of course.

Thanks, Nicey. You're a lifesaver.

I tucked the phone back into my pocket and strode to the cottage.

From your thumbs to God's inbox, Mel.

* * *

I flipped my computer open and typed Sammons's name into the search bar, scrolling past all the dozens of PR links I'd already read. Judging by Joey's reaction, Sammons had plenty to hide. But I had to sift through the crap to get to what I needed.

I skipped to the thirteenth page of results, hoping my superstitiously random selection would be lousy luck for Sammons.

Not unless you counted pictures of the millionaire owner of the Richmond Generals swinging a hammer for Habitat for Humanity as bad publicity. Damn.

I forged ahead, staring at the screen until my eyes hurt. Twenty-seven pages of results, and nothing but squeaky clean.

I clicked the image tab, but I was way more in the dark there. Parker would know who these people were, probably, but other than picking Sammons, Burke, and Parker out of the crowds, I had nothing.

I kept scrolling anyway, clicking random thumbnails up for a closer look. I was an hour in, flirting with a massive headache, and watching the clock tick closer to lunch when I spotted something.

Holy Manolos.

No.

I pulled the image up to full size, then zoomed in.

Clicking to the source, I blew out a slow breath. If I lived to be a hundred and twenty, I wouldn't forget that face. The steely eyes. The olive skin.

Two years ago, *ESPN Magazine* had run a photo of Sammons and Burke, posing with a young pitcher at Richmond American University who was likely to be a hot ticket in this year's draft. I recognized the pitcher, because I'd watched Parker bail the kid out of a spot of trouble a couple of years back. But my eyes were locked on the guy standing behind Sammons, a highball glass in his thick-fingered hand.

Joey wasn't exaggerating.

I scanned the faces again: a kid with a gambling problem, the owner of the local baseball franchise, our murder victim—and a bonafide, real-life mafia don: Mario Caccione, now-deceased favorite son of the Caccione crime family.

If Sammons was in with Don Mario, he really was a dangerous dude.

I couldn't think of a word bad enough, so I muttered a few different ones before I saved the photo and slammed my laptop shut so hard I wondered for a second if it would still work. "Dammit!" I bellowed at the soft grey walls.

Parker was supposed to be happy—this was supposed to be the happiest week of his life.

How was I going to tell him his old friend Mr. Sammons was crooked as the grapevines in those fields outside?

9

I needed Bob. Parker didn't any more murder Mitch Burke than I would wear sneakers to the ceremony next weekend, and now I had proof. Or close enough.

I dug my phone out to text him. No. Face to face would be better. I'd just go over there.

I set the computer on the sofa, shot my best friend in Richmond a quick text to check on Darcy, and stashed my phone in my pocket as I crossed to the door. Settling my sunglasses across my nose, I jerked it open to find Maisy, whose surprise at the door opening was quickly replaced by an I've-stepped-in-more-appealing-things look as she gave me a onceover.

"I see you had time to shower and change after your late night." The edge in her words could've sliced bone.

I stared. On one hand, she had the whole damned thing a hundred and eighty degrees wrong, and I wanted to set her straight. On the other, I couldn't do that without telling her stuff I didn't want anyone knowing.

"You're not even going to bother to try to deny it?" She sneered. "I can't tell if that's admirable or disgusting."

Deep breath. Lid on the temper. Wouldn't I be pissed in her plain little black ballet flats? Yes. Yes, I would. "Listen, Maisy, I'm glad you came back—"

She snorted.

"I am," I said. "I know what you saw, I know what it must have looked like, but you've got it all wrong."

"I'm pretty sure I see it just right." She shook her head, setting her ponytail to swinging. "I came back to tell you what I couldn't manage to get out this morning. You're supposed to be her friend, for Christ's sake. How could you?"

She didn't pause long enough for me to get the "I didn't" out before it was lost in the back half of her rant.

"I'm sure Mel's Casanova visits other women half-naked in the middle of the night all the time. I even figure Mel probably knows that about him. What else would you expect from a man like Grant Parker? But I'd bet she has no idea you're one of them."

"I..." I opened my mouth to defend my friend (and myself) but the words stuck in my throat. What could I even say to that? While I could relate to the suspicion and caution, the resigned disdain in her tone was more than a little sad. Sister here had more man issues than *Cosmo*.

I didn't have time to head shrink the bratty bridesmaid. What I needed was a way to keep her mouth shut in front of Melanie until the sheriff had his murderer and I had this wedding back on track.

Maisy folded her arms over her extra-helping-size breasts and fixed me with a glare. "Men are going to be men. But I have to tell you, I expected better from you."

She had to be kidding. Except her flashing eyes said she wasn't.

"Expected better than what? I have done nothing for months but bust my ass to make sure next Saturday is the fairy tale Mel has always dreamed of." I managed to keep from shouting—barely. "And you want to stand there with almost no information and jump to the conclusion that I'm screwing around with Parker," I swooped one arm toward the window, "as I'm killing myself to give him the perfect wedding to another woman? Sister, I'm not sure what your idea of a good time is, but that's nowhere close to mine. Parker is my friend. Not only am I not interested in getting tangled up in the sheets with my friend, I would never do that to Mel—or to myself. If you've ever really been Melanie's friend, you'll believe me when I tell you Parker went for an early run, and I bumped into him and asked him in for coffee, to discuss his wedding. To my other friend, Melanie. And you'll go enjoy your day, and maybe give a little thought to why you assumed the worst about your friend's fiancé, yet you plan to stand up next to her and smile while she marries him next week."

I ran out of air before I ran out of words. Her eyes stayed locked on my face until I paused for breath, then her head dropped back and she fixed them on the plant basket hook over her head.

"Then why were you still wearing your clothes from last night while he was half-dressed?" she asked, still looking at the gladiolas.

"I was in a hurry when I got up and it was the first thing I pulled back on. I was in my room, for crying out loud. If I were trying to impress a guy, or cover up an affair, wouldn't I have put on some makeup and a clean outfit?"

Her eyes skipped from the flowers to my face and back again. "Maybe you were up all night. Those circles under your eyes don't exactly testify on behalf of well-rested."

I rolled my fingers into fists, the bite of my nails on my palms helping me rein in my temper. Why I hadn't slept was none of her business. But I didn't want her to think there was even a remote chance a sex-a-thon with Parker had anything to do with it. "Has Mel ever told you how she and Parker met?"

"She said she was set up," Maisy said. "I was supposed to have a blind date I didn't really want to mess with, and she told me I'd never know if I didn't go."

"She was set up." I planted my hands on my hips and leaned forward. "By *me*. Why on Earth would I fix Parker up with Mel if I wanted him in my own bed? I'm a lot of things, but stupid isn't one of them. And Grant Parker is so crazy in love with Melanie he doesn't even know other women exist. All he wants is to get through next weekend and on the plane to Aruba."

She shook her head slowly. "If it looks like a duck and walks like a duck..."

I watched the indecision flash across her face, laying a hand on her arm and softening my voice with a fair helping of effort. "Sometimes it turns out to be a swan. If Mel is your friend, you won't spoil her wedding by casting doubt on something she has absolutely no reason to have anything but utter faith in. Parker loves her. We all do."

She stared, her forehead wrinkling, then hauled in a deep breath that came out as a sigh.

Home run.

"I'm watching," she said. "A lot closer than I was before. And if I see anything else I don't like, you'll be out of this whole thing so fast you'll be lucky to escape with those adorable shoes."

"Watch away. I have nothing to hide." Nothing that had anything to do with sleeping with Parker, anyway.

I watched her go, taking a few deep breaths to calm my racing pulse before I stepped off the porch and turned toward the bigger cabin Bob and Larry were sharing.

I rapped on the door three times. No answer. Of course.

Half-jogging to the lodge, I ran through the top of my to-do list: Lunch preparations should be starting, and I needed to chat with the chef about pushing the time and look over the setup before I could hunt for my boss, especially with Mel tied up at the airport.

I pushed the door open just as a scream rattled through the open windows from the direction of the gravel parking lot out front.

* * *

I sprinted through the building, flinging the front door into the rustic log wall behind it as I plowed toward the source of the sound. Please, God, not another body. Who could pull off a wedding if people kept dropping like characters in a George R.R. Martin novel?

Another shriek split the still morning, and this time I could make out voices to go with it. My wedges skidded on the rocks when I rounded the back end of a whole line of pickups to find the redhead who ran the vineyard's retail store, staring openmouthed at a tall blond guy in a navy t-shirt and straw cowboy hat. I pulled up short.

What? Did he steal something?

Then she moved to one side, finding her words and shouting "What is the matter with you?" at the same time I caught a glimpse of Captain

Cowboy's bare ass. Judging from the position of his arms, he was peeing. Not even trying to hide it either, Wranglers bunched around his knees as they were. Right out in the parking lot in broad daylight.

Classy.

I could say one thing for Mitch Burke's unfortunate demise: It made me way less panicked at the sight of a half-naked guy relieving himself outside Mel's bridal luncheon. This mess, I could handle.

I directed my eyes at the sky and cleared my throat as I walked toward them, the gravel crunching under my feet. "Can I maybe be of some assistance here?" I asked.

She whirled to face me, and he continued to ignore the both of us. The closer I got, the more clearly I could hear the sound of liquid hitting rocks.

"I...he...what..." The store manager—I searched my memory for her name and came up with Celia—spluttered as she turned to face me. "It's like he doesn't even hear me!"

I nodded, pasting a smile in place and trying not to laugh at the sheer absurdity of the whole thing. "I thought the property was closed for the event this weekend."

"It is," she spat through gritted teeth. "If I could get Jimmy Dugan here's attention, I could tell him that."

That was all it took. I folded my lips between my teeth to try to keep in it. Fail. Peals of laughter rolled out of me and I doubled over, hands braced on my bare knees, trying to hold myself upright as she stomped a foot and continued to rant while dude went about his rather inappropriate and gross business. He must've had a bladder the size of a 747's fuel tank.

"This is not funny," Celia barked.

I struggled to stand up, fighting to catch my breath and wiping at the first welcome tears that had welled in my eyes all weekend. "It kind of is," I choked out.

"Not. Not not not." She stomped again on each word, spinning back to the source of her frustration. "Sir, I'm very sorry for the inconvenience," her tone said she was not the least bit sorry, "but I'm going to have to ask you to return another day. We have a private event on the property this weekend."

I bit my lip, spurts of laughter still shaking my shoulders as he hitched his jeans back up. I heard the zipper close, and she leaned forward and touched his shoulder. "Ex. Cuse. Me." Her voice went up an octave.

He turned, the movements jerky and unsteady, arching an eyebrow at her. "I heard you, darlin'. But it's rude to interrupt a fella while he's taking care of business. Against the bro code."

Oh, holy hell.

The slur in the words told me he probably ought not be standing, and the chiseled features and green eyes that should be brighter out from under the influence told me he was related to Parker. One of the cousins he'd seemed so lukewarm about having in the wedding party?

Maybe this was why.

I scurried forward and laid a restraining hand on Celia's arm. "Pretty sure he's kin to the groom," I muttered under my breath.

She froze for a split second, her head swiveling between the two of us.

"See it?" I asked.

"Good Heavens," she whispered.

"I got it," I said, stepping forward. "You must be one of Parker's cousins." I started to offer a hand to shake out of habit, then let it drop back to my side, because...ew.

He nodded, the motion throwing his balance off such that he grabbed for the side of the truck bed to steady himself. "I'm Bubba. Thas' what everyone calls me. Hey—" He blinked slowly, his face pinching as he studied his knuckles. "How'd y'all get a pickup into your bathroom, anyhow?" he asked in Parker's Virginia drawl on steroids.

I coughed over a giggle and lowered my voice to a stage whisper. "They didn't. You're kind of in the parking lot."

Bubba raised his head and looked around slowly, blinking up at the bright spring sky. When his eyes met mine, and jumped from there to Celia's still-pissed tight lips, his face went red under his tan. "No." He shook his head, gripping the edge of the truck bed tighter.

"Bubba—how did you get here?" I asked. I'd covered enough drunk driving catastrophes to know there was roughly a blizzard's chance in Hell he'd driven—the fences were all intact and every car in the lot was parked perfectly.

"My brothers." He scrubbed at his glassy eyes with his free fist. "We had a lil' too much fun last night. I fell asleep in the truck. They got me up and told me I was in the can. Um. 'Scuse me, ladies. Restroom." His eyes fell shut. "I hope they've enjoyed their lives. As soon as I only see one of 'em, they're dead meat."

One—he was still this wasted from last night? Wow.

Two—I smelled more trouble than I needed if the Parker cousins were pranksters. And I had enough on my plate without having to break up a fistfight among the groomsmen.

I put one hand under his elbow and helped him take a couple of steps away from the truck, shooting Celia a glance. "Why don't we see if we can find some coffee? Maybe a couple of espresso shots? And a great big glass of water." She nodded and strode off toward the lodge.

I turned back to Bubba. "How's your stomach? Could you eat something?"

He slammed a hand down on a midsection worthy of an Abs of Steel cover from the sound when his palm hit it. "Cast iron," he said. "Haven't puked from drinking since I's sixteen."

Perfect. I led him inside and seated him at a small table in the lobby, checking the clock. Ninety minutes until the luncheon was scheduled to begin. No problem.

Telling Bubba to stay, I rushed to the kitchen. A large, spatula-wielding man lifted big-as-your-face chocolate chip cookies that smelled like Heaven off a baking sheet, moving them to a counter-sized cooling rack. "Could I bother you for a couple of pieces of bread?" I asked. "One of the groomsmen is still plastered from last night."

He grunted, turning to the fridge before he set about mixing the contents of several different bottles into a glass, finishing with a splash of red wine. He handed me the concoction, lifting bushy brows and nodding. "Bread before liquor helps body process slower. After, doesn't help so much. This will cure hangover." His accent sounded Eastern European, his voice gruff. I eyed the glass, waving it under my nose and sniffing. We were about to test that cast iron stomach theory.

"It will work," the cook said. "My grandfather's recipe. Old Russian men, too much vodka—we know how to cure hangover."

I wasn't sure Bubba had reached the hangover part of the program yet.

"Those cookies smell like they're worth every second they'll cost me in the gym."

"Food is pleasure. Life. Not tradeoff for minutes on treadmill." He rolled his eyes and shook his head. "Women. But *da*, cookies are good."

"Can't wait." I smiled over my shoulder and scurried back to Bubba, setting the glass in front of him. "The cook says this'll have you feeling better in no time."

He raised his head from its position on the tabletop and blinked. "I don't think I'll feel better before Monday, at the earliest."

"That's not acceptable," I said. "I have a wedding rehearsal that needs your full and sober attention before then."

"Booger's going to kill me," Bubba groaned, dropping his head into his hands. "Damn you to hell, Budweiser."

I stayed stuck on the first word. "Who?"

"Booger. Y'know—Grant." The words were muffled by his fingers.

I snorted, swallowing a giggle. "You...you call Parker 'Booger?'"

"Been his nickname since he was four."

"Why?"

"Why d'you think?"

My attempt to hold back laughter sent me into a coughing fit.

I got a deep breath and cleared my throat. "Drink up, Bubba."

Celia appeared with coffee and ice water.

"There. Have the shot there, then chase it with the coffee to cover the taste." I pushed the glass and the coffee cup toward him. He rolled his hazy eyes and picked up the cook's home-brewed hangover cure. Pinching his nose like a grade-schooler, he tipped his head back and poured it down his throat. He turned a dull green for about three seconds, then coughed. I stepped backward.

Bubba shook his head and blinked hard. "Damn, that burns." He grabbed the coffee cup and swallowed the contents in one gulp. "And it's gross too."

He leaned back in the chair and closed his eyes, and I turned to Celia. "Your cook swears that'll make him better."

"If anyone would know, it's Alexei. He's not the world's most pleasant guy, but he's an absolute genius in the kitchen."

"The food did smell fantastic."

"It tastes better." She smiled, shooting a glance at Bubba. "What do we do with him?"

"Leave him there for now. Have you seen or heard the brothers he mentioned?"

"Everyone who arrived this morning is on a tour of the vineyard. Melanie and Grant scheduled a wine tasting for just before lunch."

"Yeah, he can skip that."

She nodded. "Thank you for your help. This weekend is testing my limits. First Mitch, and then this...Wow."

My ears keyed on her use of the victim's first name. That implied familiarity. Celia kept her eyes on the floor, the curtain of her long auburn hair obscuring her face.

I kept my voice soft. "I'm so sorry for your loss."

"We were engaged." She raised her head, and my eyes popped wide, Hulk's allusion that Burke was a player floating through my thoughts. "But it...It didn't work out. So weird to think I'll never see him again."

An ex-fiancé? I bit the inside of my cheek to check the questions that wanted to spew out of my mouth. Slow and easy.

"I can't imagine how hard that must be," I said. "I'm so sorry."

She focused on something over my left shoulder for a long enough minute to stretch the silence to awkward territory, then shook her head and flashed a bright smile. "Thanks. But I'm okay. Let's go find your friends, shall we?"

I nodded, noting the soft snore that came from Bubba as she turned for the door. Good. Hopefully he'd sleep it off and forget he was pissed at his brothers. Following Celia, I tossed a glance at the wall she'd been so focused on.

It held a big picture window that overlooked the barn where the body was found.

Before I could figure out what to ask her next, a pair of sharp cracks that sounded an awful lot like gunfire came from the direction of the field.

10

Bubba let out a loud snore behind me as my violet eyes met Celia's gray ones. Everything seemed to freeze for a few seconds before she clapped a hand over her mouth and shook her head. "That can't be—"

I didn't let her get the rest of the words out, thankful for the wider heel on my wedges as I sprinted for the field.

She said the bridal party was taking a tour of the vineyard. My brain played a silent prayer for everyone's safety on a loop, but I couldn't help hoping the nut job who stuffed Burke in the wine barrel had just been unmasked.

I reached the end of the rows of grapevines, stuck for where to go. No noise, save for the birds. Looking around, I spied Sammons's overgrown pickup, three golf carts with Calais logos lined up behind it. That way.

Pausing at the back end of the golf carts, I let my eyes fall shut and listened.

Low voices. I kept my eyes closed, spinning slowly in the direction of the sound. Opening them, I faced a long row of vines that dropped out of sight down a hill.

If what I'd heard was gunfire, charging up into the middle of it wasn't the best idea.

My heart had to be chipping a rib or two with its pounding as I reached the top of the hill and peered down.

Jiminy Choos. A stocky man with jeans, boots, a hat, and a gun that might've been taller than him faced off with Sammons—and most of our wedding party. Including the groom.

What the ever-loving hell was going on around this place? Suddenly, the beautiful setting was way less appealing than a nice safe day at the courthouse. At least all the criminals there are handcuffed.

The Rifleman's back was to me.

I pulled my phone out and dialed 911, leaving the line connected as I slid it back into my pocket and crept forward, pushing up on tiptoe to keep my heels from crackling over anything.

Parker's wide green eyes landed on me, going a touch wider. I gestured to the little cowboy with the big gun. "Get him talking," I mouthed. The guy was probably six inches shorter than me, and unless he was hiding muscles somewhere, a well-placed *ap'chagi* kick would land him on his face. I sent a silent thank you heavenward for my daily body combat classes, still moving slowly. Edging into earshot, I froze when I heard Sammons's name, my eyes flicking to the gun. Dude wasn't aiming at the group in general—he had his Winchester leveled at Sammons's midsection.

Not that I wanted anyone to get shot, but I couldn't help the leap from oh-shit-please-no to what-the-hell-is-this-guy-into. I took another half step forward.

"You're a cheat, a thief, and a liar," he shouted. "Admit it! Admit you stole from me!"

Sammons blinked, took a slightly exaggerated look around, and tipped his head to one side. "If I do, will you put that thing down and stop this foolishness?"

"I want you to say it where everyone can hear you." He jiggled the shotgun. "Especially the sheriff."

"The sheriff's not here." Sammons's voice was calm.

My hand went to my pocket. Not yet, anyway.

Like I'd cued them up, sirens floated on the breeze.

"Say it, you thieving bastard." The words were nearly too low to make out, a chill dropping into his tone that sent goosebumps rippling up my arms even in the warm May breeze.

What the hell had Sammons done?

There'd be time to figure that out after nobody got shot.

Parker's emerald eyes darted between the two men, and I read his look like a spread in the Sunday sports section.

He wanted to be a hero.

But behind that was a blaze of curiosity. He also wanted to know what this guy was talking about.

Because he already thought Sammons might be shady.

Fascinating.

I tried to catch Parker's gaze again, but he was laser-focused on the men in front of him. I crept another two steps forward when Cowboy cocked the rifle. "Last chance," he told Sammons.

Sammons dropped his hands to his sides. "Fine," he muttered, before he looked around at the group, interested eyes lighting on me for the first time. "I stole from you, Leroy. Is that what you want everyone to think?"

Leroy let out a scream of frustration and stabbed the business end of the gun into Sammons's gut. "I want everyone to know just exactly what kind of man you are, you miserable..." He let the words trail into silence, shaking his head. "Your daddy would be ashamed."

Sammons, doubled over from the blow, raised his head, unmistakable rage in his eyes. His voice shook with it when he spoke. "I've made this place twice as successful in seven years as my father did in twenty."

"By cheating. You never were fit to clean his boots."

And then everything happened at once.

Sammons crouched and moved to spring at Leroy, who raised the gun, just as Parker leapt into the middle, his eyes on Sammons.

Doors slammed.

Running footfalls crested the hill.

"Police! Freeze!" came from behind me, and I knew without looking the sheriff and his deputies were coming in guns drawn. On a normal day, I'd have eaten the dirt, hands over my head in case everyone went batshit and started shooting.

I covered crime for a living. It wasn't unheard of.

But in that split second, Parker had every last bit of my attention, flying toward Sammons as Leroy's head twisted toward the sheriff, his eyes going wide when he saw me.

A roar rang from the end of the rifle as Parker tackled Sammons, who hit the ground with an audible "oof."

I landed on my ass when the sheriff shoved me aside in his haste to get to Leroy. He snatched the gun and whapped Leroy with the stock.

"Dammit, I told you to leave this be," he bellowed. "This. Is. Not. The answer. Why don't people listen? Is anyone hit, Reasoner?"

The words were garbled, like they'd come through a bad speaker, the bolt of pain in my tailbone ignored as my eyes scanned the commotion.

Was anyone hit?

Oh, *God*.

I blinked hard. Couldn't be.

Except it was.

I scrambled up on my knees to crawl toward Parker, a scream ripping from my throat as a dark stain seeped across his sky-colored polo.

* * *

No.

No. *Nonono*.

Even as I located the wound on Parker's shoulder, my brain refused to process the possibility. I'd seen more than anyone's share of violence, but Parker...

Parker was part of my happy zone. Funny. Friendly. Loyal. And safe. He worked in the newsroom and the press box at the ballpark.

Where shit like this did not happen.

Laying my right hand over my left, I laced my fingers together and pressed over the rip in his shirt at the center of the bloodstain.

Shouting. Crying.

From far away I heard the sheriff reading Leroy his Miranda rights.

"Parker, talk to me," I said, pressing harder on his wound.

His emerald eyes fluttered open. "Generals are going all the way this year." His voice was hoarse, but strong.

Tears flooded my eyes and I blinked impatiently, my face nearly cracking with the force of my smile. "If you say so."

"I do."

"Keep him talking," the tall deputy crouched behind me, leaning close to my ear. "Ambulance is on its way. Can I help you?"

I shook my head, my eyes still on Parker's face, which had gone pale under his summer's-coming tan.

"The cavalry's en route," I said.

"Did I actually get shot? Because...what the hell?"

"No kidding. Dead people, bullets flying, cowboys peeing in the parking lot...Is this a wedding rehearsal or an Adam Sandler movie?"

"Cowboys what?" His voice sounded strained.

"Pretty sure you know this particular cowboy." I pressed harder, watching the flow slow a little more.

"Are you goddamn kidding me? Was it Bubba?"

I nodded, choking on a laugh at his indignant tone, given the situation.

"I think you're going to be just fine," I said. "You'd better be, after all the work I've put into next weekend." I winked, the last of the tears dripping off my chin onto my shirt.

"This isn't what we had in mind when we asked you to be maid of honor. Just so you know."

"I've gained a whole new respect for my mother. I could not do this for people I didn't care about. Too much stress, man."

I heard the ambulance roll to the top of the hill and smiled. "Here we go. Just a quick detour to the hospital. That I can handle."

"Mel." His eyes went wide.

"She's not back yet." A latex-gloved pair of petite hands closed over mine and I pulled free, standing as the medics loaded Parker onto a stretcher and wincing as my spine straightened. Sheriff Jim had some muscle behind that shove.

I looked around, conflicted. I wanted to go with Parker and make sure he was okay.

I needed to stay put and make sure everything else didn't come apart at the seams.

Nobody else could handle the wedding minutiae, but surely someone wouldn't mind riding to the hospital.

My eyes lit on Larry, Nikon raised and clicking away as he spun in a slow circle.

"One minute, we're hearing about choosing a barrel made from the right kind of wood," he said, lowering the camera and ambling toward me. "The next this little guy comes up shouting about getting what's his, and now Parker's on a stretcher? What gives?"

"When you find out, let me know." I nodded to the ambulance. "Can you go with him? It doesn't look life-threatening, and I'd like to wait here in case Mel comes back. Maybe I can make sure nothing else goes wonky."

A man was dead, the bride was out of pocket, and the groom had been shot.

I didn't love my odds.

"Have you noticed nothing is ever easy for this bunch?" Larry groused, dropping the camera to hang from the neck strap as he moved toward the ambulance. "I thought all this do-gooding was supposed to stack up better karma."

"I'm a little fuzzy on my eastern religion, and never seem to have time to read up on it." I patted his arm. "Keep me posted? And thanks, Larry."

"Of course." He hustled up the hill, stopping to ask the medic where they were headed before he took off for the parking lot.

I turned to Deputy Reasoner, who was taking statements from the dozen or so eyewitnesses—enough of whom were brandishing cell phone cameras that Leroy was facing at least a year in prison, maybe more, depending on how badly Parker was hurt.

The deputy finished talking to Shelby and thanked her, and she scooted to the side to reveal Maisy, already staring daggers at me.

Dammit.

"Who wants to go next, ladies?" the deputy asked with a smile.

Maisy stepped backward. "I'll wait."

In that second, I lost the capacity to give one more damn what she thought. I couldn't make her believe me anymore than I could convince Christian Louboutin to design for Payless. I hadn't done anything wrong, and I had more important things to worry about. Since when did I have so little faith in my relationships with Mel and Parker that I thought Mel might believe such a load of crap anyway?

I didn't. Without another glance Maisy's way, I recounted what I'd seen and heard for the deputy and reeled off my phone number before I hauled my sore tailbone back to the lodge and scrubbed my hands like I was headed into surgery.

I paused outside the restroom, looking around for Celia when I spotted Bubba still snoring in the chair where we'd left him. Clock check: How was that only forty-five minutes ago? And where had she gotten off to? I'd taken off for the field assuming she was behind me.

Maybe she went to hide. Like normal people do when they hear gunfire.

I nodded to myself, a hundred questions about what Leroy had been so worked up about in the first place crowding my head. Thieving bastard, he'd called Sammons.

While brandishing a Winchester auto.

The call that flipped Ella Jane at the sheriff's office out this morning.

I studied the portrait of Sammons on the far wall, taking a few steps that way. "What are you into, dude?" I muttered.

"What he's not would be a shorter list." The words came from behind me, and I jumped, spinning on one heel.

Captain Panic from last night. Jinkerson, wasn't that his name?

I let my eyes go wide, fixing a smile in place. "Sorry. Just thinking out loud. Reporting is less what I do and more who I am."

"Sounded like quite a commotion out there." He ran one index finger along the edge of a claw-footed cherry end table, his eyes dropping to trace the smear mark he left on the practically reflective shine.

"I'm surprised half the county didn't turn out to see what was going on." I kept my voice neutral. "In my experience, small towns are good breeding grounds for nosiness."

"We're used to conflict around here." Jinkerson shrugged. "Mr. Sammons doesn't have as many friends as he'd like everyone to think."

My eyebrows shot into my hairline. I bit down on my lower lip, studying him. He wanted to talk. He knew what I did for a living and he'd started this conversation—then kept it going.

Augusta County might not be in our regular coverage area, but Dale Sammons sure was. Murder and God knows what else connected to such a powerful guy was a hell of a headline. A hell of a headline nobody else knew about—for now.

But I needed to put a hold on lunch and make sure Mel didn't hear about Parker from anyone but me.

Could I save the wedding and land the story?

"Where's a brilliant Swedish scientist when you need one?" I mumbled.

"Huh?" Jinkerson raised his head, his finger stopping near the table's corner.

I waved a hand. "Cloning joke. I could use another me today."

"Ah." His eyes crinkled at the corners with a smile. "I could use another life. They have a scientist for that?"

The words were almost too soft to hear, and I stepped toward him. "How can I help, Mr. Jinkerson?"

He opened his mouth, but before his answer made it out, a vaguely familiar baritone bellowed, "What the hell do you mean they took him to the hospital?"

11

I slapped my hands into the sides of my thighs, blowing my breath out in a *whoosh* and shooting Jinkerson a pleading look. "Thirty seconds?"

He gave a curt nod and I scurried to the porch, almost falling over my feet when I saw Maisy holding court with Parker's parents and Tony and Ashton Okerson, who must've arrived after all the ballyhoo.

Fantastic. Parker's dad's heart wasn't any stronger than Bob's, and Tony Okerson, retired football god to the masses, was the brother Parker'd never had. Thanks to the church of the internet, he was also newly ordained and officiating the ceremony.

Mr. Parker was pale, his wife holding a hand under his elbow and looking on with fear plain in her eyes. Tony looked pissed.

"It looked like he was sh—" Maisy didn't even try for sympathetic. I swallowed my temper and resisted the urge to kick her down the steps, rushing forward and cutting off her words with a too-bright "Hey, y'all!" instead.

"Nicey!" Ashton jogged up the steps and yanked me into a bone-crushing hug. "What's happened to Grant?"

By the time Ashton let me have a breath, the other three had dismissed Maisy and crowded around me, earning me an eat-shit-and-die look before she flounced away.

"Everyone calm down. He's going to be fine." I fished my phone out as I talked, checking my texts. Nothing from Larry.

How is he? I tapped.

Stowing it back in my pocket, I pasted a smile in place, laying a hand on Mr. Parker's arm. "He was cracking jokes when they left. He'll be back before you know it."

"What the hell happened?" Tony asked. "Did he fall off one of Dale's horses?"

I bit my lip. Before I could decide how to put it delicately, my phone buzzed.

I reached for it, holding up one finger.

Pretty deep gash, nicked a big vein, but it grazed him. No hole. No surgery. Stitches and antibiotics for a week. Doc is numbing him up now.

I blew out a breath I wasn't aware I'd been holding as I read, raising my eyes to the group of folks who were begging silently for some information.

I waved the phone. "See? Parker's fine. Larry's there with him. Says they'll have him stitched up and back to us in no time."

"Stitches?" Mrs. Parker's brow furrowed.

"We have had quite the newsworthy weekend out here," I said. "Bad luck on top of bad luck. There was a situation this morning where someone threatened Mr. Sammons with a gun. Parker jumped in the middle."

Tony caught a sharp breath. "Jesus, he got shot?"

I shook my head. "Larry said grazed. It's not nearly as bad as it could've been."

"Larry? Isn't that the photographer from the newspaper?" Mr. Parker pulled his wife close. "Why isn't Melanie with him?"

"She's at the airport waiting for her folks," I said, flashing my most reassuring smile. "She doesn't know yet. But I promise, he's going to be fine."

"I should go to him." Mrs. Parker shot a worried glance at her husband, who was breathing like he'd been for a run.

"Larry said they're almost done," I said. "You might not even get there before they release him, and it looks like you have your hands plenty full here."

She pinched her lips together and nodded, leading Mr. Parker to the rocking chairs on the end of the porch before she asked me where to get a glass of water and disappeared into the building.

"Someone should call Mel," Ashton said, laying a hand on my arm. "If it were Tony, I'd want to know."

I sighed. I couldn't keep Mel totally in her happy bubble, much as I'd like to. But what could she do from the airport, except worry herself sick? "I don't see any sense in scaring her when she's so far away. I'm hoping she'll be back soon and I can break it to her in person, when she can get to him quickly." Ashton nodded and I bent my head to catch her gaze. "It's wonderful to see you. How've you been?"

She tried for a smile and got halfway there. "I'm here. I get up and get dressed every day. I dote on my girls and try my damnedest to avoid letting them out of my sight. I think it's starting to annoy them, but I can't make myself back off."

Sadness flashed in Tony's famous blue eyes, so like his son's, and he put one hand on Ashton's shoulder. She covered it with hers and relaxed into the solid wall of his chest. I smiled in spite of the tragedy that still roiled around them a year after they'd lost their son, my eyes locked on their hands.

That.

That right there was what I wanted most for Parker and Mel. Tony and Ashton had been together forever, been to Hell and partway back in the last year, and whatever else they were dealing with separately, anyone who knew a damn thing about human nature could tell they were solid. Connected. Drawing strength from each other. Still so much in love.

Something I'd always dismissed as storybook unrealistic. Possible, because I could feel it, just being near them.

And I wanted it too. My mom had spent my whole life preaching that I didn't need a man to take care of me. She was right. Moreover, I didn't want a man to take care of me. Nor one who expected me to do as I was told. I wanted a partner who would be there for me just like I was there for him.

That's what marriage should be.

It's how I felt with Joey more often than not these days, but the abyss of uncertainty beyond the edge of that cliff kept me from the final leap.

My psychologist friend Emily would have plenty to say about commitment issues and paternal abandonment, but I shook off the thought. I could ponder my love life when there weren't a dozen crises vying for my attention.

I clapped my hands together. "Lunch has obviously been postponed. Though I need to talk to the staff about that."

The staff.

Jinkerson.

I swallowed a "dammit" and sighed. "Do you mind me putting you to work before you actually make it in the door?"

"Not even a little." Ashton's whole face brightened, and Tony nodded a thank-you over her head. He'd told me once things were better when she was busy.

"You're a lifesaver. Right through there," I turned and pointed, "you'll find the kitchen. I need them to push lunch back so our bride and her folks will be here and we can let the groom get patched up and returned from the ER. It shouldn't be a big issue, because the whole place is closed for the event until noon tomorrow."

"What time do you want?" she asked, already stepping toward the door.

I pulled out my phone and glanced at the clock. "Two thirty should do it."

"Got it." She strode off.

"Thanks," Tony said, putting an arm around me. His Super Bowl rings flashed in the sunlight, and I caught a breath, trying not to freak out too much that Tony Okerson was hugging me. He wasn't famous when he was with Parker. He was just Tony.

"So very happy to be able to do anything for her," I said. "For either of you. I think about y'all a lot."

"You know if you ever need anything...I'm right here. I have a bit of influence left in some circles." He winked and stepped toward Grant's folks, who both had a bit more color. "Nichelle is up to her eyeballs, and we ought to let her get back to working her wedding magic. It sounds like Dale is tied up for a while, but I've been here a few times. What do you say I show you around the place?"

"Just stay out of the fields." I shot him a grateful smile and spun back for the door with "I'm so sorry about that" already rolling off my tongue.

The words echoed through the room, Bubba's heavy snoring the only answer.

Jinkerson was gone.

I tried his office. Locked.

Rapped on the door.

Silence.

Damn.

Before I got a bead on where to look next, my phone went off again. I fished it out.

Melanie.

"Hey, Mel." I forced brightness into my voice, smiling through the stress because I knew from too much experience it was an easy way to sound happier than you were. "How's the airport?"

"About fifteen minutes behind me, thank God." She sighed. "I'm so sorry I'm late. I know how much work you've put into this day, Nichelle."

"Don't think twice about it. Lunch has been pushed, and we'll just push everything else right out along behind it. A timeline adjustment is the least of my worries." I stepped through to the back deck, my eyes scanning the field and barns for Jinkerson's gray button-down. No dice.

"Nichelle?" Mel's voice pulled my attention from a couple of squad cars that still sat at the top of the long hill.

"Sorry. Thinking about nine million things," I said. "What did you ask me?"

"Can you have Grant give me a call? He's not answering his cell and I need to ask him a couple of things."

Oh, boy. I chewed my lip. "I'll tell him you're looking for him as soon as I see him." Every word true. "How far out are you?"

"Probably another hour, if traffic is light," she said.

Perfect. Maybe I could manage to keep at least some of the magic I wanted for them.

"Everything here is under control." Okay, maybe that wasn't all true, but it was an ardent wish, at any rate. "Ping me when you get close?"

"Sure thing, honey," she said. "You win the wedding world series."

I clicked off the call hoping she'd still think that by nightfall.

* * *

A twenty-minute search of the near grounds failed to produce Jinkerson.

Of course. Because my day was giving Murphy a whole new subchapter of law to write about.

"I would gladly shred my favorite Louboutins for one. Single. Break today." I let my head drop back and stared at the sky. "Just one thing."

The last word left my lips just as my phone buzzed in my pocket. I covered my eyes with one hand, pulling the phone out and peeking through my fingers at the screen. What now?

Ah. My face split into a smile, my hand dropping to my side as I clicked open Larry's message.

The thing that hadn't gone completely to Hell today: Parker was all sewn up and they were just up the road.

I rolled my eyes Heavenward. "Point taken. Thanks."

When Larry's Explorer rolled across the gravel, slowing into a parking spot a few feet from the steps, I bolted for the passenger door, stepping to one side when Parker swung it open.

He stood, moving a little slowly, but looking not much worse for wear except for the sling decorating his right arm.

"How you feeling, slugger?" I asked, turning back for the steps.

"I'll still be just fine in my jacket by next weekend," he said. "Doc said I could ditch the sling on Wednesday. And the stitches will dissolve, hopefully before we get to the beach."

"Excellent."

Larry excused himself with something about loading photos onto his laptop, though I suspected his half-jog in the direction of the cabins had more to do with nicotine withdrawal than work.

I steered Parker toward one of the big rockers on the front porch. "Your folks just got here. Right alongside Tony and Ashton."

His eyes fell shut. "Did you tell them about this?"

"I kind of had to. Long story. But they know you're okay, and Tony's taken them on a tour of the property. Lunch is now closer to early dinner, not being served until almost three."

"You're some sort of magician," he said.

"Hold that thought." I sighed. "Ashton was pretty insistent that we talk to Melanie, and since you can't very well hide that thing," I waved to the sling, "it's not like we can keep this from her. Maybe we should just tell her everything?"

Parker nodded. "I suppose. Before we get to that, what say you tell me about my cousins and how much trouble they've caused?"

I wrinkled my nose. "I was sort of hoping you'd forgotten about that in all the injury and hospital commotion."

He snorted. "It's going to sound horrible to say peeing out in the open in the middle of the day was probably the tamest thing I was prepared for. They're—well. They're something else."

"Fun." I smiled over the word. Honestly, the Parker cousins weren't even a blip on my radar. I could put a few unruly relatives in line. It was the dead guy and cryptic comments from half the people I'd met this weekend I wanted explanations for.

"Sorry. My mom said I had to." Parker grimaced.

"It's really no big deal. Bubba said he was smashed—from last night. I gave him the chef's hair of the dog and some espresso, and he's been asleep ever since. For what it's worth, he seemed pretty embarrassed, and more than a little pissed off at his brothers."

"I'll talk to them. The only thing worse than them making trouble is them fighting. Unless you're okay with a full-scale redneck honky-tonk brawl at the rehearsal. Then I'll leave them alone." He winked.

"Talk away," I said. "Hey, speaking of talking—that was some scene, huh? What do you figure it was about?"

Parker lifted his good shoulder. "I couldn't tell." He narrowed his eyes at me. "But you have Detective Nichelle face. What do you think it was about?"

I laughed. "Well, the guy was on and on about Sammons being a snake. You've known him a long time." I paused. Deep breath. Level stare. "Is he?"

Parker sighed. "Not to me?"

Definite question mark in his voice at the end of that. I tipped my head to one side, my eyebrows drawing down. "That's a half-assed answer."

"I know." Parker kicked off with one foot, sending the chair rocking back.

"What's the other half?"

"I hear things. Things I don't love. But Dale has been really good to me. I have a hard time believing he's not the stand-up guy he makes out to be, Clarke."

"A man—" I stopped, looking around and lowering my voice as I leaned forward. "A man was found dead in his barn last night, Parker. Maybe it's time to give that some thought?"

"Yeah. But everyone knows what a prick Mitch Burke was. I mean, everyone. You couldn't be in a room with that guy for ten minutes and not get that."

Ella Jane at the sheriff's office flashed through my thoughts. Maybe not everyone. Or maybe some more than others.

"I know you don't want to answer this, but I want you to think about that whole 'Nichelle is such an awesome friend' thing you just said and trust me for a minute, okay?" I hauled in a deep breath as he nodded. "Would Sammons have had any reason—no matter how crazy you think it sounds—to be pissed at Burke?"

"I honestly don't know. I couldn't think of much else while they were fixing up my shoulder, and—I mean—maybe." He stared past me at the bright greens and splashes of color dotting the mountainside. "Maybe not. I guess it depends on who Sammons really is. The two of them worked closely enough together that if he really is sketchy, Burke would know it. Hell, Burke might be part of it. I wouldn't put it past him."

I tapped a finger on my lips. I hadn't thought of that. What if Burke had been setting his boss up?

Damn. I couldn't even figure out which proverbial goose to chase. All of them would've been my first choice, and it wasn't even about the story. Not all of it, anyway: I mostly wanted some sanity and order restored to this situation.

I dropped my head into my hands.

"What's up?" Parker asked.

I kept my eyes on the floor. "It's...too much. I'm trying to focus on the most important thing, but there are like ten life-and-death matters vying for my attention at the moment, and I don't have enough hands to juggle them all."

He chuckled. "It's kind of nice to see you like this."

"Half out of my mind with frustration?" I raised my head and rolled my eyes. "So glad I can amuse you."

"No, I mean, you always seem to have it all together. You've got all the answers, you always get the story, you're the first friend to jump in and help everyone out. Your whole thing," he waved his good hand, "is being polished and perfect. It's nice to see a human."

I snorted, forgetting to keep my jaw shut as I stared at his earnest expression.

"You're serious? You can't be serious. All the answers? Polished and perfect? Have you met me? Or are you mixing me up with you?"

He smiled, shaking his head. "Just telling you how everyone sees it."

"Everyone sees wrong. Wrong, wrong, wrong."

"If you say so."

The crunch of tires on gravel drew my eyes to the parking lot before I could ask him anything else. "There's Mel. You ready to do this?"

"Let me get to her first," he said, standing.

"Lead on."

12

Melanie wasn't mad.

She hugged me and fussed over Parker like Florence Nightingale in glasses and flip flops, settling him with his head resting in her lap on the cream satin chaise in their cabin's elegant Victorian living room.

She didn't interrupt as I offered the nutshell version of events, her fingers trailing through Parker's hair on repeat while I talked. My nutshell didn't include the parts about Parker being a possible suspect, or Sammons being up to no good. Nothing but stress lay down that path, and keeping stress away from the bride is the maid of honor's most important job.

"And you really think we should go ahead with our plans?" Mel asked, her eyes skipping from me to Parker. "We're not in the way?"

"I can double check that with the sheriff if it'll make you feel better, but they should've cleared the scene last night, and what happened this morning is the textbook definition of open and shut. We even had cops on hand as witnesses."

She nodded. "Just want to be sure." Her eyes dropped to Parker's. "I can't believe I wasn't here when you were hurt. Some fiancée I am."

He laid his good hand on her face. "Stop that. Like you could've known this would happen before you left. And if you could've, put those powers to work on the lottery and let's retire to the beach the day after the wedding."

She laughed. "You're a nut."

"I like to make you laugh."

I cleared my throat, grinning. "Still sitting here, y'all."

"Sorry." Mel winked. She was not.

I stood. "Take your moment—I have eleventy billion other things to do."

"If you see my folks, send them over?" Parker asked.

"On it."

I bounced down the steps outside wondering why Sammons didn't run a bed and breakfast with all these gorgeous cabins. He'd make a bloody fortune. Another one.

Pausing, I rested my hands on my hips and scanned the property. A Sunkist-colored butterfly worried around a trumpet vine that was eating its way up a pine tree near Bob's cabin.

Sheriff Rutledge would be back on the Mitch Burke case before too long, since Leroy pulled the trigger in front of God and everybody.

But why? What could a wealthy guy like Dale Sammons have stolen from a little country farmer? And the thing about Mr. Sammons, senior—that was interesting too. How had Sammons been so much more successful than his father in such a short time?

So many questions. I knew I didn't have a prayer of actually getting to talk to Leroy anytime soon, and the sheriff was buried under more work than he probably usually saw in six months.

Which brought me back to Jinkerson.

I turned for the lodge, stepping into the lobby to find Bubba awake and much clearer eyed, chatting with Celia, who had her own cup of coffee and wore the kind of forced-wider smile that said she was trying a bit too hard.

Bubba turned to me, one eye closing as he sized me up. "You were the other young lady from before," he said.

I nodded. "Nice to see you feeling better."

"Whatever you gave me to drink seems to be a miracle cure." He looked at Celia. "Maybe that's what you folks ought to be bottling."

She laughed. "We'll sell you the wine, then the hangover cure. Sounds like something my uncle could get on board with."

Her uncle? This place was like its own little Mayberry.

I covered the surprise with a smile, hoping my voice didn't sound too desperate when I asked if she'd seen Jinkerson.

"I actually haven't seen him since yesterday afternoon. He was coming back up from the barns."

He what?

Hulk's low, stressed voice filtered up from the night before. Had Jinkerson said he was down there at any point?

Nope.

Keeping the smile frozen in place, I nodded to Celia. "I just wanted to ask him a quick question. Could you tell him I'll be in the hall helping set up for the luncheon if you happen to see him?"

"Sure." She nodded and turned back to Bubba. "The shop isn't open because of the event, so I'll be in to help you in just a little while."

"Take your time," I said. A giddy young woman who was half-thinking about Parker's cute cowboy cousin would be more likely to be chatty. And Celia knew something, even if she wasn't aware of it. So chatty was exactly how I wanted her.

* * *

Twenty minutes of digging through closets for lilac tablecloths I knew good and well had been delivered on Tuesday later, my patience looked like it might pay off.

Celia found the linens and helped me shake them out over the round tables for eight. We had five scattered around the room.

"We've done weddings out here for five years now, but this is the biggest rehearsal I've ever seen."

"Most of their friends and family live in driving distance, which is one of the reasons they liked this location," I explained. "Since Mel's parents were really the only part of their inner circle who had to travel far and Mr. Sammons was so nice to offer the place for the weekend, they just invited everyone."

She surveyed the room. "I guess when you're Grant Parker, your inner circle is a little wider than most people's. I don't know that I have forty people who would show up for a party. Let alone so many who might be hurt if they missed it."

"I bet your uncle does."

She snorted. "Only because they want the free food and booze."

I dropped my eyes to the table, fussing with a crease in the cloth as I lined it up with the white satin underskirt. Let her talk.

"You don't get where he is without screwing a few people over," she said. "When you're the kind of person who can do that without really caring, you don't tend to have many friends. Not these kind of friends, anyway. People seemed pretty upset that Mr. Parker was hurt earlier."

I blinked. I thought she'd disappeared in the middle of all that. "Grant is a good guy." I kept a light, inviting tone. "No one wants to see him hurt or unhappy."

"Maybe it runs in the family. His cousin is very charming."

"And you were ready to string him from one of the trees just a couple hours ago." I winked.

"Anyone would've been more than a little shocked." She laughed. "But his backside is...a pretty nice one. And it seems like he's more embarrassed about the whole thing than I'd even think about being."

"Speaking of embarrassed, I'm sure your uncle is feeling his share of it this weekend." I smiled. "I hope he knows how much Parker and Mel appreciate him hosting their wedding."

"How much they did before everything went crazy here, anyway."

"How is that his fault?" I let the words float out, not wanting them to drop like the loaded question they were.

"He should've left old man Fulton alone." The words no sooner hit the air than she pinched her lips together, turning to a wheeled cart and lifting a short vase stuffed with rosebuds in three shades of purple and setting it in the center of the table before she dipped her hand into a bowl of silver confetti and scattered it around the vase.

I pulled plates from a cabinet in the small hallway between the kitchen and the dining room, breathing deep to steady my hands when the china rattled in them. Celia wouldn't look at me, hiding her face behind a curtain of rich red hair as she pretended to fidget with the flowers.

I'd wheedled enough information out of people to know she thought she'd said too much, even though I had no idea why. Clearly, Parker got hurt because Fulton had a beef with her uncle. Everyone in the county had to know that by now. But fishing for elaboration wouldn't get me anywhere except alone setting up for this party.

If I let her be, I could go back to her later: Family loyalty is strong, but human decency will usually trump it, given enough time. I needed her conscience to work on her for a few hours.

I pulled out my phone and clicked Kenny Chesney up on my playlist, laying napkins and silver alongside delicate white Royal Daulton as Kenny crooned about lying to women he wanted to pick up in bars.

Everyone lied. Every day. I myself had told (outright or by omission) at least a half-dozen since I woke up. It was separating the white lies from the more serious ones that could be tricky when you were looking for secrets—and the more I learned about Calais Vineyards, the surer I became that secrets were there for the finding.

But how deep were they buried, and who would kill to keep them that way?

13

The luncheon was the first thing to go off without a hitch.

Parker got a few *oohs* and *ahhs* over his injury, but he handled it like a champ, laughing off the "way to be a hero"s and turning everyone's attention back to Melanie with a toast that had half the room misty eyed by the end of the first sentence.

"I'm going to need stock in Maybelline if I go through any more mascara today," I muttered to Shelby as Parker bent to kiss Mel, who was also weepy.

Shelby shook her head, returning her attention to her chicken salad. "You ever wonder what's wrong with us?"

"Us, who?"

"Us, you and me." She stuffed a forkful of chicken, bleu cheese, and some kind of magical house vinaigrette into her mouth, looking at me expectantly as she chewed.

"I have a moderately expensive shoe habit and a phobia about dark parking lots," I said. "I once had someone tell me I'm too nice, but I disagree." I wasn't going into my list of what was wrong with Shelby. A short year into our truce was too soon for that conversation, especially when she'd been tolerable for months now.

She rolled her eyes toward her spiky black hair and laid her fork down.

"I mean, why is everyone else paired off, and here we are skating around thirty, no closer to finding Mr. Right than we were five or ten years ago? What's wrong with us?"

Ah. I knew from hours of long-distance analysis via Emily that my psychologist friend thought I had commitment issues thanks to having never met my father. She said I was afraid to open up to a guy completely, because I was sure I'd get hurt.

Maybe she was right. As happy as I was with Joey, there was still a wall there. I just couldn't tell how thick it was. Or how to scale it.

I smiled over my introspection. "I work too much for romance. Who am I going to meet? A cop? A lawyer? Another reporter?"

"There's that hottie at the ATF you have all the history with," she said. "I even heard he was interested in picking things up with you. Why aren't you with him?"

"Work and love don't mix well." Brisk, because my friendship with Kyle was starting to feel comfortable, and I wasn't up for "what if" road with Shelby Taylor as the tour guide.

She ignored the drop-it tone, nodding toward Parker and Mel, back in their seats and laughing at something Tony was saying. "All evidence to the contrary."

"Yeah, well—neither of them tries to get killed for a living on any kind of regular basis." I paused. It wasn't like Joey had a desk job.

But he was on the other side of Kyle's justice line. He didn't have to play by the rules. Terrible, of course. But true.

Before Shelby could get another word out, Parker's dad stepped to the mic, welcoming Mel to their family and thanking everyone for joining the celebration.

"I know we've had some delays today, and we're so glad you're all still here," he said. I tried not to snort my water, thinking about our Rifleman wannabe and poor Mitch Burke. I was glad everyone was still here too.

Parker's dad informed the crowd that we'd moved the ceremony rehearsal back to seven, since there would still be plenty of light, and that dinner would be served buffet style instead of plated since lunch was late (Ashton's brilliant idea—she had some party planning chops, that lady).

"The bars are both stocked with Calais wines, including the Riesling that will soon be this year's Governor's Reserve," a voice boomed from the far end of the room. I turned to see Dale Sammons, who raised a highball glass half-full of amber liquid. "And plenty of top-shelf Kentucky bourbon. To Grant and Melanie, many happy returns."

I twisted my head back to Parker like I was watching a tennis match. He smiled and nodded to Sammons, raising his flute of seltzer (champagne and painkillers don't mix well) in return.

By the time I looked back, Sammons was gone.

I nodded and laughed through a dozen more conversations after Shelby excused herself, and though I made the rounds of the room until the last champagne glass had been cleared, I didn't catch another glimpse of Dale Sammons. Or Jinkerson.

I watched all seven of Parker's cousins stumble out into the long shadows of early evening, wondering who'd be the first to puke bourbon all over someone. All told, our groomsmen had behaved themselves, though things had gotten a bit rowdy when Celia whispered to Bubba that the largest one in the bunch needed to take his Marlboros outside the second time he lit up during dessert. A broad-chested man who looked like a Xerox enlargement of Parker's dad had gotten in the middle of that and led Smokey Smokerson out to the deck while everyone returned to their mousse and conversation.

I spotted Celia in the far corner, but she disappeared into the kitchen before I made it halfway there. Pressing up on tiptoe, I peeked through the high glass circle in the swinging oak door. Her back was to me, but she looked to be in deep conversation with chef Alexei. Worry over something going wrong with dinner got the best of me and I pushed the door slightly and leaned into the crack, ears open.

"He was just supposed to get sick," Celia hissed. "I didn't want him to die, dammit."

* * *

I blinked, the words playing on repeat in my head.

I wanted to charge through the door shouting "A-HA!" and haul Celia to the sheriff, but I couldn't move. Which was probably a good thing, because while the comment was damning enough on the surface, I covered crime for a living: She hadn't said anything that would do more than get a warrant and maybe have her brought in for questioning. And then there was the whole pesky witness issue where I hadn't seen her because of the door. I'd only heard her. Any decent defense attorney would shred me in four seconds with an argument that someone else entirely could've said the damning words—possibly even the radio or the TV.

My brain spun through thirty scenarios in as many seconds and I stepped backward, out of sight of the door behind a seven-foot potted palm outfitted with twinkle lights.

Deep breath, Nichelle.

Did the sheriff need this information? Hell yes. However, I'd seen Celia clam up earlier, and though I was pretty sure that had been a show designed to toss some suspicion on her uncle, I knew the sheriff wouldn't get anywhere with her.

But maybe I could.

The conscience is a funny thing. There were about a million and one ifs in this, but if she was talking about Burke, and if he'd been poisoned, and if the sheriff would listen to me, Celia should feel guilty because she didn't mean for Burke to die. Which meant a little of that wine her uncle mentioned could get me more of the story.

I spun for the back doors, my eyes scanning the throng of people on the deck for Parker. I needed Bubba to make sure Celia would be at the party we'd planned for after the rehearsal.

Catching a glimpse of my reflection in the glass on the door, I winced. I also needed a shower, some makeup, and a dress so I didn't trash Larry's photos of the ceremony run-through. A glance at my phone told me I had just enough time for some express primping.

And a text from Joey.

I slid my finger across the screen, trying and failing to banish Shelby's probing questions from my head, wishing things could be different. Not like I hadn't known what I was getting into from the first night he turned up in my living room with a story tip and scared the hell out of me.

My eyes fixed on the little gray bubble on my screen.

By my watch, it's about time for me to remind you to leave Dale Sammons the hell alone.

I rolled my eyes, moving to click out of the messages when the little gray dot-bubble that meant he was typing popped up at the bottom of the screen. My heart skipped as I focused on the dots.

Bing.

I mean it, princess. You'll never touch him. But he can get to you.

I tapped a finger on the side of my phone. I knew he could see on his screen that I'd read the messages.

No chance you've reconsidered sharing what you know? It'd be so much easier and safer than digging for it myself. Send. *Wish you were here. Miss you.*

Can we make a deal? I'll handle Sammons. If he's your guy, I will find a way for you to hand him to the cops. If you'll stay out of his way.

I blinked at the screen. The last time Joey had been that much help with a sticky story, he'd had a lot riding on the outcome.

But...he hadn't brought me this one. Could it be he just wanted to help me? Maybe all my do-gooder instincts were rubbing off.

Consider your hand shaken, I tapped. *And thanks.*

I was more curious about Celia than her uncle at the moment, anyhow. And less than interested in winding up in a wine barrel myself.

Bing. *Excellent. Miss you too. Have fun.*

Stowing the phone back in my pocket, I grabbed Parker, who shrugged his good shoulder and nodded when I asked him to get Bubba to keep Celia around for the evening.

I was still thinking about Joey's words when I stepped into the shower. Too much experience had taught me that when Joey worried, it was for good reason.

But no one had warned me away from the quiet little shop manager. And if Sammons grabbed my attention again...well, that could surely wait until I was back in Richmond and had some help.

* * *

Practice be damned, I had to reach for the tissue I'd stowed in my ribbon bouquet when Parker and Mel recited their vows an hour later. And these were just the regular ones for the rehearsal—they'd written their own for the real show, but wanted to keep them a secret until then.

I told myself I was happy for them, not sad for me.

It was mostly true, too.

Thankful I'd remembered the waterproof mascara when I redid my makeup, I blotted my eyes at the corners and smiled for all thirty zillion of Larry's photos. The more he picked at each nuance of every frame, the more I thought he was going to be the kink in my to-the-minute schedule for the big day. I'd have to talk to him—gently—sometime this week.

I added it to my growing mental list, scanning the crowd for Bubba's dark blond head when Larry finally dismissed those of us who weren't about to tie the knot. He led Parker and Mel out toward the barns as I spotted Bubba and Celia. She had a glass of white wine, a smile lighting her pretty face as Bubba leaned close to her ear. Whatever he said looked to be hilarious.

Good. Let her have a little more wine, get a little more relaxed. And then I'd get her alone. A girl doesn't spend nearly a decade chasing crime stories without learning a trick or two for cornering sources. Enough wine would equal a trip to the ladies' room, and I'd noticed when we toured the facility months ago that its main door locked from the inside.

Happy with that plan, I moved to the bar for a glass of my own. "White, please," I said when the bartender smiled an inquiry at me from under a cloud of ash brown curls.

The first sip hit my tongue with an explosion of sweet and tart I'd never tasted in a wine. "Wow," I murmured, holding the glass up to the light like it would make the pale liquid reveal some kind of secret.

"It's good." That baritone could only belong to Hulk. Er, Franklin. I turned and smiled up at him, swirling the wine in the glass.

He raised a short glass half-full of bourbon and I lifted mine to it. "Cheers. It's freaking amazing. I'm no aficionado, but I know what I like, and I'm pretty picky. This is the best wine I think I've ever had. How do I go about taking some home? Or is it like three hundred bucks a bottle?"

He smiled, his eyes lighting for the first time since I'd walked into him the night before. "Not even close. They'll have it in the shop and in the local grocery stores in a couple weeks for nine. Though I imagine the price will go up if we win."

"Win?" I lifted my eyebrows. "Oh—what Mr. Sammons was saying about the Reserve whatever? It's a contest?"

He nodded, shoving his big hands into the pockets of his jeans as he stared out the windows toward the barns. "Quite a contest. But from the look on your face when you took a sip of that, we've got it on lock."

"I've never had better." Every word true. "If there's one that can beat this, I want in on the taste testing."

He chuckled, leaning against the post behind him. "I imagine I might be able to arrange that."

Something in his tone hinted at more than helpfulness. I sipped my wine and studied his profile over the rim of my glass. He was good-looking—proportional, symmetrical features, a tan that spoke of hours in the fields, a shock of wheat-blond hair, and bright, sky-colored eyes. No wedding ring. Well put together.

I had plenty of men in my life at the moment.

But I wanted him to open up to me about this place and its people.

I cast my eyes down at my shoes. "Tell me how you go about creating an award-winning wine."

I expected him to launch into a story about how complicated the process was, how the grapes need just-right tending, what a genius he was. You know, the stuff a guy says to a comment like that if he's trying to impress a girl.

I expected a hundred and eighty degrees wrong.

He sucked in his cheeks so far it widened his eyes, blew out a deep breath, and tossed back the rest of his bourbon in one swallow.

"Normal people study, hire smart folks, and pray."

My brow wrinkled, and I sipped the wine again. Best to stay quiet and let people talk when they start blurting out the unexpected.

"Not Dale Sammons. No respect for craft. No time for an honest win." He fell quiet, his eyes roving the crowd under the lanterns on the wide lawn. Shaking off his reverie, he held his glass up, three fingers around the base. "I think it's time for another round."

Brilliant idea, except I didn't want him to walk away. "When you say 'honest win...?'" I let the sentence trail off, lifting the last word into a question.

He shook his head and pushed off the post. "Mr. Sammons isn't exactly what anyone would call a stand-up guy."

"How do you mean?"

"Better question might be how I don't."

Three for three with the employees alluding to Sammons being shady, which made me itch to dig deeper. But pouncing was a sure way to shut him right the hell up.

I lowered my voice. Softened my tone. Laid one hand on a forearm bigger than my thigh. "Is there something you need to talk to a friend about? I've been told I'm a pretty good listener." There. My best Emily Supershrink impression.

His eyes came to rest on the pale curve of my fingers around his arm. "I'm just so tired, ma'am. So tired of all the bullshit. This wasn't what my grandfather wanted when he bought this place."

Time. Out.

Hulk was related to Sammons? That meant he was related to Celia too.

And that changed the whole game.

14

My brows jumped so high so fast they must've given me a new wrinkle, and I hoped the smile I practiced in the mirror at least a couple times a week flashed up in time to cover my shock.

Hulk shrugged, his eyes half-focused on the wall behind me in a way that said he'd had more than the one glass of bourbon.

Phew.

I kept the smile in place as my thoughts pinged in seven thousand directions at once. My brain hurt from the effort of trying to pick a trail to follow.

If Celia had been talking about her former fiancé when I overheard her in the kitchen, and this guy was family—well, hell. He "found" the body.

I studied him, the brooding in his glassy eyes making me wonder suddenly if he'd deposited Burke in the barrel and then come looking for help to cover it up.

Wouldn't be the dumbest idea I'd ever heard.

Or maybe he was just frustrated that Sammons was getting away with something.

He shook his big head and dropped his eyes to his empty glass. "I wish things were simpler."

"I can relate to that," I said.

He chuckled. “It does look like you’ve been running your tail off this weekend.” He cut his eyes toward me and let his full lips turn up at the corners. “I imagine Burke made things a little difficult for you.”

“Can’t blame the guy for getting killed, but the gentleman this morning definitely threw a wrench into my day. What was with him?” I kept my tone light.

Hulk nodded to me, then moved his gaze back out to the fields, which were slowly being gobbled up by the deep indigo twilight. “Mr. Fulton was a good friend of my Granddad’s. All the way back to when they served together in Korea. It was actually him who got Granddad interested in making wine in the first place. Fulton inherited his family’s farm and started growing grapes before the wine industry really came to Virginia. Listening to him talk about the craft, the fruit, the mystery of the process—that sparked my Granddad’s love of a challenge.”

I looked around as I sipped my wine. Didn’t seem like anyone was paying us the slightest attention, but a room full of newspaper people can pick up on an interesting conversation through walls, traffic, and screaming babies.

A server walked by with a tray half full of shrimp cups and half full of bourbon shots, and I waylaid him, handing Hulk one of each with my best saucy grin. “It’s too beautiful here to stay inside,” I said. “Any interest in moving out to the deck?”

He shoved off the pillar he was leaning against and nodded. “Outside is probably a better place for me to stay, anyhow. Mr. Parker was nice enough to invite me up this afternoon when I went by to check on him, but Mr. Sammons probably wouldn’t care too much for me being here.”

The “Mr. Sammons” stuck in my ear like an icepick every time he said it. If Sammons’ father was his grandfather, then the man was his uncle. Why the formality? Moreover, why the unease about his opinion? I’d yet to meet the man who should be able to intimidate Hulk, just on the basis of sheer mass.

Curiouser and curiouser. And I was a big old sucker for curiosity. It’s what drove most of my eighty-five-hour workweeks.

He waved a ladies-first and followed me out to the wraparound porch, pointing to an empty sofa at the far end.

"You were telling me about your grandfather and how he got interested in winemaking," I said as I sank into the deep blue cushions and set my glass on the table in front of me. On the lawn, servers were setting up a tapas buffet and Larry was trailing Parker and Mel, taking candids of them chatting with guests. The cousins were locked to the bar at the far end of the deck with bourbon and cigars, and seemed content—and quiet. Good. I returned my attention to Hulk.

"Granddad loved any kind of a puzzle," he said. "Anything that challenged him. He got an engineering degree from VMI and served in the Air Force for three tours. When he came back, the military was just starting to get into computers. Back when a computer took four large rooms and its own air conditioner."

"Must have seemed like quite a challenge to a young engineer back then."

"He started playing with how to make them do things in his free time." Hulk nodded. "Eventually his hobby became his career when he'd written enough programs to start his own software company."

"Wow." I sipped my wine.

"Orbitron? All Granddad."

"Holy Manolos. I played that for hours growing up." I looked around, somehow more impressed with my surroundings knowing where the Sammons money had come from.

"He sold it all to Microsoft about twenty-five years ago."

I didn't need to ask to know that was a seven-figure deal. Maybe eight. Hulk kept talking.

"He'd been growing grapes in his backyard garden—they lived in the DC suburbs, and the winters are just enough colder there to be troublesome. Then the Generals' owner went bankrupt." He sipped his bourbon.

I knew that story. Big scandal, complete with gambling and whispers about organized crime.

Wait.

The photo of Sammons with the former head of the Caccione family flashed through my head and I snapped a mental puzzle piece in place. Had the scandal gone away? Or were the Sammonses just luckier than their predecessors?

"Granddad had been looking for something to do—a place to put all that money, and something to occupy his mind. His old man was a baseball player when he was young—three seasons with the Dodgers—and he loved the game, even though he didn't play too well. So he put in a bid for the Generals at the court auction and won it. Six months later, he bought this place on a tip from Mr. Fulton. He talked a lot about a blessed life. Said he always got to do what he loved, and even in his old age, he was getting to learn something new and do something great. He was forever reading about new techniques and tinkering with his process."

His eyes went misty and I tipped my head to one side. "You miss him."

"Eight years gone now, and I really do. It's a good thing we had him cremated. He'd have found passage to China rolling in his grave at what Dale Sammons has done to this place."

Which was?

I sipped the wine again, waiting for him to go on.

Two more sips and an officially awkward pause later, my head felt swimmy from the wine, and Hulk still stared in the direction of the fields, the look on his face telling me he saw something I couldn't.

"It doesn't sound like you have a super high opinion of your uncle," I said finally. "Why keep working for him if that's the case?"

Hulk furrowed his brow and then shook his head, a rueful smile pinching his lips together as they turned up.

"I owe it to my grandfather to try to keep some of what he loved about this place alive. He was a great man," he said softly. "But Mr. Sammons isn't my uncle. He's my father."

* * *

"I. Um. Huh?" Anyone who's known me for ten minutes could testify that it's damned hard to render me speechless—yet that little revelation managed it. I pulled in a deep breath and tried again. "But you said—your name..." Not much better, but I got part of my point across, anyway.

He chuckled. "Dale Sammons is a first-rate prick who walked out on my momma when she was four months along. I wouldn't take his name if it were plated in platinum." Another head shake. "I suppose it kind of is, at that. Not worth it."

I blinked, roughly thirty thousand questions vying to tumble through my lips first. "Wow. Okay," was all I managed.

"My grandparents were friends. My mom was in her senior year of college when Sammons set his cap for her, and she fell hard. Hard enough that they made a mistake. Pretty good size one." He waved toward his massive chest.

Ah. "Sounds familiar."

"You have a kid?" His eyebrows lifted with interest.

"My mom was seventeen when I was born."

He nodded. "They get married?"

"Nope. But because she didn't want to." And that was all I had to say about that. Talking about the tangled mess that was my family was hard enough with people I'd known my whole life or had blood ties to.

He cocked his head and drummed his fingers against his thigh. "My mother made the mistake of believing that Sammons was in love with her. Until she told him she was pregnant and he pitched a screaming fit that included the words 'get rid of it' and 'I'm not the marrying type.'"

My nose wrinkled. The guy really was an ass. But just a regular old ass, or something more sinister?

"Harsh," I said.

"My mom's dad called Dale's father, and the two of them agreed that my parents would be married." He waved a hand. "Here, as a matter of fact. They put it all together for a quiet wedding as soon as they could pull it off."

I waited, figuring I knew what was coming, but not really wanting to believe it.

"He disappeared. Not even a note. I didn't meet him until I was twenty-two: the summer my grandfather died and he showed up to claim his inheritance. I know it hurt my granddad that I never took his name, but I couldn't do that to my mom."

His mom. Boy, did I ever want to talk to her.

"Does she live nearby?"

"She passed away two years ago. Breast cancer."

Shit. I put a hand on his arm when his voice thickened. "My mom is a survivor."

He cleared his throat, managing a half-smile. "We seem to be two peas in a pod, don't we?"

Indeed. I'd never met anyone with a story so similar to mine, but I didn't have time to consider much of anything past I really didn't want this dude to be wrapped up in Burke's death. He was nice. And it certainly seemed he'd had a rough go of it.

The more I heard, the more I wanted it to be Sammons, just because he sounded like such a miserable excuse for a human being. But wanting it to be him didn't mean it was. Franklin here had shed some light on Sammons's character, but clearly had a t-rex-size bone to pick, so it wasn't like his opinion of whether his father was a murderer would be worth anything.

I studied his profile as he downed the rest of the bourbon, his glassy eyes crossing slightly.

"You're not driving anywhere?" When you've seen as many accidents as I have, you don't play around with the possibility of a DUI.

"I'll crash on the couch in the tack room. His highness will want my help with the horses tomorrow." His tone made me sad. He nodded, the gaze trailing to the barns. "That's about the only thing he's done with this place that Granddad would approve of—those horses still get treated better than most people. Dale Sammons will have only the best of everything, but for my granddad the horses were always that way. All organic feed, designer drugs—top of the line across the board for his babies."

Something tickled the back of my brain.

"Speaking of the horses, I heard a few people talking about the Governor's Cup. Does Sammons race them?" I asked.

He tipped his head to one side, his brow furrowing. "That's not a—well, okay. No, he doesn't race them. They're pets, really—though he hosts a polo match for his buddies every Sunday."

"Polo? Like 'sport of kings' polo? In Virginia?"

He chuckled. "It's the royalty reference that he likes. Ego the size of Gibraltar. But also, the Governor's Cup isn't a horse race. It's the contest in the wine industry Mr. Sammons mentioned earlier. Vineyards from across the Commonwealth compete in the Governor's Cup for the right to bottle and label the Governor's Reserve wine for that year. Competition is fierce. People bet on who'll win for months."

Ah ha. I raised my glass. "Lots of people betting on y'all this year?"

He smiled. "It's a big deal. Gambling isn't my idea of fun, but the cup is always a hot ticket. Even Mr. Jinkerson has money on Calais this year."

"So he likes your odds?"

"I do, too." He nodded to my glass. "I was checking another barrel of it last night when I...well. You know. Burke."

The green pallor I'd seen on him and the sheriff's comment about hoping he was okay skated through my thoughts.

"How do you check a wine? I mean, it's bad for it to be exposed to the air, right?"

He nodded, holding his glass up and turning it so the light glinted off the heavy crystal in dancing rainbows. "Right. We use a wine thief. It's a small siphon you tap into the bottom of the barrel to see if the wine is aging properly."

"By..." I let the word trail, my eyes going wide.

"Tasting it." He nodded slowly.

Sweet cartwheeling Jesus. "Oh, tell me you didn't."

"How I wish I could. I mean, I spit it out, it was rancid. So I opened the barrel to see why. Not that I don't still feel sick. I even went to the hospital to get checked out—Mr. Jinkerson insisted."

Ugh. I'd have demanded a stomach pump, spitting be damned.

As much as I shuddered at the ick factor, I was glad to hear the story—I liked him. Surely he hadn't known Burke was in there and then taste-tested the barrel. And his camo-green pallor the night before provided decent evidence he wasn't lying.

I shook my head and rested a hand on his arm. "I might have to give up wine for good in your shoes."

"My shoes would swallow your feet twice." He winked. "And I like whiskey better anyway. I'm just gifted at picking out notes in a wine. Though I may have Celia try her tastebuds at that."

Celia. Wine.

Oh, yeah.

Popping to my feet and scanning the crowd, I smiled. "Thank you for a lovely talk. I should go check on the bride and groom."

He nodded. "My pleasure, ma'am. I think I'll head on to bed in a minute."

I crossed the deck, my eyes hunting long auburn hair or a straw cowboy hat. Parker and Mel and a half-dozen other folks swayed to "Time of My Life" under the stars. Skipping my eyes over the dancers, I spotted Tony, Ashton, and both sets of parents. No Celia. And no Bubba.

Tapping a foot, I stared into the distance, so lost in wondering I didn't hear Shelby come up behind me. "You looked cozy with the big guy over there," she said. "He's cute. Too much of a mountain for me to climb, but cute." She giggled. "I bet you could handle him."

I shrugged, not about to take that bait. "You haven't seen the little redhead who works in the gift shop, have you? I need to confirm a couple of things for tomorrow."

Shelby waved to the encroaching darkness. "She went that way with one of Parker's relatives and a bottle of wine about a half-hour ago."

Damn. I couldn't corner her in the ladies' room out there.

So be it. No time for being choosy. "Thanks, Shelby."

Surveying the horizon, my gaze settled on the barns. Where better to be alone on a pretty spring evening? I charged off, ready to dig a few answers out of Sammons's niece.

* * *

Metal squealed across metal when I slid the half-ton door to one side. Slipping through the opening, I was too distracted to shut it behind me.

Wow.

The ceiling was easily thirty feet up, the floor covered with sawdust and hay. Spaced around aisles wide enough for two people to walk were wood and metal racks filled with barrel after barrel. Floor to ceiling, I counted seven barrels in one stack. Times...I looked around. Times a lot. I bet there were almost a thousand barrels in the building.

At the far end of the center aisle that stretched in front of me, I spotted a door and hurried to it, ogling barrels as I walked.

Holy Manolos, that was a lot of wine. And a lot of money.

Almost nine years into my stint at the crime desk that was supposed to be a stepping stone to politics, I could testify that the Charles Mansons and Ted Bundys of the world were a pretty rare breed. Most murders could be traced back to one of two things. Money was the first.

And it sounded like the second was going on in that room.

I tiptoed three steps closer, my eyes on a little plastic rectangle proclaiming "Employees Only," fastened to the door at eye level.

I listened.

Yup.

That was a zipper.

Followed by a soft moan.

I guess everyone grieves in their own way.

Bright side: I was sure they didn't any more hear the squalling door than the man in the moon. Downside: I wasn't interviewing Celia tonight.

Shaking my head, I scurried back out into the frost-touched evening air, wondering if I'd packed a sweater that went with my dress as I decided against shutting the barn door. No sense calling attention to myself twice.

I pulled my phone out of my cream satin wristlet. Almost eight thirty already. I quickened my pace, out of breath before I reached the steps of my little cabin.

Fumbling the key out of my bag with shaking fingers, I wondered whether that was from cold or fatigue. Anyone's guess, really.

Before I could get it into the lock, a long shadow stretched across the porch, the floorboards squeaking their protest to footsteps. I jumped, a small scream escaping my throat as the key fell to the woven blue and white doormat with a soft jingle.

15

"It's just me, kiddo." Bob's familiar scratchy baritone froze my hands and feet halfway into their punching stance.

I sagged against the door. "Jesus, chief. There seems to be a murderer running around out here, you know. Lurking in the shadows might not be the wisest way to spend your Saturday night."

"I saw you take off for the barn and figured you were chasing a lead," he said. "Wanted to talk to you, so I waited until you came back. You still pissed at me?"

I sighed. "I'm not mad. But you are wrong, Bob. I tried to come find you earlier to explain why, and got sidetracked by about seven thousand things. I'm sorry I yelled. You hurt my feelings—on Parker's behalf, I suppose—and disappointed me." My voice fell soft on the last words.

He plopped into one of the rockers on the porch and gestured for me to take the other. When I shivered as the cold wood touched my bare back, Bob shrugged his dinner jacket off and tossed it to me.

"Thanks." I pulled it on. "I was going inside to get a sweater."

He drummed his fingers on the arm of the chair. "You know how much I love you, right?"

The backs of my eyeballs pricked at the sincerity in the simple words.

"Right back at you, chief."

"You very rarely actually say the words, you know."

"What words?"

"I love you."

"I say them all the time!"

"To whom?"

I paused, considering. "My mother."

"And?"

While I'd have liked to say "my boyfriend," it would've been a lie. "My best friends."

"But not your mystery man."

I blanched. "My what?"

"I'm not stupid, kiddo. I have competing theories for why you're keeping the guy a secret, and I have to admit, I'm rooting for the fairly benign Nichelle's-too-driven or she's-just-guarded."

"Did you come here to lecture me about my commitment issues? Because my friend Emily does that enough for everyone, I promise."

"Nah. That's just a fun bonus. Big picture, more important topics."

"Like?"

"I love Grant almost as much as I love you, Nicey. However much it hurt you to hear me this morning, it hurt me more to say those words out loud. You can bet on it."

"Then why the hell did you?"

He leaned forward, pulling a folded packet of papers out of his back pocket and flattening them. I reached for the stack, but he held them just out of my grasp.

"What are those?" I asked.

"What I was trying to tell you about this morning, before you told me off and kicked me out. Emails. I started getting them about the time the wire syndicated Parker's column. Just one nasty one every few months. Ryan and our other computer geeks traced them pretty easily."

Oh, shit.

"Burke," I whispered.

Bob nodded. "Day before yesterday, when their wedding announcement ran in Lifestyles, I got four in the space of a couple hours. Same return IP address as always." He handed me the stack.

I scanned the pages, my stomach freefalling to my shoes. I stammered, a minute or so passing before I remembered how to make my lips work. "How could someone even think up doing things like this to another human being? Someone who's not Jeffrey Dahmer, anyway?" Burke's vivid words conjured blood-soaked images that rolled through my head on replay no matter how hard I tried to shut it off. I handed the papers back to Bob. "Jesus, Bob. Did you call the PD?"

"I had a long talk with Aaron White yesterday morning. He sent a detective named Landers by the office."

"And did Landers say Burke was psychotic?"

Bob nodded. "I never thought he was terribly stable, really. That's why this shook me up the way it did. But shook up is not the term I'd use to describe Grant."

I caught a shallow breath and held it for four beats, my eyes falling shut. "You showed them to Parker."

"I had to. He's in the best position to keep her safe."

I dropped my head into my hands. "You showed them to Parker, and there's a police report about it in Richmond. Oh, shit, Bob. What are we going to do?"

Even seeing the revolting slasher-movie things Burke threatened to do to Melanie, I couldn't believe Parker killed the guy. I knew now why he'd been on Mel like a Kardashian on a sequined-bikini sale, but I couldn't believe he'd actually hurt anyone.

The chances that I could convince anyone who wasn't blood related to my friend I was right?

I didn't like my odds.

"I waited this morning, wanting to see if Grant would bring them up. He didn't."

See? I couldn't even convince Bob.

"I have to figure out who did this," I mumbled into my fingers, rocking the chair. "Getting to the bottom of it is the only way to fix it. Once the sheriff gets ahold of these, he'll think he's got it all wrapped up and stop looking."

"I wish that were our only problem," Bob said.

"Huh?" I sat up and stared.

"This is tricky, Nichelle. We've got a member of our own staff who will certainly be a person of interest in a murder investigation—and that's if he's not the prime suspect. As a bonus, the victim has ties to two of the most influential men in Richmond. It's a huge story, and the only reason we're not already behind a day is because the body was found in a media dead zone. As soon as Burke's obit hits the internet, it'll be open season. You have to be ready."

Be ready. Because I had to cover it. Like things weren't already screwed up enough? It was one thing to chase a headline about Sammons being up to his neck in a murder investigation. But Parker?

There went my stomach again. "How can I write about this?"

Bob nodded. "I know it's a lot to ask. You've never been this close to a story, and you have to be absolutely impartial. If Charlie gets even a hint that you're spinning the story in Parker's favor, she'll flay you alive on the eleven o'clock."

I nodded. Charlie Lewis at Channel Four was my biggest rival for queen of the Richmond crime news scene, and months of losing to me on every big story in town had her unusually hot to make me look bad. One more land mine for this field.

"Andrews would just love that," I said. The publisher's crusade to force Bob into early retirement was the reason I'd been killing myself to stay ahead of Charlie.

"Exactly. One misstep will send him running to the board, and we'll both be out on our asses." Bob leveled a hard look at me. "Can you do it? Tell me now if you can't, and I'll go talk to Shelby."

Over. My. Cold. Corpse.

Except...could I? Being balanced was one of the things I prided myself on. But a thousand percent honest, way down in the dark places in my heart? I wasn't sure I could this time. Dammit.

"Andrews loves the money Parker's column generates. He doesn't want him in jail any more than we do."

"He doesn't love Parker as much as he hates me." Bob barked out a laugh. "Trust me."

There was something sad about how automatically my head bobbed at those words.

My eyes fell on the emails in Bob's hand again. "Parker didn't do this, Bob. I can't even tell you how I know, because I don't have words for it, but I just know. Like, down in my bones certain. He's flat ass not capable of it."

Bob didn't blink for a full minute before he sighed, running his fingers through his always messy white hair. "I want to believe you, Nichelle. Hand to God I do. But..."

I waited, the doubt on his face hitting me square in the heart.

"I've never seen anyone as in love with a woman as I was with my Gracie. Not until Parker fell for Mel. And in his shoes, seeing this?" He waved the printouts. "I can't say for sure I wouldn't have killed someone."

Damnation. That easy answer I'd been wishing for all day had fallen flat into my lap. Trouble was, it'd get Parker twenty to life if I couldn't figure out why the easy answer wasn't the only one.

I knew I was right. How the hell could I convince everyone else?

Very carefully wording the hardest story of my career could be a start.

I scrubbed my hands over my face, blowing out a deep breath. "When do you want to run it, and how much of our hand are we tipping?" I asked.

"That's my girl." Bob patted my knee. "I called the office this afternoon —the obit will go live Tuesday morning. We'll post the story Monday night, print on Tuesday." I nodded, and he squeezed my hand. "You're sure? It won't be easy."

"The really good ones never are."

"Ain't that the truth?" He stood, offering me the papers. "You want to hang onto these? I suppose we should go back to the party."

I shook my head, handing his jacket back. "I'm not likely to forget that mess. And while I'm suddenly not in the mood to party, the maid of honor can't bail on the rehearsal celebration. Besides, I could use another glass of wine. Or four." I fetched the keys and opened the door, frowning when the knob turned ahead of the key. "Just let me grab my sweater."

Flipping the light on, my eyes fell on the coffee table. And my laptop, slightly angled in the center of it. I paused.

Bob, from the doorway behind me, asked, "What's wrong?"

I took in the rest of the little cottage. Neat as a pin. But—"My laptop. I left it on the sofa when I took off this afternoon."

He stepped up beside me, scanning the small living area. "You're sure?"

"I have a stupidly specific memory of shutting it and putting it on that cushion." I pointed, taking a step that way and pausing. I didn't have time to get into that, and it was probably still safer in here with the door locked than it would be out in my car. "It didn't feel like the door was locked just now."

Bob's lips disappeared into a thin line. "It seems unlike you to leave it open."

I snatched a white cable-knit cardigan off the back of a chair and turned for the door. "Unlike regular me? Sure. Unlike overstressed wedding maestro me? Maybe not as much. I wonder if there's a maid?"

"Maybe." Bob's tone said he was thinking the same thing I was: Possible. But not likely.

* * *

The rest of the party passed in a blur of forced laughter, too-cheerful conversation, and too much wine.

By the time I walked Parker and Melanie back to their room at midnight, I was doing good to stay upright, and the wine was a close second to exhaustion on the list of reasons.

I let myself into my cabin and reached into my bag for the mace Kyle had forced on me last year when I refused to take the handgun class.

Walking through the charming little structure, I flipped on every light, checked every closet, and looked in both kitchen cabinets, under the bed, and behind the shower curtain.

Satisfied that I was alone, I slid the chain on the door into place and turned for the bed, pausing as I passed the table where my laptop lay. I knew good and well I'd left it on the sofa. And while a better reporter would probably open it and check it out, maybe even do a little more research on the main players in this nightmare my perfect wedding was rapidly deteriorating into, I physically could not. I didn't even have the energy to take my makeup off, pulling back the covers and falling asleep almost before my head hit the pillow.

Seven hours of fitful dreams about Mitch Burke and trophies and wine barrels later, I took the world's fastest shower, glad I hadn't felt up to checking my computer the night before. What if the answer to all my problems was sitting right on that table?

Yanking my hair into a ponytail, I pulled on a soft white lace skirt and a lavender sweater and shoved my feet into my new jewel-toed Jimmy Choo sandals. I found a plastic grocery sack in the bitty pantry and used it to pick up my computer.

A fifteen-minute drive, and I stared through the sheriff's department safety glass at Ella Jane. Pasting on a smile, I asked if the sheriff was in.

"He's rarely anywhere else," she said with an eye roll, deepening her voice to imitate her father. "'Price of being the law in a small town.'"

I nodded. "Folks don't often get up to no good between eight and five on weekdays."

That got me a smile. "What can we do for you?"

"It seems I have a police matter of my own this morning." I held up the bag containing my computer. "I think someone might've broken into my room last night."

She furrowed her brow. "A deputy can take a report. The sheriff is pretty busy right now."

"Of course." I nodded. "I just have some information I want to pass along to him, too, and I didn't get the chance to talk with him yesterday."

"Information about Mitch?" Her voice caught, her eyes going shiny. "Just a minute."

I smiled, studying the variegated colors of the brown brick wall while she buzzed Rutledge. When I heard the phone clatter back into its cradle, I turned back to her.

"He says he'll be with you as soon as he can."

Ella Jane started to look back at her computer and then shot me another glance. "This has been the craziest weekend."

I nodded. "You can say that again."

She blinked hard and I noticed the red outlining her blue eyes for the first time. She was pretty handy with a concealer brush—it was scarcely visible even under close scrutiny.

"It's rare for this place to see so much action in just a few days, huh?" I dropped my gaze, trailing one finger through the fine layer of dust on the counter in front of me. It was a practiced tone, one that often came in handy: not really interested, just making conversation.

"Now it's your turn to say that again. Most of the calls we get are either for the EMTs or people bitching about one of three things: gunfire after bedtime, kids busting mailboxes with bats, or grapes."

Grapes? Her first two things were standard-issue rural law enforcement staples. But that last one could be interesting.

"Did you say grapes?" Still carefully half-interested.

She nodded, an annoyed sigh heaving her generous chest. "Old man Fulton has rung this phone off the hook since the wine expo. I guess at least now he's in a cell. I have to feed him three times a day, but he can't call me from in there."

I smiled and nodded, puzzle pieces flying together in my head.

Fulton.

He'd been calling the PD. About grapes. And was pissed at Sammons for stealing from him.

Hulk's voice floated through my head: "Why *that* barrel?"

I'd thought he meant it like "why us?" when he found Burke. But what if he didn't?

What if whoever put Mitch Burke in the wine set to take the big Governor's honor picked that one on purpose?

Celia, yesterday: "He should've left old man Fulton alone."

Just exactly how far had Sammons pushed Fulton? Moreover, did Burke have anything to do with it?

Jiminy Choos.

The answer to this whole mess might already be back in their lockup.

"Why would anyone call the police about grapes?" I tried for the same careful tone, but my thoughts were zipping in so many directions at once that I wasn't sure I hit it.

She didn't seem to notice, picking up a Sharpie and popping the cap off and on as she talked.

"Mr. Fulton is a science whiz. Does everything himself, including breeding his own fruit hybrids. He's convinced Mr. Sammons swiped the seeds for a new varietal he's been trying to perfect for years. The sheriff told him, I told him, we all told him: He needed a lawyer, not the police. But he kept calling. Until yesterday."

Hot damn. My fingers itched for a pen.

The door buzzed next to me and she smiled. "I guess he's ready for you. Nice talking to you."

I met her smile with a bigger one of my own. "You too, Ella."

Maybe nicer than I ever could've hoped.

* * *

The sheriff looked annoyed.

"In case you missed the nuances yesterday, I'm a little busy this weekend," he said, one eyebrow popping up as he eyed the grocery bag I'd set on his desk.

"I understand, and I'm grateful for your time," I said, words tripping through my lips so fast they nearly tumbled over each other. "I'm helping with an event at Calais Vineyards, and I've heard a couple things I think you might like to know about."

"Is that a fact? You know, we're not as backward out here as folks from Richmond and DC always seem to think. I know who you are." He flipped open a manila folder on his desk, glancing at the contents and then back up at me. "Miss Nichelle Clarke, cops and courts reporter for the *Richmond Telegraph*."

I nodded, not surprised. They ran my name because the 911 call came from my cell.

"Nice to meet you, sir." I put out a hand.

"I don't have much use for reporters." His tone had a wary edge. "You're only sitting there because I appreciate your quick thinking yesterday—calling the emergency line and leaving your phone on was smart. And I'll be polite about telling you I'm not giving interviews about Mitch Burke."

"I'm not asking for one." Yet, anyway.

He nodded, then angled his head toward the sack.

"So what's in the bag?"

"My laptop. I'm staying in one of the guest houses at Calais, and I know I set it on the sofa when I left the building yesterday afternoon. I could swear I locked the door. When I came back last night, the door gave pretty easily when I went to unlock it, and my computer was sitting in the middle of the coffee table. Normally, I wouldn't be rattled by something so small, but this weekend has been at least two realms outside normal, and experience poking around a handful of murders has taught me 'better safe than sorry' is a cliché for a reason."

"Anything else out of place?"

"No, but anyone who knows what I do for a living..." I let the words trail.

"Would know whatever you know is in the computer." He pinched the edge of the bag with two fingers and lifted it. "You didn't touch it?"

"Not even the edges."

"I can dust it, but it'll take a week for us to run them. Maybe more. And that's if there's a match."

Huh. I bit my lip. "I may know someone who can expedite that."

He shrugged and opened a drawer, pulling a little plastic box from it. "Good for you. At least this is easy. I'll take easy today."

"I'm sorry to give you more work, and it might be nothing, I know."

"No, you're right to wonder. Something's definitely off out there."

He slipped on latex gloves and opened the box, taking out a tiny brush and a jar. Shaking the jar, he unscrewed the lid and rolled the brush in the fine powder that had collected there, then spun it across the surface of my laptop. I leaned forward and watched the prints appear like magic, a silvery sheen clinging to the ridges and whorls.

"Lots of prints." He pulled a piece of tape from a roll inside the fingerprint kit and touched it to the edge of the computer, using a thick card to smooth it down. "Probably mostly yours, but let's see if we get lucky."

"Thank you, Sheriff. I appreciate it."

"Any idea who might want to know what you've been working on?" He lifted the print from the computer and stuck it carefully to a glossy card he pulled from the box, then started over with the tape on another one.

Many ideas. But should I share them? Small-town politics can be a bitch, and with his daughter possibly tangled up with the murder victim and him appearing to know (maybe even like) Sammons, this thing was complicated on all sides.

I twisted a strand of my hair into a knot. "What about Mr. Fulton? Is there any chance Mitch Burke was caught up in whatever grievance he has with Mr. Sammons?"

Rutledge stuck another piece of tape to another card. "You'd make a decent detective, young lady," he said. "I asked that question myself. But five hundred people can put Fulton at a conference in Napa Valley all week, and his flight didn't land in Charlottesville until almost midnight Friday. So unless he can be in two places at once, he's only on the hook for yesterday."

He put the brush back in the box and picked up his phone, snapping photos of the fingerprint cards. "Speaking of yesterday, we took a statement from Grant Parker at the emergency room. Getting married next week, I understand. Seems like I remember him and Mitch Burke playing at the same time, years ago." His voice was light, but I caught the probing undertone.

"I understand they did." Light. Breezy. Nothing to hide.

"You're friends with Mr. Parker, aren't you? They still talk to one another?"

"Not from what I hear." Every word true. I met his eyes with a smile when he looked up.

"Uh-huh." His gaze lingered before he handed the laptop back to me. "Damn shame, having something like this happen in the middle of your wedding."

I kept silent.

He picked up the cards. "You want a copy of these to take with you?"

I nodded, watching him print photos and slide them into an envelope. "Thank you."

"Anything else I can do for you?"

"Not at the moment, but there might be something I can do for you."

He leaned back in his chair as I told him about Celia's conversation with chef Alexei.

"She also told me they were once engaged," I finished.

He snorted, tipping the chair upright as he leaned forward. "I don't doubt it. Boy made his rounds. Hell, my daughter thinks she was in love with him too." A shadow crossed his face for a second so split I might've imagined it. "Good thing he wasn't the marrying kind. I'd have had to ship Ella Jane off to my sister in Texas or some such nonsense."

I kept quiet, hoping he'd say more, but he shook his head and stood.

"I'll let the lab know I want an expanded tox panel on Mitch. Right after I get some more coffee." Rutledge snagged a Virginia is for Lovers mug off his desk and led me to the door, shaking his head as he opened it. "I never would've seen Celia as capable. Her momma was the gentlest soul you'd ever meet. Dale's older sister, Jolene. Lovely woman."

"Was?" I stepped into the hall.

"She passed on just days before her daddy. I still say he plain gave up when she died." Rutledge's voice dropped an octave as he walked to the tiny break room. "Poor little thing struggled with demons most of her life. Ended up taking her own."

"How..." I paused and shook my head. "Tragic."

"I hope I don't have cause to worry that I'll regret this conversation." Rutledge's eyes said he meant that in more than one way.

Me too, Sheriff.

I shook my head. "Unless you'd care to comment on the record..." I let the sentence trail and he smiled.

"Open investigation. You understand."

I sure hoped so.

"I appreciate the tip. If you think of anything else I should know, give me a call," he said when I smiled and thanked him for his time.

I walked back to my car in a daze, his words looping in my head.

Celia's mother struggled with mental illness, which can be hereditary.

She also died right before her father—leaving her estranged brother to inherit a fortune.

Convenient time for a suicide.

Did Celia's mother really kill herself? Because Sammons...well. People who got away with murder once were more likely to try it again.

16

Hooves thundered over the lush emerald lawn, the thoroughbreds kicking up divots in every direction as their riders navigated sharp turnabouts, waving mallets and shouting.

I didn't enjoy the polo match nearly as much as I wanted to, mostly because I couldn't bring myself to pay attention to it for more than thirty-seven seconds at a time.

I'd looked everywhere I could think to look for Jinkerson when I returned from the sheriff's office and found bupkis. No one had seen him since Saturday morning. I went to the kitchen hoping to chat up the Russian chef who was (possibly) supposed to have made Mitch Burke sick, but found only trays of muffins and a really good cup of coffee.

Questions spun through my head faster than I could consider them, trying as I was to be covert about watching the folks around me. Most everyone's eyes were on the horses: magnificent, well-muscled and expertly cared-for animals that would've been just as at home carting royalty on a fox hunt as they were in the Virginia countryside.

The matches appeared to be an all-hands event. Though Sammons and some of his friends were on the field, I caught several familiar faces in the crowd. Chef Alexei, for one. His thick arms folded across his barrel chest, he kept his eyes on the riders as Celia hid behind her sunglasses and tried to be unobtrusive about talking to him. She leaned closer, gesturing to the field and getting a nod from him, but was she really talking about the action?

I followed her pointer finger to a massive stallion carrying a tall broad-shouldered man with silver hair and an elegant seat that spoke of a lifetime of riding. He knocked the ball easily from Sammons's reach, pulling the horse up sharply to turn him the other direction. I studied his profile. Familiar, I thought, but couldn't tell from where. Most of these people were probably regulars in our business pages.

My eyes strayed back to Celia. Her conversation with Alexei looked like it had grown more serious.

I didn't have a prayer of deciphering actual words, so I settled for watching their body language, thankful for my oversized Kate Spade shades.

Their exchange from yesterday was certainly the most damning thing I had, but it also wasn't the only off-base thing at Calais, and my gut said there was more to this story. Old man Fulton, the sheriff, Sammons, even Hulk, to a lesser degree: I knew just enough to be suspicious of nearly everyone, but not enough to prove anything. And the sheriff's bit about Celia's mother had me itching to learn more.

My eyes lit on Parker and Mel, his good arm pulling her into his side, her head resting on his shoulder. The letters Bob had shown me crept into my thoughts, and I shook them out like a bad Etch-A-Sketch creation. Mel pointed at something on the field and Parker laughed, his head falling back.

They were happy. I would keep it that way.

At the top of my list of questions sat our murder victim. I knew Parker's association with him was just waiting to blow up in my face. But if Burke was such an asshat, he had loads of enemies. Boil that down, and it was both good and bad. Good, because Parker couldn't be the only one with motive and/or opportunity. Bad, because more suspects equaled more complications, and I had a time constraint with their impending happily ever after officially less than a week away.

It was a darned good thing I did my best work under pressure.

Getting information without raising eyebrows in a crowd this size would be almost impossible, so my best bet was to get everyone the hell out of here and dig deeper into Mitch's life when we got back to Richmond. So far, no other news outlet appeared to even know he was dead. But the obit would run Tuesday, and the quiet wouldn't hold three seconds if Parker was named a suspect. It might not hold 'til then with Charlie so hot to beat me to a headline.

Journalism in the Age of the Internet 102: Get it first has a whole new meaning.

Journalism in the Age of the Internet Master Class: You still have to get it right.

Never had I been so desperate to get to the bottom of a story. I just needed a few (okay, a lot) more pieces of the puzzle.

I scanned the crowd again, lifting my sunglasses on the third pass. Celia was gone.

Chef Alexei still stood in his same spot, with the same stoic look on his face.

I tapped one sandal on the grass. Go talk to him, or hunt for her and Jinkerson? I scanned the crowd again.

Parker's parents and the Okersons were half a football field away, chatting and watching the match. Maisy stood behind them to the left, sneering at Parker. Not that anyone noticed. What I wouldn't give for the bratty bridesmaid to be my biggest problem.

I could catch up with the chef anytime—especially if Burke's tox screen turned up poison.

I slipped through the back of the crowd and behind the stable, wishing for a second as the sounds of the match faded into the distance that I had a normal life. What would it be like to have Joey here, arms around my waist, making jokes in my ear as we watched Sammons and his friends attempt to play a game they appeared to know next to nothing about?

Meh. What-If Avenue was generally my shortest road to sadness and frustration. Lucky me, my brain veered right off of it when I caught sight of Celia's dark hair vanishing into the barn where Burke's body was found.

* * *

As much as I'd wanted to chat with Celia the night before, I wanted to see what she was up to today. Innocent people didn't usually pop over to the scene of a body discovery while everyone else was occupied.

I slipped off my sandals as I stepped onto the hay-strewn floor, padding quietly to the first corner and peeking around.

No Celia.

Creeping along the wall, I listened for footsteps in case I needed to dive into a corner. Quiet as a church on Monday morning.

At the end of the row, the door from last night was ajar.

Cleaning up evidence of her tryst with Bubba?

Maybe.

I tiptoed closer, and got almost two-thirds of the way there before the door swung open and she stepped out.

I froze, but she turned toward the other end of the building without noticing me. Hugging the wall, I stared at her hand, closed around an L-shaped silver object that bounced a reflection of the sunlight onto the ceiling with her every step.

Just what I needed: another question. Two, really: What the hell was that thing, and what did she want with it?

* * *

I stayed a safe distance back, sliding my shoes on as I stepped outside. Before I could get a bead on what to do next, my phone started buzzing.

I pulled it out and smiled at the screen.

"Hey there." I put it to my ear.

"Good morning, beautiful." Joey's warm voice made my stomach tickle, a tingle shooting all the way to my toes. His wake-up line was as standard as Bob's meeting dismissal, but I never tired of hearing it.

"You staying out of trouble?" he asked.

"Of course." I stopped at the corner of the barn, looking around. Not a soul in sight. Damn. I leaned on the wall and focused on Joey.

"Why don't I believe you?" he asked.

Because he knew me. When I kept quiet, he sighed.

"Listen, Princess, Sammons has an awful lot to lose. People with that much at stake don't play by the rules."

My stomach twisted. He knew more than he was saying. And after what the sheriff said about the sister, that made me more than a little nervous. "Like what?"

"Like prison." Long pause. Muttered string of swearwords. I could almost see his tight jaw, his hand floating up to his temple. "Sammons wasn't always the wealthy beacon of respectability your newspaper makes him out to be. He's still not, I suspect, but he's got a couple of skeletons in his wine cellar that could snatch his whole life away. He had a sister. A sister who was set to inherit everything his father had. Who supposedly committed suicide days before their dad died. And right after he reappeared in their lives."

I froze.

I'd come to that conclusion on my own a couple hours before, of course, but it wasn't Sammons I was focused on.

Joey was sharing secrets. About a murder suspect.

I've gotten too deep in my share of stories—and a few times, Joey tried to keep me away because he knew things about the players. He was a great sounding board, and a heck of a decent bodyguard.

But spilling details willingly like that? Never.

I let my head fall back against the cool siding of the barn.

He trusted me.

Deep breath.

"And no one thought that was odd? Why didn't he go to prison?"

"That part I don't know. I'd say money is a safe bet though." He paused, his tone sharpening. "You know I'm telling you this so you'll understand why I asked you to let me handle him for you. Not so you'll go get yourself stuffed in a barrel being Nancy Drew."

I nodded, a wave of fatigue making my knees sag. I slid down the wall onto my rear almost involuntarily.

"We made a deal," I said. "I have no plans to back out."

"So you're on your way home?"

"I'm almost ready to head out. I have a story to put together for Bob when I get home."

"Drive safely, please," he said. "You sound tired. How about dinner one night this week?"

"That would be lovely." I smiled. "You coming to town?"

Joey lived in Baltimore, but spent more time in Richmond lately than he did in his own town. Which was more than fine by me.

"For you? I'll make the drive." I could practically see his dark eyes crinkle at the corners with a smile.

"I can't wait." I outlined three circles in the dirt with my finger.

His voice deepened and softened with a warmth that made my knees watery all over again. "See you soon."

I clicked off the call with the smile still in place, but it faded when I looked around the fields. From the noise coming my way, the polo match was wrapping up, and I'd lost Celia and still hadn't seen Jinkerson. My personal life might be batting a thousand today, but I was striking out in the crime-solving game, with no time for extra innings.

Falling in step with the crowd, I chatted with Larry and Shelby all the way back to the cottage, then loaded my car and pointed it home, wishing I'd thought to get Jinkerson's cell number as I pieced together a lead for the Burke story in my head.

17

By the time I'd gathered my little toy Pomeranian from my best friend's house, I had a long list of questions and eyes fighting to reopen after every blink. The last three blocks to my house were dicey, Bob's warning about overworking myself floating through my head as I turned into my driveway on autopilot.

I bent over the fence and set Darcy on the back lawn before I climbed the kitchen steps, every thought of Mitch Burke replaced by my cherry four-poster and fluffy pillows.

"Sleep, Darce," I mumbled, pushing the door open. "Then all this will make sense." Okay, so a nap doesn't generally equal a miracle, but it would at least help me have the brainpower to see what to do next.

I spooned half a can of Pro Plan into her little pink porcelain bowl and dropped clothes through the house on my way to the bed. Burke's cat-canary smile and the nasty words in his last letter to Bob floated through my head as I drifted off.

It was dark when my eyes opened again.

I blinked, turning my head toward the clock. 8:40. Dammit. More of a nap than I intended, and I couldn't call people looking for information at nine o'clock on Sunday night. Not if I wanted them to talk to me.

I groaned and flipped over, pulling a pillow over my face. "Why does everything have to be so damned complicated?"

"Nichelle?" The voice came from the hallway, and would've scared the hell out of me if I didn't know it so well. As it happened, I bolted upright, very aware that I was a lacy bra and a thong from being naked under the quilt.

Footsteps. *Tap. Tap. Tap.*

"You okay?" My door squeaked open a crack and I tightened my grip on the blanket, clearing my throat.

"Hey, Kyle." I flashed a smile. "Um. What're you doing in my house?"

He grinned and stepped into the room, light flooding in behind him when he opened the door. "Hazard of the job. I was in the neighborhood and wanted to talk about your murder vic. The car was in the drive, the dog was raising hell, but you didn't answer the door. I went around to the side and found the door unlocked and..." He shrugged. "It scared me."

I felt my lips tip up in a smile. "I appreciate the concern. My crazy weekend caught up with me all at once, and I barely made it in here before I passed out."

"You should take better care of yourself."

"Look who's talking." I laughed, nodding to his wrinkled, untucked shirt and shaggier-than-normal facial hair. "How many nights this week did you sleep on the couch in your office?"

He shook his head and half-perched on the end of the bed. "I'm going to take the fifth on that."

"It's good to see you." I cleared my throat and wrinkled my nose. "I wish it didn't always involve dead people."

"They do seem to populate the majority of our conversations." He shrugged. "Perhaps we should take up a hobby?"

His easy smile shot straight to the special place in my heart Kyle would always occupy. Whatever else was going on in my crazy world, my friend was firmly in my corner. Nice thing to know. So nice I reached for his hand—and let go of the covers.

Everything slowed to a crawl. Kyle's eyes dropped from my face to the scraps of pink lace and satin covering my skin, going wide as I tried to remember how to make my hand close around the damned quilt and pull it back up.

It probably took five seconds, but they were longer than that predawn hour before little Nichelle was allowed to get out of bed on Christmas morning.

My cheeks heated, instinct telling me to dive under the blankets and refuse to look him in the eye ever again. Stupid, if you consider that Kyle had seen me in much less than a bra more than once. But this was different. The friend thing was just getting comfortable.

My fingers finally found the edge of the quilt and resettled it, my lips hunting a word that would make the air in the room less heavy with awkwardness. "I..."

Darcy started yipping as his eyes returned to mine. "Maybe I should just call next time?" He stood, running both hands through his hair and sending the curls sticking up in thirty directions.

"I'm glad you came over—" I began, keeping a purposeful death grip on the edge of the quilt.

The dog's yipping stopped.

Just as Joey appeared in the doorway.

Joey's eyes skipped from the rumpled bedclothes to my nearly bare shoulders to Kyle's mussed hair in half a second, the smile on his face flashing to disbelief, then to hurt as his gaze came back to me. "Forgive the interruption. Doesn't look like you were expecting more company." The words were strangled, his stoic drive-Nichelle-nuts expression settling over his face like shutters closing.

"No! You've got—"

He didn't let me finish the sentence before he spun on his heel and disappeared.

* * *

Kyle spread his hands wide. "That didn't really just happen."

"Out." The word slid between my teeth.

He scurried from the room and shut the door.

A pair of yoga pants and a faded *Telegraph* comics t-shirt later, I'd chased Joey to an empty driveway, no sign of his car on my street. I shuffled back into the house brushing away tears and found Kyle waiting in the kitchen with a glass of Moscato and a smile that looked sincerely apologetic.

I swallowed the wine in one gulp and put the glass on the counter, leaning both hands on the edge and letting my eyes fall shut. "Whatever I've managed to set off-kilter in the universe really needs to right itself. I'm tired of being some kind of karmic punching bag."

He rested a hand on my shoulder and I flinched, the hurt on Joey's face playing on a loop on the backs of my eyelids. Kyle's fingers faltered, then squeezed. "I'm still your friend. Right?"

I sniffled and nodded, letting my chin drop to my chest and pulling in a deep breath. "I just wish everything wasn't so..."

"Ridiculous?" Kyle chuckled, sinking his fingers into my knotted shoulder. "Me too." He produced my iPhone and laid it on the counter in front of me. "You should call him. He knee-jerked, but he'll listen to you once he cools off. Trust me."

My eyes popped wide. I snatched up the phone and turned, tipping my head to one side. "Who are you and what've you done with Kyle Miller?"

He shrugged. "As your friend, I want you to be happy. I've been watching this for a while now—for the most part, you seem happy with him. And I'm around to keep you safe. So...call him."

I patted his arm, punching my favorites list up on the screen. "Excuse me for a sec?"

He nodded and I gestured a help-yourself toward the fridge on my way to the living room, holding my breath as I listened to the ring buzz in my ear.

One.

Two.

Three.

Voicemail.

Damn.

"I know you don't think you want to talk to me, but you have to let me explain," I said. "What you saw wasn't at all what it looked like. Please call me. Or just turn around."

I clicked off and tapped my messages, texting him a "Turn around. Not what you think, I promise. I was napping, he's helping me with Burke, I left the door unlocked, he panicked and came in the house." I clicked send with a silent thank you that at least Joey hadn't been ten seconds earlier, because I never would've sold him on this story without the covers, truth or no.

Staring at my phone, I tried to go go Gadget psychic power the little gray dot bubble into existence.

No dice.

I kept my eyes on the bottom corner of the screen until it faded into a blur, then flung the phone on the couch just as Kyle poked his head around the corner. "It's awfully quiet in here."

"He won't answer me." I blinked, trying to smile. Maybe if I pretended everything was okay, it would actually get that way somehow.

Kyle stepped into the room, uncertainty rolling off him in waves as he shoved his hands into the pockets of his flat-front khakis. "I'm sorry?" I wasn't sure he meant for it to sound like a question, but that's how it came out.

I curled my hands into fists at my side, pulled a deep breath through my nose, and fixed a smile on my face. "I appreciate that. It doesn't look like there's any more to do for it right now, and I'm starving. Why don't we eat something and talk about what you came to tell me?"

I moved back to the kitchen, pulling a loaf of bread from the pantry and turkey, cheese, and a tomato from the fridge.

"Can I help?" Kyle asked.

"You can grab drinks, then take a seat and tell me you have a plan to save this wedding."

He popped two diet Dr Peppers and dropped his long form into one of my little bistro chairs, crossing his legs at the ankle and settling his hands behind his head.

"Burke had some questionable friends. The Caccione kind."

I sliced the tomato and kept my face carefully neutral. I'd figured that, both from the photo I'd found and Joey's freak-out when he heard Sammons's name. Not that I was telling Kyle. "Awesome. Which one of them put him in that barrel?"

Kyle chuckled. "I wish I could tell you. I'm not sure. Not yet. But here's what I do know: the guy he had the most contact with? Runs their bookmaking operations."

Jiminy Choos.

I almost dropped the knife, my jaw unhinging. "Holy..." I steadied my hands and turned to Kyle. "A guy who works for a major league sports team betting... that's a huge big deal."

Kyle nodded. "Pete Rose, anyone?"

I nodded, my eyes still wide. If Burke was in too deep with a bookie—a bookie for the mob, no less—well. Parker wouldn't even be a blip on anyone's radar.

I drummed my fingertips on the counter, twisting my mouth to one side. "We need more. Solid proof."

Kyle's brows went up. "I deliver a key to the candy store and you ask for the code to the register? I can't have you chasing off after the Cacciones alone, Nichelle. They're..." something dark flitted across his face and he cleared his throat, "...they're dangerous."

I couldn't tell if the weird look had to do with Joey, or something else entirely. I let it go for fear of the former.

"I'm not alone." I smiled. "I have you."

"Always glad to be of service."

I rolled my eyes, turning back to the sandwiches and considering my next words for half a second.

"The easy road is going to lead the cops to Parker," I said around a sigh, resuming my tomato slicing. "And the local sheriff out there is a nice guy—pretty sharp one too—but I'm not sure how far he's willing or even able to dig into something involving Dale Sammons."

"Just because Grant had an old rivalry with this guy..." Kyle paused as I piled honey-roasted turkey, smoked gouda, and tomatoes on fresh wheat bread from a bakery around the corner, shaking my head. "What are you not telling me?" he asked.

I put the plates on the table and snagged a bag of Doritos from the pantry. "Burke wasn't an 'old' rival. Bob has been getting emails from him for years, bashing Parker."

Kyle shrugged, lifting his sandwich. "That's not motive."

"The one he sent last week threatening to cut Mel up and feed her to his dogs is."

The sandwich froze halfway to Kyle's mouth and he flinched, shutting his eyes. "Jesus, Nichelle."

"Sorry. But now do you see?"

"Who knows about the letters? Besides you and your boss?"

"Landers and Aaron. Bob said he called them because he was afraid to blow it off."

Kyle put his sandwich down, one hand going to his forehead. "Damn."

"Yup." I bit into mine and chewed, letting my brain wander. Sometimes the best way to focus is to not.

"And Parker knew about this email? And where it came from?" Kyle said, his fingers massaging his forehead.

"Bob said he was worried about Mel and Parker was in a position to keep her safe."

Kyle nodded. "That's true. And it seems she's okay."

"But Burke is not." I took another bite, the weekend playing in my head as I chewed and swallowed. "Parker clung to her like a Valentino on a supermodel." I picked up a chip and tapped it on the edge of the plate, something just under the conscious surface of my thoughts. "Except..."

"What?"

Oh, shit.

"Except on Saturday morning." The words were a hair above a whisper, my stomach doing a full somersault.

"Come again?"

My chip dropped to the floor and Darcy's paws scritched across the linoleum toward it.

Kyle waved a hand in front of my face. "Nicey. What?"

I shook my head as the words tumbled from my lips.

"He left her sleeping in the cabin and went for a run. Before we told him Burke was dead. Why the hell would he do that, unless he already knew?"

18

Kyle's forehead dissolved into a folded mess of lines, his finger tapping on the back side of his sandwich as he chewed.

"I couldn't say. But I still don't buy it. If there's one thing I know, it's people," Kyle said, taking a long swallow of soda. "Grant Parker isn't any more capable of stuffing a guy into a wine barrel than Darcy is. I know you know that too."

I nodded, trying to tamp down the traitorous thought. "Like I told Bob the other day, I thought the worst of Parker once and was a hundred and eighty degrees wrong. When someone comes up with a video of him offing Burke, I'll reconsider."

"Video can be manipulated." Kyle winked before his face fell serious. "Here's the thing—that email you mentioned and your guys at the PD knowing about it is a problem. If the local law enforcement out in BFE hasn't yet talked to the Richmond cops, they will shortly. And if no one else is on the hook for this by then, Parker will be in a world of trouble."

I took another bite of the sandwich and chewed slower, mostly so I didn't have to talk. I knew Joey had ties to the Caccione family, even if I wasn't sure how tight they were. I also knew Kyle at least suspected as much, and I didn't really want to know exactly what he knew. He'd produced a surveillance photo of Joey about a year ago, and spent months pleading with me to stay away from him. I'd managed to keep his suspicions at bay by telling him to talk to me when he had proof.

But.

I had to keep Parker out of prison and save the wedding.

Had to.

Hopefully it wouldn't come at the expense of everything that had become important to me over the past ten or so months. Crossing my fingers under the table, I swallowed and locked eyes with Kyle.

"Tell me about the Cacciones."

His eyes widened, his turkey and cheese going down the wrong pipe. He coughed and sputtered for a minute as I popped out of my chair to pound between his shoulder blades. Wiping his eyes, he watched me resettle in my seat and cleared his throat. "Warn a guy before you drop a bombshell like that, huh?"

"Sorry."

He tipped his head to one side. "Are you sure you want to hear this?"

No, I was not.

But I straightened my shoulders and nodded. "I can't let Parker go to prison because I'm afraid to ask a question. I ask questions for a living and I like to think I'm a better friend than that." I shot Kyle a warning glare. "But I'm not looking for grandstanding or theories about my personal life either. Start with the bookmaking thing."

He nodded. "What do you say we move to a more comfortable seat? This may take a while."

My eyes found a window, the indigo twilight outside it fading to inky black.

Maybe I could still manage it all. Carefully. I stood, picked up my glass, and waved Kyle to the living room.

I had just settled on the sofa when my phone binged.

Bob.

"Charlie Lewis called Andrews looking for a comment about the paper's position on Parker's ties to a murder victim. He's pissed. Wants to see us both first thing in the morning."

"Of fucking course he does," I muttered, shooting Kyle an I'm-sorry smile and tapping the Channel 4 site up in Safari.

I scrolled, cursing myself for sitting on this and wondering where the hell Charlie got her information. And what she was playing at, calling our publisher for a comment.

Nothing on the site. "So she's digging, but she's not sure what she's looking for yet," I said the words aloud, though I didn't really mean to, my teeth closing over my bottom lip as my fingers floated up to loop my hair into knots.

"What's up?" Kyle stretched one arm along the back of the couch from his spot in the far corner.

"Charlie. Somehow she found out about Burke." I tapped one finger on the edge of my phone. "And she knows I know about the murder, or she wouldn't have tipped her hand. Fantastic. Charlie being a pain in the ass is about the last thing I need this week."

"What'd she say?"

"Nothing publicly yet." I waved the phone, more annoyed with Charlie than I could remember being in a long time. She knew Andrews had it in for Bob. "But she called Andrews and got him all hot and bothered. Bob and I get to start Monday with an ass-chewing from the jackass who calls himself our publisher."

"Always nice to have something to look forward to." Kyle smiled. I knew he was trying to lighten my mood, but Andrews was the last nail in this weekend's coffin. There was nothing for it.

"For months, I've worked like a dog to keep Andrews in his cave and get this wedding off the ground, and now they're both going to fall apart over this one dead guy? I never met Mitch Burke, but I don't love him right now, I have to tell you."

Kyle chuckled. "From what I've found on this dude, I'd be surprised if many people did."

"Tell me about it—I hit on several folks this weekend who could well and truly be our killer. But I have nothing concrete."

"Welcome to my world." Kyle flashed a sad smile, and my heart squeezed. He'd been working on the Caccione family for years, even before he'd come to Richmond. With what Kyle suspected about Joey, it had to be like rubbing a whole stack of disgusting in his face, me dating him.

"I like mine better, generally speaking." I smiled, and got a chuckle from him. "So."

"So." He pinched his lips into a thin line, clearing his throat and trying for a smile that came across as more of a wince. "No surprise, the Cacciones run the most extensive bookmaking operation on the Eastern Seaboard. From Bangor to Miami, if you're betting on something, chances are you're doing it through them."

"Wow. And Burke?"

"Was a frequent guest of the Caccione bookmakers, according to our surveillance." Kyle propped his left foot on the opposite knee and ran one hand through his still-unruly curls.

"In debt?" Any moron knows owing the mafia money could land you in a wine barrel.

Kyle shook his head. "Plenty of money in all his accounts."

"Huh." My foot ceased bouncing. The first symptom of a gambling addiction is usually being broke. The house always wins, eventually. "I wonder how." My fingers returned to worrying my hair, my brain flipping this new puzzle piece every which way, trying to make it fit.

No dice. I added it to my pile and looked up at Kyle.

"How does a gambler avoid the poorhouse?" I reached into a basket on the end table for a pen and notebook, scribbling that down. "Maybe he owed someone else money?"

"No large deposits from mystery sources that I noticed," Kyle said. "But I can check again."

"And his credit report was clean?"

"As a preacher's sheets."

I wiggled my eyebrows. "I suppose that depends on your preacher." Kyle's grandfather was a Baptist minister—who had five children.

"Gross."

"You started it."

"Anyway."

I giggled, poising my pen again. "Who else didn't like our guy?" I held my breath, thankful I'd made it through the bookmaking discussion without some sort of attack on Joey. Maybe we could get away from the Cacciones for a bit.

"He filed a police report last year about threatening messages he was getting. They were coming from a woman in the Generals' front office."

I snickered at the hypocrisy of Burke complaining about threats, considering his history with Parker, then focused on Kyle's words. "Another woman. How did this guy have time to do anything else?"

"Huh?" Kyle's brow furrowed.

"I used to think Parker was Richmond's Casanova. Before he met Mel, that is. But this Burke fellow—I bet his bedpost has been notched right the hell into sawdust."

"Sex—or something related to it—is often a good motive for murder," Kyle said.

"Money, too." I scribbled a note about the woman who worked for the Generals. Maybe Parker knew something about her that Kyle's file might not show.

"Indeed," Kyle said. "So who are these other women? And how'd you find them?"

I told him about Ella Jane and Celia, and his eyebrows disappeared into his hairline when I got to the part about Celia's conversation with the chef. "That's pretty damning, Nichelle. Does the sheriff know about that?"

"I told him. But things out there are weird. I can't put my finger on why, and my gut says this guy is a good cop, but...everyone knows everyone else, and I can't figure out where Sammons and his family slash staff fit into the sheriff's social circles. I don't know what he'll do with it. Like, he told me this morning that Celia's mom—Dale Sammons's only sibling—committed suicide right before their father died."

The widening of Kyle's blue eyes said he wasn't sure he bought that either. "Convenient."

"That's what I thought. I mean, if Sammons is our guy, maybe what happened to his sister could help us figure out what happened to Burke."

"Maybe. Without the coroner's report on Burke, it's hard to say anything, but it's certainly worth some research."

Research. "Oh!" I dove for my bag, retrieving the fingerprint copies and handing them over. "While you're volunteering for stuff, could you run these and see if you get a hit?"

He tucked them into his pocket. "Where'd they come from?"

I told him the laptop story and he shook his head. "Watch yourself."

"Trying. But I'm fighting the bad guys and the clock. I'd like to drive back out there and see what I might have missed. Maybe find someone to talk to about Miss Sammons while I'm at it."

"Can I come with?"

My heart skipped, Joey's face flashing through my head. He wouldn't love that. But Parker and Mel had to come first this week.

I smiled. "Absolutely. Let me get through my ass-chewing and check my calendar in the morning. I'll call you."

* * *

Kyle left with a promise to call if he found anything earth shattering, and more assurances that we'd figure it out. I brewed a cup of coffee and opened my laptop, coming down to the wire on this story I really didn't want to write.

"I've made an executive decision, Darcy," I said as she flopped her head onto my bare foot. "If I ever get married, I'm eloping. Surely it'd be harder for dead people to find me at an unscheduled event."

I opened my file on Burke, skimming the info I had. Couldn't say he had mafia ties, even with the photo evidence, unless I wanted to risk a lawsuit. That kind of accusation about someone not alive to defend themselves better come with an autobahn-sized paper trail. Plus, I didn't know what Charlie had.

So I'd hit the highlights of Burke's career and the open police investigation. I would not mention Parker unless or until the police did. Period.

The Virginia baseball community is mourning the loss of one of its own this morning: Former Virginia Tech pitching star Mitch Burke. Augusta County authorities are investigating the circumstances of Burke's death and the discovery of his remains, and declined to comment on the record about an open investigation.

There. I reread the lead a half-dozen times. All the facts, plus right up there at the top I said Rutledge didn't comment. Surely that would earn me a few trust points with the sheriff.

I added more about Burke's career with the Generals, plus a space for a statement from his family, who I'd have to call in the morning (Joy. Asking people in mourning to talk to me was the suckiest part of my job), and Rutledge's plea for people with information to call his office.

Nice. Neutral. I attached it to an email to Bob and clicked into my browser, the thing with Sammons's sister, plus Franklin's comments about Sammons, swirling in my head. I had less than no experience with cold case investigations. Probably hunting a toothpick in a pine forest.

But that didn't stop me from wanting to try—for Celia, maybe for Mitch Burke, and certainly for Parker.

First stop: the local paper. Yes, it had closed the year before. Lucky for me, the internet is forever.

Though a few quick clicks proved that the paper's website (and archives) were indeed gone, a search of the county's online birth and death certificate database and a trip to the Wayback machine got me a screen full of coverage of Jolene Sammons's death.

"Thirty-six. Too young," I muttered as I looked at her long wavy red hair and inviting smile. The cutline said the photo was taken a month before she died. She didn't look depressed, though I knew that didn't mean much. Many people are good at hiding problems, especially in the age of social media.

I scrolled through the coverage.

The first story said she was discovered unresponsive in her own bed.

Six days later, a follow up said the coroner's report showed respiratory depression as cause of death, and toxic levels of oxycodone hydrochloride in Jolene's blood.

Four days after that, Rutledge's predecessor closed the file, stamping Jolene's death a suicide. The story quoted him as saying Oxycontin had been prescribed to her father, who'd died two nights after her.

"Ten days. They looked at it for ten days, Darce."

And it didn't appear from my screen that they looked terribly hard.

Maybe Kyle and I could remedy that. I could tell from the clips there'd been an autopsy, and if they used the Richmond lab now, they probably used it then too. If I could get hold of the file, maybe we could find something they missed.

Next on my list was chef Alexei. I clicked to the Calais webpage and found his full name, then up to the Google bar to see if the internet had anything past what Facebook could offer.

More than a thousand hits. On a tiny country vineyard chef? I scrolled.

An Instagram feed chock full of food porn, a Facebook page locked down to friends only. Normal.

Fifty-four video links: not so much.

I clicked the first and found a younger, less round Alexei lined up in a cavernous kitchen listening to a tiny man in a not-tiny chef's hat bark orders in Russian. He stopped, and Alexei and the other chefs ran for individual cooking stations.

A Russian *Hell's Kitchen*?

I clicked through more clips, watching the Calais chef prepare a second-place borscht, trays of exquisite sugar lace cookies, and a horrifying stew (by the facial expressions and volume of the little judge chef, who ended up cutting the only woman on the show even though he spit out Alexei's concoction).

Next clip.

No Alexei.

Huh? I scrolled back up, checking episode numbers with Google translate.

He didn't get voted off. In episode ten, the woman went home.

In eleven, she was back and Alexei was gone.

Why?

I clicked to news results and found a dozen articles from Moscow papers, all in the entertainment sections.

Staring at the type, my eyes started drifting shut. I copied two leads into the translator and got a word salad I needed to be more awake to un-toss.

Saving the links, I made a few notes and shut the computer just before one, taking Darcy out for her bedtime game of fetch before I crawled back under the covers trying not to think about what morning had in store. Settling into my pile of down pillows, I drifted off half-dreaming of Andrews yammering nonsense about cookies and stews and stealing wine.

19

"Who died?" Shelby asked as I stepped off the elevator into the newsroom Monday morning.

I glanced down at my black tank dress and cropped black jacket, my eyes coming to rest on my favorite Mary-Jane-style Jimmy Choos as a giggle burst from my lips. "I suppose this shows you how excited I am to have a meeting with Andrews first thing in the morning."

Shelby's head tipped to one side as she fell into step beside me. "What for?"

"Charlie." I practically spit the word. My story would be ready to go live on the web as soon as I could track down Burke's family and Bob gave the green light. As of thirty minutes ago, Charlie had nothing online, so hopefully I could still beat her to the punch and shut our publisher up. For today, at least.

I knew that as well as I knew my shoe size (Nine and a half US. My feet aren't what anyone would call dainty), Parker would be the sticking point. Andrews understood what a family the newsroom was, and he was just douchey enough to try to make me cast suspicion on my friend. I wouldn't. But at the same time, I didn't want to pull more heat onto Bob.

How to get around the publisher's demands without causing trouble for my boss had me twisting my hair into knots as I turned back to Shelby and filled my coffee cup. "Charlie called Andrews looking for a comment on a story I've had since Friday, but Bob and I decided not to run until today. And he'll take any excuse to bitch about either of us. He must be positively giddy to have us both in his crosshairs today." I pulled a bottle of sugar-free white mocha syrup from the cabinet above the sink and tipped it over the coffee, stirring in a little milk from the container I kept in the fridge and taking a sip.

Shelby laughed. "Tell me how you really feel about our head weasel."

"Rick Andrews isn't mammalian enough to be called a weasel. I've stepped in things I like better." I was so annoyed I didn't even care that on a normal day I wouldn't badmouth Andrews to anyone but maybe Bob, simply because it wasn't professional. To hell with it. He'd been a festering sore on our collective limbs for nearly a year, and I was about tired of killing myself to make him happy. I couldn't stop, because of Bob. But I didn't have to be nice and pretend I liked the little snot either.

Shelby nodded. "I'd love to see that in a tweet. Or a book."

I smiled, genuinely glad to have her around for the first time since I met her. "Stay tuned." I picked up my coffee, striding back to my desk.

Flipping my screen open, I clicked into my search bar and typed Richard Burke's name.

Google, don't fail me now.

The top hit was a bio. Click.

The victim's father had taken over his family's construction empire and spun it to follow his passion—BurCo was the only construction company in Virginia that specialized in restoration of historic properties. Exclusively.

Lucky for them, we had plenty of old buildings to go around.

I found a number and dialed, knowing Richard Burke probably wouldn't be in the office today but hoping someone could get him to call me.

A chirpy receptionist transferred me to the public relations desk when she heard the newspaper's name. "PR, this is Jonas," picked up on the third ring.

"Hi Jonas, this is Nichelle Clarke over at the *Telegraph*, and I'm working on a story about Mitch Burke for tomorrow's paper. I'm so sorry to have to call about this, but is there any way I could get in touch with the Burke family today? I'd like them to have a chance to talk about their son."

"The family isn't taking calls or visitors at this time, but I have a statement I can fax you if you'll give me the number."

I reeled it off and thanked him, smiling as I put the phone down. Easiest family talk I'd ever had to do about a murder.

I grabbed my coffee and the fax and hurried to Bob's office, tapping on the doorframe as I poked my head around it. "Morning, chief." Andrews wasn't due in for another fifteen minutes.

Bob sat back in his chair and sighed, gesturing to his monitor, which was dominated by my story on Burke. "Not a word in here about Grant."

I settled myself in my usual Virginia-Tech-orange velour armchair and crossed my legs at the knee, sipping my coffee. "There is not."

"Charlie called asking specifically about Parker, Nicey."

"So I hear."

"What does she know?" Bob leaned back in the chair and laced his fingers behind his head.

I met his hard gaze with one of my own. "I haven't the first damned clue. Not enough to go on air with it, is all I can tell you. She's fishing. And I'm not offering my friend up as a sacrifice because she might beat me on a story. I've been ahead of Charlie for months. I'm not afraid of her."

The crease in Bob's brow said he might be, which took a bit of the wind from my sails.

"We know there's a chance..." he began, his strained tone belying tried patience.

"No, we do not," I snapped, closing my eyes and hauling in a deep breath. Bob was being difficult, but he wasn't the actual enemy here. Just one hell of an irritating devil's advocate. "We actually know nothing anyone could prove. Here's the only thing I have for sure—Mitch Burke was a first-class dick, and a borderline disturbed one, at that. He had enemies by the truckload, including some with mafia ties, probably." I paused for a breath when Bob's eyes widened. "I'm sorry. I'm not trying to shout," I said, more controlled. "I also know Parker. He did. Not. Kill. Anyone." I punctuated the words with a pound of my fist on the arm of the chair. "I'm not saying in the paper and all over the damned internet that he might have, Bob. I'm just not."

"You're not what?" Melanie's voice came from the door and I felt my eyes fall shut as she stepped into the room. "Everything okay in here?"

She tucked her phone in her pocket with a smile and I realized she hadn't heard anything else. Phew.

"Just arguing tomorrow's headlines," I said.

She shook her head. "You have more passion for this job than anyone I've ever met."

I shrugged. "Keeps me out of trouble."

Bob snorted and I shot him a shut-up look. He straightened his face and turned to Melanie. "What can I do for you, Mel?"

"I have a couple of councilmen who want to use the paper to grandstand on the new ballpark proposal, and I'm having a hard time with it," she said. "On one hand, it is news. It's big news."

Bob nodded.

"But I'm getting a lot of pressure from both camps, and I don't want it to look like the paper is biased." Her lower lip disappeared between her teeth.

"That would be easier if you weren't, I suspect," Bob said.

My eyes volleyed between the two of them as Mel sighed.

"I'm trying to stay out of it and just do my job, but it's hard when Grant feels so strongly about something." Mel's eyebrows drew down and her tone gained a defensive edge. "And I agree with him. Progress is important, but so is history."

Bob ran one hand through his thinning white hair. "Listen, Melanie, every one of us has issues we know in our gut are right a certain way. This isn't any different than last year when they wanted to cut the funding for the inner-city after-school arts program. You knew it was wrong, but you reported the story fairly. Do it again here."

She sighed. "I suppose. Thanks, Bob. I'm a little all over the place right now."

"Of course you are. But you can do this. I wouldn't have hired you if you couldn't."

"Put a hard eye on it when I turn it in, okay?"

"Sure thing."

As she disappeared into the newsroom, Bob turned back to his monitor, tapping one finger on the edge of the keyboard. "This is good solid reporting, Nicey. It's a thousand percent impartial, except for the failure to mention Parker, and I know how hard that is for you." He gestured after Mel. "Boy is causing me all kinds of trouble this week."

I smiled. "He wouldn't do that on purpose."

"My point is this, kiddo: Think about what Melanie said. If you're really keeping his name out of it because of a lack of evidence, I'll run it like this. Andrews will live. But you need to ask yourself what it would look like if the dead guy had sent threatening letters about anyone else's fiancé last week, only to show up on the same property in a wine barrel less than forty-eight hours later."

I was still pondering that when Andrews stepped into the room and shut the door.

* * *

"Morning. I won't say good, because it isn't." Rick Andrews flashed an attempt at a withering look at each of us and stomped across the room to take the chair opposite mine.

"It's definitely Monday, but we all woke up this morning. Given the subject matter I work around, that's usually a good enough reason to be happy." I put all the sunshine I could muster into the words, mostly because I knew it would annoy the fire out of him.

He pursed his lips. "How lovely for you." Snide contempt practically dripped down his chin.

I widened my eyes and smiled my best clueless smile at Andrews, which set him to muttering and scowling. And it hadn't even been five minutes.

I shot Bob a wink as he coughed over a snicker.

"What can we do for you this morning, Rick?" Bob asked.

"You can explain to me why in the sam hell you two were out celebrating the wedding of a murder suspect all weekend, apparently in the thick of the action, yet Channel Four has beaten us to the story." He crossed his legs at the knee and swung his polished black loafer back and forth, a quarter inch of fishbelly white shin peeking out above his dark sock.

"I haven't heard the sheriff name a suspect, have you, Bob?" I asked.

Bob shook his head. "Don't believe I have."

"Then why is Charlie Lewis convinced our sports columnist is headed for prison?"

I spread my hands. "I honestly have no idea. To my knowledge, they haven't even questioned anyone in the wedding party." I wasn't fool enough to think that would hold with Charlie on this trail, but it was technically true.

Andrews' gaze flicked to Bob, who nodded. "Nichelle has been all over this since Friday night."

"Then why hasn't it been in the paper?" Andrews practically roared.

"It happened forty miles outside our local coverage area, and the only thing we know for sure is that a body was found in a wine barrel. There's no coroner's report yet. No cause of death. No solid suspects. I don't even have a police report," I said. "I have no idea what the heck Charlie is up to or where she's getting her information, but I promise you one thing: If she had anything on this, especially anything explosive about Parker that would make me and the *Telegraph* look bad, she'd have run it already."

Andrews tipped his head to one side, moving his right index finger to his chin. I talked faster.

"The sheriff is still piecing together what happened to this guy. There's no story here yet. The facts I have are only good enough for 'suspected foul play' with a few details. She called you because she's fishing. Don't fall for it."

I sat back and took a breath, my eyes skipping over Bob, who nodded so slightly half a blink would've obscured it. Andrews folded his hands in his lap, his face flicking from indecision to annoyance. He didn't like me, and really had it in for Bob. But if there was one thing a narcissist hated above all else, it was being made a fool.

Bob cleared his throat. "I've been wondering all night why Charlie didn't call me. I run the newsroom. Parker works for me. It seems she thinks you're gullible enough to force Nichelle to give up an exclusive, Rick."

"Well, she's wrong," Andrews snapped.

"Bob has a story with the facts—only the facts—as we know them," I said. "We should post that before the obituary hits, and the family has scheduled it for tomorrow. We're still ahead on this because the local paper out there shuttered last year, and none of the TV stations were close enough to get wind of what was going on this weekend, so they're playing catch up. That's all Charlie is doing. Trying to catch up. Think about what it would do to our ad sales if we accuse Parker of something so heinous."

Andrews nodded, and I knew I had him. Appeal to the bottom line. "The facts don't support it. Not today."

He swung the foot some more, tapping his index finger against his lip before he spoke. "Put it on the web. Have Ryan tweet and post it to our Facebook with an 'exclusive' slammer." He stood, turning a glare on each of us in turn. "But if the TV station ends up with something on this story we don't have, you'll both be sorry."

I pinched my lips together and nodded, wise enough to stay quiet since we'd won the battle at hand.

Now all I had to do was make sure Charlie didn't have anything—or that I beat her to the headline if she did. Simple (not).

Andrews strode out, pulling the door shut hard. Bob sighed, dropping his head into his hands.

"You ever miss our nice normal drug wars?" he asked the carpet.

"I do today." I stood, resting one hand on the doorknob. "Don't worry, chief. I have a whole sled team of dogs in this, and I'm not letting anyone down."

I had five hours before the noon broadcast to make sure of it.

20

My brain flicking through what circumstantial things I knew, I stepped out of Bob's office and smack into another human. My bag flew out of my hand and scattered lip glosses and tampons across the mottled brown seventies chic carpet.

"I'm so sorry!" I stooped to grab the bag, blowing my hair out of my face. "That's twice in a week. I don't know what's wrong with me."

"Looks to me like you're in a hurry." The honey-butter voice stopped my hand cold as I closed it around an Urban Decay lipstick tube.

I raised my head slowly to find the warmest brown eyes I'd ever seen shining above a grin that could give Parker a run for his charisma.

"Hey, Miss Clarke."

"Troy!" I shot to my feet and yanked him into a hug. "What on Earth? And why didn't I know about it?"

He swooped all my stuff into his long fingers and stood, dropping it back into the bag when I opened it.

"Mr. Parker got me an internship. I'll be here all summer." He grinned. "We thought it'd be fun to surprise you. I want to work in TV, sure, but I'm not going to get very far without knowing how to find a story, am I?"

"You are not." I couldn't have lost the smile threatening to crack my face open if I'd wanted to. Troy Wright grew up in a rough neighborhood and lost his older brother, Darryl, a couple years back in the drug wars Bob had just mentioned. A bright kid with a passion for sports and a personality that screamed ESPN, he'd stayed on the straight and narrow, winning a National Merit scholarship and becoming the first person in his family to go to college.

"How's school?" I asked, slinging the bag over my shoulder and motioning for him to follow me to my little ivory cubicle.

"Great." He fell into step beside me. "I got A's in both my journalism classes this year, and the professor in the freshman reporting class offered me a position at the campus paper in the fall. He gave me special permission to get credit for working here this summer too—usually they don't let you do internships for credit until you're a junior."

I dropped my bag under my desk and grinned. "They do when you're an overachiever."

He chuckled and leaned one thin shoulder against the edge of my cube. "And you wouldn't know anything about overachieving—shot, stabbed, surgery, all manner of crazy folks. But you get your story." He shook his head. "My momma prays for you every night."

My breath stilled for half a second. "That means more to me than you could possibly know." I had massive heaps of respect for Joyce Wright, a single mom who'd raised two boys working as a housekeeper and seamstress after she booted their deadbeat father out of the house. Losing her oldest son had nearly killed her, but she was so proud of Troy it practically seeped from her pores. "How is your mother? I haven't talked to her in a while. Tell her I promise I'll remedy that soon."

He nodded. "She'll be so glad to hear from you. She won't ever forget what you did for Darryl, Miss Clarke—and neither will I." He cleared his throat, ducking his head.

"Nichelle. Please. And it was truly my pleasure."

He nodded, wiping at his nose. "I saw the trial coverage. Couldn't bring myself to go down there. But y'all really got the bastards, huh?"

I nodded. "DonnaJo is a hell of a prosecutor. They'll stay right where they are for a long time. Things a little quieter in your neighborhood these days? I haven't seen a murder out there in months."

"It's almost like they've figured out shooting other folks only makes it more likely they'll get shot themselves."

I flipped open a notebook and scribbled that down. Interesting, the violence that had plagued Southside for so many years dying a rather sudden death. I wasn't sure what to make of it, but as soon as I had time, I'd ask around. What a fantastic feel-good feature—and I wasn't exactly swimming in those, working at the crime desk.

I glanced at my calendar and saw that I was due in court at noon for an assault case involving a football player from Richmond American University. Damn. DonnaJo had been prepping for months—I couldn't skip.

Before I could ask Troy to elaborate any more, my phone rang. He raised both hands and stepped backward. "Don't let me interfere with your work, Lois Lane." His dark eyes took on a teasing sparkle and I grinned, my spirits bouncing back from the depths of a meeting with Andrews to something resembling normal. I liked Troy. A lot. It would be fun to have him around for the summer. I laid a hand on the phone and nodded. "We'll catch up later?"

"You got it." He pointed to my coffee. "Where'd you find that?"

I waved in the direction of the break room. "Go that way past Parker's office, and look for the ugly orange cabinets on the right."

He nodded and stepped away, and I snatched up the phone just before it clicked over to voicemail. "Crime desk, this is Clarke."

The other end of the line was silent for half a second, followed by a heavy sigh.

"Hello?" I leaned my elbow on the desk, retrieving my pen. Eight times out of eight, when people call a reporter and are reluctant to talk, what they have to say is pretty damned interesting.

"Hey."

My stomach twisted into a knot. Just one word, but I knew my favorite detective well enough to read in his tone that whatever followed was going to be bad. And I had a hunch I knew what it concerned.

"Good morning, Aaron," I choked out, pausing to clear my throat. "What's up?"

"I've got a Sheriff Rutledge in my office, Nichelle, and I'm wondering if you'll do me a favor and bring your friend Grant Parker down here to talk to us."

My eyes fell shut, the plastic of the handset biting into my fingers as they closed tighter around it.

"Y'all are wrong, Aaron," I whispered.

"I'm sorry, Nichelle. I can't tell you how sorry. I know the timing is shitty, but we have evidence here we can't ignore." He sighed. "You know how this works. It'll be easier all the way around if you can get him to come to us, but Landers will be there with a warrant in an hour if you can't."

"I'll see you in forty-five minutes," I bit out. "Do me one favor and don't call Charlie—or anybody else—until I've had a chance to talk to you."

Another sigh. "Nicey, I know he's your friend..."

"I'm good at what I do, Detective White. And so are you. Just trust me."

Long pause. "Text me when you get here and I'll meet you downstairs."

I cradled the phone and bit my lip, curling my hands into fists and pulling in enough deep breaths to keep from chucking my stapler across the room.

Whatever was going on here, Parker didn't have anything to do with it.

I couldn't believe it.

I wouldn't.

Not with nothing more than a few emails and some circumstantial crap to go on.

So how was I going to convince Parker of that when I'd been elected to drag him through an Aaron White interrogation?

21

I found Parker at his desk, phone pinched between his cheek and good shoulder, taking lightning-fast notes and grunting "uh-huh" at thirty-second intervals. I paused in the doorway and he waved me in, pointing to the gray chair on my side of his desk.

"But Dale—" He fell quiet, tapping the pen on his notepad. "Agree to disagree. But in that case, why not use someone with a better reputation?" he asked, his hand poised to write again. "Got it. Thank you, sir."

He plunked the phone back into the cradle and flashed me the famous megawatt grin. "Morning, sunshine. You look very Audrey Hepburn today. What's the occasion?"

I bit my lip. His tone was so...up. What karmic contest did I lose to be the one to bring it down?

He ducked his head and caught my eye. "Nichelle?"

I opened my mouth, but couldn't force my lips around the words.

"Oh, God." Parker leaned back in his chair, toying with the strap on his sling. "What now? Did the baker get the flu? The flowers come in dead?" The color drained from his face. "Did Mel change her mind?"

A laugh escaped my lips despite the utterly shitty reason I was sitting across from my friend. I shook my head, giving him a few more seconds of thinking a problem with the wedding was his biggest worry.

"Mel is over at City Hall listening to people argue about the new ballpark. Potential new ballpark."

He nodded and opened his mouth, but I plowed on before I lost my voice again. "And as far as I know, everything is golden for this weekend. But..." I faltered, clearing my throat. "Parker..."

I had to tell people hard things on the regular. You'd think I'd be better at it after so many years. But Parker wasn't just anyone.

"What's up? I'm not sure I've ever seen you look like that when you weren't mired in some insane web of a story that would end up landing you in the hospital." He paused. "You're not, are you? Because one of us getting shot the week of the wedding is enough." He winked.

I would take that bullet in place of what I was about to tell him in two taps of a Louboutin.

"Parker, I just got a call from Aaron White at the PD. They want me to bring you down there. They have some questions about Mitch Burke."

Parker blinked. "What kind of questions?"

I sighed. "Bob showed Chris Landers the emails he got from Burke last week. He was worried about Melanie. The police think—" I sighed. "They think the emails give you motive, Parker."

Parker's face went blank. "Motive." His eyes fell shut, his voice going monotone. "So what do we do now?"

"I know you didn't do this." I leaned forward and laid a hand on his arm. "But Aaron has to ask. It's his job."

Parker nodded, his face more wooden than I'd ever seen it. "Can you drive?"

"Of course." I stood, pulling my bag over my shoulder and taking his arm.

"Nichelle? Does Mel know about this?"

"No," I said, leading him to the elevator. "Chin up, Captain Charisma. We'll fix this. I'm not letting all the work I've put into this wedding go to waste." I smiled up at him as the elevator doors closed.

He nodded, staying quiet until we were turning out of the *Telegraph*'s garage.

"I didn't hurt Burke." His voice was low, with a hard edge that made it sound like someone else was talking. "I wanted to. But I couldn't find him."

* * *

My fingers tightened on the steering wheel. "You—you couldn't find him?"

Parker's golden head dropped into his hands. "God, Nichelle. Did Bob show you? What he said? I've never been so...Angry's not the right word. Furious? I'm not sure that covers it, even. I think I went a little crazy for a few minutes. I jumped into my car and stormed over to Burke's loft."

Oh.

Shit.

I swerved into a parking lot and cut the engine. "You what?"

"I went over there. Wouldn't you? Bob told me the whole story, how he'd been sending these BS emails about me for years, and Bob had the tech guys look into it and decided to ignore him. He's tried a hundred times to make it hard for me to do my job—having him in the Generals' PR office was the only thing I didn't like about this gig for a long time. But I got around it because the coaches and players and Dale, they all like me, so I just didn't deal with the PR folks. Burke purposely left me out of the loop on two press releases a few years ago, and the second time Dale almost canned him."

My brain was still back on Parker going off to Burke's home in a blind rage.

Talk about damn to the hundredth power.

He was still rambling. Focus, Nichelle. "I really thought we were past all this. It was such a long time ago," Parker muttered to the floorboard.

My eyes fell shut. Something in his voice said there was more than a few lost baseball games between them. "What was so long ago?"

"Mari." The single syllable held so much sorrow, I reached for Parker's hand. If only I had clue one what the hell he was talking about.

"I think I'm behind on background, here, Parker," I stage-whispered.

He let out a shuddering breath. "Burke's sister. Younger sister, by a year. A couple of the guys decided it'd be a good way to get under his skin to ask her out. Having his sister cheering against him would mess with his head, we thought, with our high-school understanding of sports psychology."

I nodded, my stomach closing around the Pop-Tarts I'd scarfed in the car a lifetime ago. Something told me I wouldn't like where this was going.

"So I 'bumped into her' at this pizza place near her school. Asked her to a movie."

"Oh, Parker." I sighed.

He nodded, not looking at me. "She turned me down. Not because of her brother—she didn't know who I was. Because, she said, I wasn't her type."

I arched an eyebrow. I'd bet the number of women who would turn Parker down flat could be counted on one finger. If you counted Miss Burke.

"She was pretty, but not super into her looks." He leaned his head against the back of the seat, his face softening as he talked. "She didn't need a ton of makeup and hairspray. And she was so quiet, but she had the sweetest voice when you listened to her."

I watched his profile, my ears tickling at the familiar softness in his tone.

Because it was how he talked about Mel.

"I kept after her, and the more times she told me to beat it, the more I liked her. She was funny and honest and didn't care what anyone else thought. Smart too."

I glanced at the clock, wanting to ask where the "but" in this story was coming, yet not wanting to pull him from the memories that were clearly all he could see at the moment.

"Three weeks of begging, and she finally agreed to dinner." He sighed. "I fell for her, Clarke. Harder than I thought I'd ever fall for a girl in my whole life."

"Why is that a bad thing?"

"It was a wonderful thing. My dad and coach kept saying she was distracting me, but I played better that spring than I ever had. I was happy, and it came through in my game." His hands went back to his head. "We won State that year."

Ah. Against Burke. "Did she find out why you'd asked her out?"

He shook his head. "She..." His Adam's apple bobbed with a hard swallow as he shook his head. "She died. In an accident. I couldn't save her. Mitch never forgave me." The last word nearly disappeared into a half-sob, and he put a hand over his eyes and took a few deep breaths.

Oh. My. God.

I wanted the rest of that story, but wasn't sure what kind of rabbit hole it would lead to, and the clock said I had to move. There'd be time to pry after we got through this police interview. I patted Parker's arm and put the car back in gear. "Oh, Parker. I'm so sorry."

Fighting to keep at least part of my attention on traffic, I white-knuckled the steering wheel. This would up everyone's conviction that Parker had motive. It's possible to explain away threatening letters from an old sports rival. Even messages as horrifying as the ones Bob got about Mel. A joke gone wrong, a prank in ridiculously poor taste. But if Burke had spent years blaming Parker for his sister's death, Melanie had been in very real danger. And that made it more likely that Parker—who knew this other part of the story—might kill Burke to protect her.

I glanced over to find pleading emerald eyes fixed on my profile. "I didn't do this, Nichelle. I never saw him."

"I believe you." And I still did. But could I convince Aaron? Right then I wasn't sure I'd be able to convince my own mother. The fact that Kyle was on our side for the moment was just about all I had going for me.

Kyle.

I stopped at a red light and dug in my bag for my phone. "Let me see if I've got one more miracle rescue in me," I mumbled, patting Parker's hand.

Truth be told, the wedding had just officially become the least of my worries.

* * *

Kyle must've made every light and sped too, because he was pacing in front of Police Headquarters when we pulled up.

"I'm not sure I can pull this off, Nichelle." He ran one hand through his burnished bronze curls.

"You can bluff with the best of them, Agent Miller. All I need you to do is misdirect the conversation such that they believe there's an open investigation into Calais Vineyards and you're interested in this case." My smile was more confident than I felt.

Kyle rolled his eyes at me and nodded to Parker, who still looked dazed. "How you holding up, Grant?"

Parker shook his head. "Saturday's supposed to be the best day of my life." He snorted, and my heart squeezed at the broken note in his voice.

"It will be," I said. "Today's only Monday. We got this." I glanced at Kyle. "Don't we?"

"I'm going to give it my level best shot."

I gestured to the door with one hand and took Parker's arm with the other. "Aaron's waiting inside."

I hadn't had time to tell Kyle much, just that I needed his help keeping Parker out of a cell. But my gut and years of experience with Aaron told me Parker's best bet was to tell them about his relationship with Burke's sister before they dug it up. It was almost always better to be honest with the police—when you were innocent, especially.

"Nichelle." Aaron waved from the other side of the metal detectors, raising an eyebrow when he saw Kyle behind me. "Agent Miller. Grant."

The men shook hands all around and Aaron gave everyone an apologetic shrug as he punched the elevator button.

"This isn't awkward or anything, right?" I chirped, drawing a chuckle from everyone but Parker, who only managed a half-smile.

"I'm sorry to have to drag you down here." Aaron was looking at Parker, but his face told me he was more focused on wondering why Kyle was in the elevator with us. I don't suppose too many people bring a federal agent to a police interview, to be fair.

Parker nodded. "Nichelle tells me you're just doing your job."

"But that doesn't make it feel less insulting," Aaron said with a nod.

"Just a few things that need clearing up," I said, pleased that the confidence in my voice didn't falter. Aaron caught that, I knew. And if he walked into the room with his mind leaning toward misunderstanding, this thing would be a lot easier.

He nodded and put a hand in front of the elevator doors when they opened, waving us off in front of him. "My office," he said. I led Parker and Kyle that way, wondering how the four of us plus I'm sure Landers and Sheriff Rutledge would fit in Aaron's cluttered little closet of an office.

I strode past the rows of cubicles, feeling every eye in the room following us. Good cops were way nosier than any reporter ever thought about being. Well. Most any.

I rounded the corner and saw that Aaron had indeed squished four chairs between his desk and the wall. I might bump knees with Landers, long legged as we both were, but I kind of liked that Kyle would have to stand. His height would make him that much more imposing if everyone else was sitting.

Landers nodded a hello, not bothering to hide his surprise when Kyle stepped aside so Aaron could shut the door. "What're you doing here?" he asked.

"Tactful as ever, Detective," I said.

"The location of the body discovery is interesting." Kyle shrugged, and I bit down on a giggle, wondering how many times he'd rehearsed that in his head. I shot him a wink while everyone else turned to Parker.

"Mr. Parker, I'm Jim Rutledge, the sheriff out in Augusta." He drummed his fingers on the brim of his giant hat, which rested across his knees. "I understand you're getting married this weekend." He shot me a look that said he wasn't happy I'd played dumb about this connection, and he knew I'd done it on purpose. Yay.

I smiled at the sheriff as I put reassuring pressure on Parker's arm. Small talk was a good sign. They didn't know much, or they'd start with questions instead of trying to get him comfortable enough to feel chatty.

"Yes sir." Parker cleared his throat. "We're so sorry about the tragedy out at Dale's place last weekend, but everyone so far has told us there's no need to relocate the wedding. I'd like to know how you feel about that."

"I can't imagine why you'd need to. Unless being there makes you uncomfortable for some reason." His eyes strayed to the sling on Parker's arm, but the words were calculated. Tread carefully, Parker.

Parker wasn't stupid. "I'm sad for the Burke family's loss, but that's it," he said, meeting the sheriff's gaze straight on.

Landers opened the folder on his knees. "According to Bob Jeffers, the victim didn't like you very much, Mr. Parker."

My eyes followed Parker's to the emails.

"He didn't seem to, no."

"Why is that?" From the sheriff, who sat back with an interested smile.

My brain flicked to Ella Jane. Didn't seem like the sheriff was too big a Burke fan himself. I pinched my lips together to keep from asking him about his daughter's relationship with the victim and the potential conflict of interest there. Rural departments often have cases concerning people the cops know—it's one of the things you just have to accept if you live in a smaller jurisdiction. And this wasn't the time or place for that question.

Parker sighed. "It started with baseball. I beat him in a couple of important games back in high school and college." He cut a sideways look at me and I nodded ever so slightly.

"It's hard for me to fathom someone writing threats this graphic over a decades-old sports rivalry," Landers said. "I told Bob Jeffers as much last week."

"Burke didn't have a reputation for being the most stable guy around," the sheriff said, and Kyle nodded.

"Or the most reliable," he added.

Kyle's tone made it sound like he knew more than what passing interest would dictate about Burke, and Aaron's face said he didn't miss that. Good. That's exactly why I wanted Kyle in the room—if my local guys and the BFE sheriff thought the feds were investigating the victim, Parker wouldn't look so interesting.

"He was...different," Parker said, an I'm-not-speaking-ill-of-the-dead way of calling Burke an ass that nobody in the room missed.

Landers rested his elbows on his knees and bent his head to catch Parker's eye. "Explain this to me, Mr. Parker. Why was Mitch Burke so focused on you? And why did my forensic team find your fingerprints all over the door to his apartment this morning?"

Landers's tone was low. Dangerous. He knew something he wasn't saying. I glanced at Aaron.

"Marilyn." Parker sat back and opened his arms. Nothing to hide, Detective.

Landers relaxed his posture in response. Watching body language was fascinating stuff.

Aaron looked confused, and Rutledge laced his fingers behind his head and nodded to him. "Vic's sister. Killed in an accident when she was sixteen, my research says."

"His parents already lost one child?" Aaron shuddered.

Parker, who was still nursing Tony and Ashton through the loss of their son, flinched at the mention of Burke's parents. "They were devastated." His emerald eyes searched an aerial photo of the city that covered most of the wall behind Aaron's head, taking on a faraway memory-lane sheen. Everyone in the room leaned in.

Parker shook his head, flicking moisture from the corner of his left eye. "She said she felt free for the first time in her life. Wanted to do all the things she'd read about and daydreamed about and never tried. Growing up with all that money sounded great to me, but to hear Marilyn tell it, the restrictions that came with it were stifling. Not worth it. She'd had enough."

Landers opened his mouth, but thought better of speaking as Parker went on. "It was a Sunday. We went skinny dipping, made love in a field, climbed a mountain—she was seriously up for anything. Wanted to go for a walk after dinner. It was so cool out. Weird for July, even at night. She was wearing a sundress and this little blue sweater. We got to talking and didn't realize how far we'd gone until we were way out by the train tracks. She hopped up on the rail, walking along it like a balance beam. I kept telling her to get down, but she was laughing, calling me a chicken. I swear I begged her not to go out on the bridge. She said she'd always wanted to, and she was teasing that the rush was better than sex, telling me I had work to do—" His voice cracked and the lawmen in the room exchanged uneasy glances. None of us wanted to hear what came next.

"A train? Jesus, Parker. I'm so sorry." I'm not sure the words made it out loud enough for him to hear them.

He sniffled. "She was right in the middle of the bridge when we heard the whistle. She was wearing these ridiculous shoes," he shot me a look, "and she couldn't run. It was a forty-foot drop to a rocky creek bed below. She screamed..." He put his hands over his ears like he could still hear it.

I put a hand on his back and Kyle laid one on his shoulder. Landers shook his head, speechless for the first time since I met him.

"So Burke blamed you because you were with her." The sheriff didn't bother with the question inflection at the end of his sentence.

"That would certainly explain these." Aaron waved to the folder full of emails and sat back with a heavy sigh. "Damn."

Parker pulled in a hitching breath. "I knew Mitch hated me. For a long time, I hated myself. I pushed so hard, trying to make her proud of me. But I took everything that went wrong in my life as punishment. For not protecting her. My shoulder. The fact that I never felt that way about another girl. It was all just what I got for not being able to help her."

"You're in love with your fiancé?" Landers asked, and I widened my eyes his way. What kind of question was that?

Parker nodded. "I never thought it'd happen for me again, you know? I guess I'd decided people only get one. And then Mel...she's amazing."

"So Burke threatening her," Landers cast a disgusted look at the papers in his lap before he returned his eyes to Parker, "that's why you went to his home, banging on the door and screaming obscenities? The lady down the hall described you pretty well."

Parker spread his hands. "Look, gentlemen, I'm not proud of my temper fit, but when Bob showed me those emails—I mean, I knew Burke had been after me for a lot of years, but...whatever. He couldn't possibly be as mad at me as I was at myself, you know? But I knew from way back that he was kind of messed up. Marilyn told me a story once about a stray cat that I'll spare you. Suffice to say, I hadn't been as scared as I was reading those in years. Not since I stood there that night watching that train come and knowing there wasn't a damned thing I could do."

Landers hit on that. "But this time, there was something you could do. You knew where to find Burke."

That was his best moving-in-for-the-confession voice. I patted Parker's arm.

"But I didn't. Find him. He never came to the door, and he wasn't at the ballpark, and by the time I got through looking those two places, I had regained some measure of sanity. I went to gym and blew off some steam, and then I went back to the office and picked Melanie up and stayed with her. We were leaving the next morning to go to Dale's for the rehearsal anyway."

Something tickled the back of my brain, but I couldn't pin it down. I focused on Aaron. If he wasn't convinced Parker had done anything wrong, I still had time to figure this mess out.

"And what time did you arrive at Mr. Sammons's place?" the sheriff asked.

"We stopped at Sugar Shack for breakfast. Mel said she'd had it with low carb. Probably ten? Dale's niece showed us the cabin and we took a walk, then had some lunch." Parker smiled. "It was a nice day."

"And when did you first see Mr. Burke?" Rutledge asked. He tried for nonchalant, but he wasn't nearly as good at that as Aaron.

Parker shrugged. "I didn't. I told you, I didn't find him. I kept watching for his truck to turn up at Dale's, but it never did. I watched Melanie all weekend—even when I wasn't with her, I made sure she was safe. I went for a run Saturday morning, but I stayed where I could see the cabin. Until Nichelle told me he was gone."

I was so relieved to hear that I almost yelped when he said it, but managed to keep quiet.

There was that tickle again. What? I closed my eyes and tried to focus, but not too hard. Trying to grab an elusive thought only ever made it float further away from me.

I let the conversation around me fade into background noise. The sheriff kept dogging Parker about his whereabouts, and Parker kept the same calm, even tone in his answers.

Burke.

Burke wasn't at his apartment Thursday afternoon. Or at work, Parker said.

Nobody I'd talked to had seen him at the vineyard Friday.

Hulk discovered the body because he was checking the wine.

How often would one do such a thing?

Leaping Louboutins.

My eyes flew open and I shot a hand up.

"Nichelle? You okay?" Aaron's Virginia drawl had an interested uptick in octave.

"When was the last time anyone saw Burke? Y'all keep asking when Parker saw him, but what if Parker couldn't find him because he was already dead?"

22

Parker's chiseled jaw went slack and everyone else in the room fell quiet. Kyle found his voice first. "Sheriff? You have a time of death yet?"

The sheriff shook his head. "The folks at the lab say it's tricky because of the alcohol. It does something or other to the tissue and they have to work that out." He shrugged. "I'm not a scientist."

"But it is possible that he was there for more than a day?" I leaned forward, excited about my little epiphany. Everything was going to be okay. Aaron wouldn't arrest Parker on a maybe.

"I suppose it is." The sheriff tapped his fingers on his hat again. "Hopefully I'll know more about that in the next few days."

"I have a friend at the lab," Kyle said. "I think. If she'll still talk to me, I'll see what I can do to push that along."

I shot him a grateful smile.

"So then we're done here?" I asked, moving to stand.

"For now," Rutledge said, shooting me a glare.

Aaron got up and moved to the door. "Thank you for coming in."

The sheriff followed Landers into the hallway, the two of them seemingly making plans to head over to the diamond. Kyle ushered Parker out the door, making small talk about baseball.

Aaron laid a hand on my arm when I moved to follow. "The county where this happened has limited resources, but the Burke family does not. I got special orders this morning to send my best homicide detective to accompany the sheriff on his investigation. But I got the distinct impression the investigation was mostly supposed to consist of this interview. Because I respect you, I'm telling you off the record, my gut says Richard Burke wants Grant Parker in a jail cell. I didn't hear enough today to warrant that, and I'll stand firm there. But if you know or can dig up anything on who might deserve that spot, it'd sure be a help—to me and your friend both."

I smiled and hugged him, dropping my arms and stepping back after a quick second. "Sorry. I just—" I swallowed over a lump in my throat. "Parker is a good guy, Aaron. He didn't do this. I know he didn't."

"Your gut is usually as accurate as mine. I'm going with you on that for now. But stay with this."

"I have no intention of doing anything else. Hope the rest of your week is quiet." I winked and turned for the door, then paused. "Aaron? Has Charlie called you about this?"

He settled in his chair and looked up, shaking his head. "Nope. I assumed she hadn't caught wind of it, with it being so far away and no reports on it. Though I don't expect it'll stay that way. Especially not if Burke doesn't get his way here."

I nodded a thank you and strode after Parker and Kyle, my brain clicking through possibilities. Charlie had called our publisher asking specifically about Parker, but she hadn't called Aaron about a murder investigation, and she had no story on it. What the hell did she know?

And what was she up to?

* * *

Kyle followed us back to the office, where we sent Parker upstairs with assurances that this would blow over and the wedding would be great. Kyle opened the passenger door of my little red SUV and climbed in, and I slid behind the wheel arching a questioning brow at him. "Where are we going?"

"I need more coffee, and we need to talk. So I'm thinking Thompson's."

I started the engine. "I always need more coffee."

"And the company is nice too." Kyle winked. "You don't have to say it."

I rolled my eyes. "Feeding your ego can be dangerous." I stopped at a light and turned to him. "But seriously—thank you for coming this morning. It means more to me than I can say."

"Why?"

The question caught me off guard and I shrugged, putting my foot back on the gas. "I guess I feel like you should have plenty of reasons to dislike me. Or at least to not be so nice. But you're always there when I need you. Thanks."

Kyle sighed. "Heavy for before my third cup of coffee." He ran a hand through his hair. "Listen, Nicey, you have to stop being so hard on yourself. You're not the girl I used to know—you're more confident, and so much stronger. But you're still such a damned perfectionist when it comes to how you think you're supposed to be. Why should I dislike you? Because you'd rather date someone else? I guess there are guys who would, but that's not me. You're my friend. Is there a situation you can fathom where you wouldn't be there for me if I called?"

I shook my head.

"Exactly."

I blinked hard as I pulled into a spot at the coffeehouse. "You're something else, you know it?" The throaty ring in the words put a furrow in his brow.

"What's up?"

I shook my head, brushing impatiently at my eyes. "Too much stress. Sorry."

"Don't apologize. That's part of what I was talking about. Why should you be sorry my eloquent little speech moved you to tears?" He sat back and puffed out his chest and I giggled, swatting his arm before I grabbed my bag and opened my door.

"Thank you. Again."

"I like to make you laugh."

I held the door for him and followed him to the counter, paying for his latte before he could dig out his wallet. "You're doing me a favor. I can buy your coffee," I said when he protested.

He rolled his eyes. "I like Parker too. But fine. Thank you."

We commandeered the overstuffed mocha-colored armchairs in the back corner of the shop, and I pulled a notebook and pen from my bag.

"So the biggest question is when Burke actually disappeared. If it was before Thursday afternoon, Parker had no motive," Kyle said. "The sheriff is right that it'll be hard for the lab to nail that down though. I worked a case once where a body was left in the dumpster behind an IHOP, and the syrup caused all kinds of headaches. Sugar makes tissue decompose faster."

"Shit. And Hulk told me the wine they found Burke in was that sweet Riesling I liked so much." I shook my head. "Between me and you, Aaron stopped me on the way out to tell me Richard Burke wants Parker to answer for this. Though I suspect, listening to Parker this morning, that Burke blames Parker for his daughter's death and just can't stick it to him legally."

"Of course," Kyle said. "Though that's a problem for us."

"Why's that?"

"We don't just have to prove it wasn't Parker. Or that it's not likely to have been Parker. We need to find out who it was. Otherwise, Burke could still pull strings and cause trouble for Grant. Lab reports can get lost—or falsified—for the right amount of money."

I rolled my eyes. "And here I thought I was getting out of this particular frying pan."

Kyle grinned, sipping his latte. "Welcome to the fire."

"So far, the best lead we have is at the vineyard. You still up for driving out for a chat with Celia? I'm interested to see what you make of her. I have court at noon today, but we could go tomorrow."

"Sounds like a plan."

I grabbed my coffee and my keys. "Thank you for offering to call Bonnie." I hoped it wouldn't be too awkward for Kyle to ask the forensic biologist he'd recently stopped seeing for help.

He stood and motioned an after-you. "Don't thank me yet. She might tell me to go to Hell."

"I know better." I winked. "Holler if you find anything?"

He held the door for me and nodded. "Thanks for the coffee. See you tomorrow."

I started the car and pulled away from the curb, wondering how in the world I could hold Charlie—and everyone else—off of Parker for another twenty-four hours.

* * *

Parked at my desk with forty-five minutes to spare, I pulled out my notes from the weekend.

Sammons's name was the most popular word on all my lists. I snatched up the phone and called the medical examiner's office, crossing my fingers around my pen as I asked for the autopsy file on Jolene Sammons. Surely they kept a copy, even though the exam had been done at someone else's request.

The bureaucrat on the other end of the line was silent, clicking keys as he checked for the file. "I'm sorry, ma'am," he said finally. "Looks like that one was moved to storage about three years ago."

"Storage where? Can I go get it?"

"Not sure. We had a fire out there nine months ago. Many files were destroyed, and the ones that weren't have been shuffled all over creation. I can put in an order for it, but it'll be eight to ten weeks if it's there at all."

I slammed my hand down on my desk. I didn't have two months.

I also had very little choice. I gave him the contact information he asked for and hung up, the file I'd created for chef Alexei last night catching my eye.

Clock check: six minutes.

I pulled up the translations I'd copied and studied them. Behind three cups of coffee, I still couldn't follow a story, but I picked out keywords.

Poison.

Illness.

Judge.

Cheating.

Holy Manolos. Stuffing my laptop and a notebook into my bag, I snatched up my cell and texted Kyle as I rushed to the elevator.

What are the chances you have any friends in Moscow?

23

DonnaJo's backboard-shattering slam dunk of an opening statement barely left shards and splinters for the defense to work with. By the time court recessed for the evening, I had a hand cramp—and a pretty good hunch Ironfists up there was going to prison for a good long while.

I stopped DonnaJo in the hallway and asked if her office might have a copy of an old autopsy report. Of course not. She took Jolene Sammons's name anyway, promising to see if she could find anything.

Ducking Charlie in the parking lot, I sped back to the office to file the day-one story before six.

I walked in to find Bob sitting in my chair.

"I have a trial for the metro front," I said, dropping my bag. "Good stuff. The RAU sports assault. DonnaJo is going to nail this guy to the wall."

Bob, who had approved us printing the graphic photos of the defendant's girlfriend's patchwork of bruises, nodded. "Excellent. I'll tease it on the front."

He didn't get up.

"What?" I asked, an edge of defensiveness creeping into my tone.

"Just checking to see if you've thought about my question from this morning. Are you proud of your Burke story like it is?"

I puffed out my cheeks, then blew the air out slowly. "I need to add a statement from the family. But that's it."

"There's something you're not saying." Bob stood, his brows drawing down into a stern glare.

There was indeed. But sharing Parker's trip to police HQ would just cause another fight, and there still wasn't enough for me to change the story.

I sank into the chair, tapping my foot and fighting to keep my tone even. "I've always said people come before the story for me. Just by a hair. But this time, it's by a football field. I did my level best to report the facts for you on this, and the facts do not include Parker. Not today. This is about so much past the headline, chief. And if we start it off giving everyone else reason to smell blood in the water, the sharks are going to eat Parker for lunch. Scandals get ratings. I will not be party to opening that vein."

He watched my face for a minute, and I set it in my best I-won't-budge glower.

"Okay." He turned. "For today."

I nodded, flipping my laptop open and pulling up a screen for the trial. Today was all I needed right then.

* * *

I'd just turned onto my street when my phone erupted into "Second Star to the Right." I reached for it slowly, unsure I wanted to know what else could go wrong.

Emily, the caller ID announced. My face relaxed into a smile.

"You have no idea how glad I am it's you. On so many levels," I said in place of hello.

"I figured you'd need me right about now." She laughed, which made my smile widen. Em has the best laugh—big and loud and brimming with joy. It'd been one of my favorite things about her since she loaned me her Strawberry Shortcake eraser in third grade and became one of my best friends. "The wedding is this coming weekend, right?"

Ah. She had her psychologist hat on. "It is. Though I'd bet what you're calling about is the least of my worries today. The rehearsal weekend included a dead guy, and at least half the people I know think Parker killed him."

A full minute of silence followed.

I turned into the driveway and cut the engine. "Em?"

"I can't even. How?"

"I don't have time to bother with how. I need the who and the why before Saturday."

"You need to talk?"

"Like a little black dress needs the right pair of heels." I unlocked the door and stooped to pat Darcy's head, filling her food bowl and reaching for the wine rack. "Get comfortable."

"Shoes off. Hair down. Wine open," she said. "Go."

By the time I'd finished the story (again), she'd been quiet for so long I'd have thought the call dropped if it weren't for the occasional clicking of her earring against the receiver as she nodded. Snuggled in the corner of my overstuffed sofa with my bare feet curled under me and Darcy in my lap, I sipped my Moscato.

"Wow," Em said.

"Yup."

"Not only do you seem to have yet another killer to hunt down, but that might not even be your biggest issue." She clicked her tongue. "It seems everything you try so hard to keep compartmentalized about your life is on the verge of crashing together. How are you holding up?"

"I'll take vague psychoanalyzing for two hundred, Alex."

"I'm not trying to be vague. I've been listening to you talk about this wedding for months, and I love you, sweetie, but you are fooling yourself if you think being in the middle of this lovefest isn't getting in your head. Making you wonder what you want."

"Right now I want a fairy to appear in my living room with irrefutable evidence of who killed Mitch Burke."

"For your life. You can't live the job forever. You've been doing it long enough that you have to know that by now."

I tapped a finger on the stem of my glass. "Funny, Bob said the same thing last weekend. So did Larry."

"Maybe you should listen to them."

"And what?" I let my head fall back into the cushions. "Be as depressed and down on myself as Shelby is that I don't have a one-and-only to cook dinner for every night? No thanks."

Her voice softened. "I think if you look a bit harder, you might see that something in your basic belief system is evolving. Having a front row seat for Grant and Melanie's happily ever after has been chipping away at your commitment phobia for months."

I set the dog in the floor and got up to pace. "You think?"

"The real question is always do *you* think?"

"I think maybe you're right. But I don't know what to do about it. Yet."

"We all know how much you love situations you can't control," Emily said.

"Right this second what I need to control is digging up what the hell happened to Mitch Burke."

"That I might be able to help with. Your victim was a narcissist. Which means there should be a diary of his every move online. Check his social media. A new pair of shoes says the profiles are public."

Damn. Social media hits are usually in the top returns when you search anyone on Google. Except when the person in question is even a G-list celebrity—then they get buried in news clips and official websites. And in all the craziness, it hadn't even occurred to me to look. Some detective I was.

"You are a genius." I strode to the kitchen and dug my laptop out of my bag.

"Just a bit smarter than average," she said. "Good luck, sweetie. Call if you need me."

"Thank you, Em." I flipped open the computer and clicked off the call, arranging Burke's Facebook and Instagram feeds side by side on my screen.

The grin on his face in his profile photo was of the things-go-my-way variety.

"Something definitely didn't last week," I murmured to the screen, scrolling down. "Let's see if you can tell me why."

* * *

Mitch Burke's online life depicted a bachelor's dream.

Just in the week before his body was found, he'd checked into six restaurants and five nightclubs with thirty different people, more than half of them beautiful women. Work was hanging out at the ballpark. Lunch was meeting his dad for sandwiches and a walk along the James. They took a selfie with the old Lucky Strike statue in the background a week ago today.

My heart twisted, looking at Richard Burke's easy smile. Whatever kind of person Mitch was, I felt terrible for his family. Richard's hazel eyes, crinkled at the corners from the grin and the sun, were happy. And his face was familiar, though I stared for a good three minutes and couldn't place why. Probably just from the general "around"—the head of the state's historical league had to pop up in our society pages often, and Lord knows I'd spent enough time poring over them last fall.

I kept scrolling, building a timeline of Burke's last week and thanking my lucky stars for friends like Emily.

The last photo on his Instagram was taken Wednesday evening in Richmond. I held my breath, crossing fingers and toes as I snapped a screenshot. Clicked over to Facebook.

Damn.

He'd checked into a fancy five-star restaurant in Charlottesville at six thirty Thursday evening, which washed out my theory that he'd been in the wine barrel for more than a day. I stared at the screen.

Wait.

Scrolling back down, I checked entry after entry. Burke never went anywhere alone. But no one was tagged in this dinner check-in on Thursday.

So who did he meet that he didn't want anyone to know about?

I had to leave the room to keep from hurling my laptop into the wall.

Every road I thought would lead to an answer produced more questions. Always more questions.

My phone binged a text arrival and I scurried back to the kitchen, hoping Kyle was finally answering me about Moscow.

Not Kyle.

Joey.

Three little words that shot straight to my heart.

I believe you.

I slid my finger across the screen, my thumbs flying as soon as the message screen opened.

I will never lie to you. He is my friend. Absolutely nothing more.

Gray dot bubble.

I'm glad. Your day OK? I hit an interesting wall asking about our mutual friend.

So we were speaking in code?

Interesting good?

Bing. *Interesting weird. Can I tell you about it over dinner tomorrow night?*

So not an answer, or he wouldn't wait. I blew out a frustrated sigh. At least he wanted to tell me. And I missed him.

I'd adore it.

I put the phone on the charger and shuffled to the bathroom. Peering at the purple craters under my eyes in the mirror as I waited for my clawfoot tub to fill with steaming water, I shook my head. I was no stranger to stress, but this week was piling it on too thick. A hot bath and a good night's sleep sounded like Heaven. So did a remote cabin where no one could depend on me for anything ever again, but I bored easily. Bath it was.

I stayed in until my fingers shriveled, Parker's story about Marilyn playing on a loop in my head, images of smiling Mitch Burke flashing over top of his words. I was missing something. I had to be.

I'd almost dozed off in the tub when it hit me.

I sat straight up, sending water all over the floor.

Richard Burke.

He stood out in the photos—not because of the society pages I'd stared myself blind over last fall. Because I'd seen him. On a horse in Sammons's field on Sunday. Richard Burke was the tall silver-haired man with the impressive skill.

What the hell kind of man plays polo two days after his only son is found dead?

24

Wide rays of light danced across my quilt by the time I opened my eyes, yet I didn't feel rested as my feet touched the sun-warmed hardwood floor. Grabbing my phone from the charger, I texted Bob.

Skipping the meeting, so sorry, have to track something down if you want ahead of Charlie. Will have follow on Burke by five.

I hit a Starbucks drive-thru on the way to Kyle's and had his caramel macchiato waiting in the cupholder next to my white mocha when I picked him up at eight.

"Sorry I didn't answer you yesterday—I could tell you how crazy it was, but you might not believe me," he said as he slid into the passenger seat. "The short answer is, the odds aren't good. I've never worked on anything anywhere near Russia."

Of course. I set the GPS for Calais and pointed the car toward the interstate as I filled him in on chef Alexei.

"Nice work," he said. "I like that scenario. A lot. Will we see this TV cook today?"

"I sure hope so." I sped up and merged onto I-64, flicking a glance at him out of the corner of my eye. "What do you know about Richard Burke?"

"Mostly that his family life is pretty tragic, based on what Parker said yesterday." Kyle picked up the latte and smiled a thank you as he sipped it. "Why?"

"I talked to Em last night—she said to tell you hey—and she told me to check Mitch Burke's social media. There was a photo of Mitch and Richard from last week and he looked familiar. I finally realized why: I saw him on Sunday, playing Polo at Calais. Who does that?"

No answer.

I cut my eyes his way. "Hello?"

"Well, I guess I'm wondering where you're going with that," he said. "I mean, everyone grieves in their own way, right? Didn't you tell me even Ashton Okerson had to stay busy right after their son died?"

I tapped one finger on the wheel, images of Ashton making lemonade and delivering trays of snacks to everyone in her house flashing through my head. He had a point.

"True, but..." I didn't really have a place to take that.

"But what? You can't really think this man was somehow hung up in his own son's death?"

Not when he said it like that.

"I guess not?" I didn't really intend the question mark, but it came out all the same.

"That's rare. Like, one in a million rare when the kid in question is grown."

Right again. "And we don't need any more geese to chase," I said.

"Not on the strength of slightly odd behavior in the wake of a tragedy anyway. I think we have enough likely suspects to keep us busy for today."

I nodded, turning my attention back to the vineyard we were speeding towards. "So here's the plan..." I began. By the time I turned onto the driveway at Calais, Kyle was the assistant florist looking over the property because his boss was out with a cold. And I'd given him the full rundown on the players as I knew them, including what I'd found on Jolene Sammons's very quickly glossed-over death.

"From what I found, Sammons only spends time out here on the weekends most of the time," Kyle said as we parked the car. "Though it seems he's been out here more than usual lately. You see anything that gave you an idea why?"

"The scuffle on Saturday where Parker got hurt had something to do with grapes. The old guy says Sammons stole seeds for a hybrid varietal from him."

"Did he?" Kyle furrowed his brow at me.

"Entirely possible."

"Anything to do with Burke?"

"Sheriff says no. Mr. Fulton was out of town until after the body was found."

Kyle surveyed the field, opening his door. "Let's go see what these folks know."

I started with the lodge, checking Jinkerson's office first.

The whole place was empty.

"Are they closed on Tuesdays?" Kyle asked.

"The gates were open," I said.

"True."

I looked back toward Jinkerson's office. The door was closed, but not locked. "You know—if you wanted to play lookout, I might be able to find something in there," I said.

Kyle pursed his lips. "I can't use anything procured in a search without a warrant."

"But I can. And you won't be doing the searching."

He nodded slowly. "This is the guy you said acted like he wanted to talk to you and then disappeared?"

"He knew something about Sammons, it sure seemed. I'm kind of hoping he knows what happened to the sister. But I'll settle for any answer I can find."

"Do you have any idea what you're looking for?"

"Not a clue. Figured I'd start with Mitch Burke and Sammons and go from there."

"Did Burke even work here?"

"Not that I know of. He worked for Sammons with the baseball club. But he was out here enough to have broken a few hearts around these parts, and nobody seemed too surprised that he'd been murdered."

Kyle nodded, waving me toward the office. "Good luck. Hope your haystack isn't too big."

I slipped inside and surveyed the room. It wasn't huge, with a giant carved dark wood desk in the center of the floor and two low matching file cabinets behind the chair.

I moved to the first one and knelt in front of it, pulling on the top drawer. Locked. Shit. The bottom one opened, as did the two in the other cabinet. So anything interesting was probably in the one I couldn't get into. I flipped through tabs in the other three anyway: utility bill files, county board of supervisors meeting records (Sammons was a frequent agenda item, it appeared. Worth reading, but I could get the minutes myself at the courthouse) and sales records by wine label. I wished I knew how to read the latter, but I had no idea if the summer Rosé selling seven hundred and thirty-nine cases was great or terrible.

So how to get into the locked files?

I stood and moved to the desk, sliding the top drawer out in search of a key. A dust bunny, a pen, and a couple paperclips. Strike one.

I'd just edged the side drawer open when the knob on the door that led to the back hallway where I'd eavesdropped on Jinkerson and Hulk a hundred years ago (how was that only Friday?) rattled. I only had a lookout in the lobby. Should've locked that one. I glanced around.

No time—or place—to hide.

I slapped the drawer shut, throwing my bag over my shoulder and snatching a pen off the desk just as Celia pushed the door open.

* * *

"What are you doing here?" she asked, her eyes wide, voice trembling.

I gave her a onceover. Miss prim and polished gift shop manager was looking a lot rough around the frills this morning. Puffy eyes, sallow skin. Her hair, stuffed into a crooked ponytail, could use some shampoo. And her jeans and sweatshirt were a far cry from the designer pencil skirts and silk blouses she'd worn every other time I'd seen her.

Her eyes skated around the edges of the room, flicked back to me, and resumed wandering.

Nerves.

Was she worried about what I might find in the office? Worried that I'd seen her there? Or something more pressing—like, maybe, a murder charge?

No way to know.

I brandished the pen. "I brought the florist to look over some things and I couldn't find you or Mr. Jinkerson. I was leaving him a note that we'd gone out to survey the property in case he came back."

I was a lousy liar, and my eyes dropped to the desk as I talked, but she seemed too wrapped up in whatever was bugging her to notice.

"I took the day off. I'm not feeling too well." Her voice was scratchy.

"I'm sorry to hear that," I said, wondering if she had a regular bug or the guilty-conscience kind.

She tried for a smile and managed a wince. "Thank you."

"Is it okay if I take him out to look around?"

"Sure." She waved a hand and I turned for the opposite door, her voice stopping me with one hand on the knob.

"I thought their florist was a woman?" Celia's tone had an undercurrent of accusation.

I smiled, turning. "She's out sick today so her assistant is filling in. Must be something going around." I winked and dropped my voice to a conspiratorial whisper. "Between me and you, I'm glad he got to come look at the venue. He's a genius."

She held my gaze for a moment before she nodded. "I hope the wedding is everything it should be."

Something in the way she said it made the hair on my arm stand up as I nodded and walked back out to Kyle.

* * *

"Maybe she really is sick," Kyle said as we passed the guest houses on our way to the barns. I'd blurted out the whole thing so fast I was gulping air, my chest tight.

I tried to slow my breathing. "Maybe. But something is weird. I don't think that's all, how's that?"

He shrugged. "Maybe. Nothing good in there, either way?"

"Not that I had time to look too hard. But her going in the back door when the place was empty makes me think she felt pretty sure she'd be alone in his office. Which means there's something going on with him. Google had zip, save for a bunch of wine industry magazine articles and blog posts, but my gut says there's more."

Kyle's eyes popped wide. "You think he's our guy? What about the chef?"

"I don't know. Conspiracy? Celia mentioned that she saw Jinkerson near the barns Friday afternoon, but who the hell knows if she's trustworthy? What I think is I want to find him, and it looks like he's not here. Can we look for an address and stop by his house before we head out of town?"

"No harm in trying."

"You're a gem. Now if you can come up with a reason I'd need to show the florist this building, we'll be all set."

Kyle grinned. "You suck at lying, Nicey. Always have." He raised a hand toward the tops of the huge red doors. "We need boughs of greenery out here for photos, obviously. This would make a killer portrait. Um. You know what I mean."

I nodded to the scrap of crime scene tape still clinging to the doorway. "Tactful."

"Sorry."

I looked around as I slid the door open, the screech setting my teeth on edge. "They really ought to oil that. Also, are you sure you're following your true calling? Because you're totally right about the portrait and I'm ordering greenery for this door the minute we leave here."

Kyle snickered and stepped inside. "Happy to help, but I like my job, thank you."

I followed him and began chatting a bit too loud about the wedding, keeping it up in a steady stream until we reached the offices at the far end of the building. No lights. I tried the door that had concealed the Debbie Does Calais noises Saturday. Locked.

I sighed. "Damn. Strike two."

Kyle looked around. "I think it's safe to say we're alone." He walked back toward the racks of barrels. "So this is where they found him, huh?"

"Indeed."

Kyle stood at the bottom of a rack and looked up. "How'd someone get him up there?"

"I imagine the barrel was on the ground..." The words trailed off, the mental image making my stomach turn. "Ugh. Gross, Kyle."

"No, I'm serious. These things have to be heavy. How could anyone move one that had gallons of wine and a fully grown man in it?"

Hulk flashed to mind. "The guy I told you about—Sammons's illegitimate son. He's a house."

"Even a house isn't lifting like five hundred pounds of big awkward barrel alone, Nichelle. Certainly not with enough precision to set it in one of these racks such that no one would notice it was different."

I surveyed the ceiling beams, spotting a pulley rigging. "There. I bet that's how they place them." I followed the beams down and saw a rope lift in front of each rack.

Kyle touched his chin, studying the ropes and the rack. "Still not a one-man job. You'd need one to lift and one to position, at the very least. Where was the barrel when the cops got here?"

I opened my mouth and then stopped. "I don't know. I heard Hulk panicking, but then...no one ever said specifically. And the report isn't done."

"Still?"

"Far as I know."

Kyle shook his head. "That's weird too."

"It's only been four days." Four of the longest days in the history of the world. But four nonetheless.

"How much crime you figure they have around here? It shouldn't take one day to write an initial report on something like this. The further we look into what's going on here, the less I like it."

"Like what?"

Kyle and I froze for half a second. The deep bass coming from the direction of the doors wasn't unfriendly, but it was guarded.

"Hey there, Franklin." I waved, forcing brightness into my tone. "This is Ryan from the florist. We were talking about taking photos in here this weekend, but we think perhaps with everything that's happened..." I let the words trail and shrugged as he closed the space between us in a half-dozen giant strides. "We think we'll stick with outside."

Scanning my face carefully, Hulk relaxed his shoulders as he nodded. "Probably for the best." He stuffed his big hands half into the pockets of his faded Wranglers. "I'm glad I bumped into you, actually. I seem to remember getting carried away with the bourbon on Saturday and being a little too loquacious. Hope I didn't scare you off." His shy smile drew a loud throat clearing from Kyle.

I shot one heel back into Kyle's shin and smiled at Hulk. "Not at all." Every word true.

The smile widened. "Good." He let out a deep breath I didn't realize he'd been holding. "Now that I've apologized, can I show you folks anything else while you're here?"

I cast my eyes down at my lavender Manolo sandals. Indeed he could. But I had a feeling the answers all depended on the asking.

25

I tucked my arm through Hulk's as we walked back out of the barn, chirping about garlands in the doorway and photos as he nodded and Kyle stayed close on our heels.

We were halfway down one of the rows, surrounded by vines heavy with sweeping green leaves, Hulk pointing out spots in the field that would look nice in sunset photos and me trying to pretend to note them, when Kyle popped up with "Could we use cuttings of these vines in some of the arrangements?"

I spun on my heel and shot him a what-the-hell-is-wrong-with-you look. Had he forgotten he couldn't actually commit to things on behalf of the florist? I had no doubt Lorraine would be around this weekend, and didn't want questions over something so silly.

Hulk turned and nodded to the leaves, which obliged by rippling in a gentle breeze. "These?" His voice was a full octave too high.

I furrowed my brow as Kyle kept his face perfectly blank, waiting for an elaboration. He was a good cop. And that look told me he was onto something. I scanned the field.

Hulk let the awkward silence stretch for as long as he could bear before he shuffled one extra-large boot in the dirt. "I'm not sure Mr. Sammons would be onboard with that, but you're welcome to ask."

Kyle held the silence for three beats before he smiled his easy smile. "Sorry. I know next to nothing about wine outside which kinds I like to drink. I didn't know that would be a sensitive question."

Hulk nodded and shrugged, nodding to me. "Have y'all seen enough? I should probably get back to work."

I thanked him for the tour and followed him back to the barn, more questions plunking on top of the others already ground into my brain. Why would Sammons care about donating a few cuttings to Parker's wedding? And how could I find out what had Hulk so antsy without him asking why I wanted to know?

I practically tapped a foot through the pleasantries, whirling on Kyle as soon as Hulk was safely out of earshot.

"What the hell was that?" I hissed. "You have something's-up face, and he got weird when you asked about cutting those plants. Why?"

Kyle lifted one eyebrow. "Deep breaths, Nicey," he drawled.

"We do not have time for meditation advice. What did I miss?"

He laid one hand on my shoulder and turned me back toward the field. "Look at the vines. The ones I asked about."

"They look like grapevines."

He nodded, pressing my shoulder and turning me another thirty degrees to the left. "Now look at these."

I squinted for a second, then skipped my eyes back to the first batch. "The leaves are bigger."

"They are."

"Why is that bad?"

"Do I look like a farmer? This is about the closest I've ever been to food actually growing out of the ground." He shrugged. "I don't know that it's bad. I found it mildly interesting until I asked and he clammed up. Now I find it very interesting."

I leaned my head on Kyle's shoulder, watching the wind skate through the leaves and enjoying the peace of the moment before I straightened my shoulders and sighed. "There's too much that's very interesting."

Kyle patted my back. "We'll figure it out, Nichelle."

"Before or after Parker ends up in jail?" I bit my lip, shaking my head.

Kyle didn't answer, moving his hand to the small of my back and turning me toward the lodge. "Let's go see who else we can find."

* * *

Nobody. That was who.

"How can the gates and the door be open and there not be anyone up here?" I asked after we'd scoured the lodge and the grounds around it a second time.

"The sign in the shop window says it doesn't open until three today. Maybe the rest of the place isn't supposed to be open either," Kyle said.

"That's really damned annoying," I snapped, rolling my eyes and softening my tone. "I'm sorry to drag you all the way out here for this."

He shook his head. "I got a feel for the place, and something's off. Several things, actually. I just can't figure out how—or if—they go together. But it wasn't a wasted trip in any sense of the word."

Resting my hands on my hips, I turned a slow circle, my eyes coming to rest on the lodge. Celia's comment about someone getting sick floated over what I'd read about Alexei. The kitchen was dark and empty ten minutes ago. "I wonder if we could find something in the kitchen," I mused.

"Something like whatever your chef and the sick girl were talking about the other day?" Kyle twisted his mouth to one side. "Would you leave evidence laying around at work if you poisoned someone?"

"No. But criminals aren't usually terribly smart."

He waved a hand. "Might as well have a look."

I strode back to the steps and glanced around before I opened the door. Still a ghost town.

Stepping into the kitchen, I surveyed miles of stainless steel. Everything spotless.

"This would work better if we knew what we were looking for," Kyle said.

"You don't say?" I smiled and crossed to the fridge, pulling it open.

"No skull and crossbones labels?" Kyle asked, opening a cabinet.

"Darn the luck," I murmured, scanning the inventory of the massive Samsung. "About a million eggs, twenty pounds of butter, at least a dozen kinds of cheese, and half a dairy worth of cream and whole milk. No wonder his stuff is so good."

Kyle chuckled as he moved to the trash can. "Empty."

"Of course." I shut the fridge and turned, picking up a sheet of paper off the end of the counter. Last week's menu. I scanned the words. "Facebook says Burke was in the area Thursday, but he didn't have dinner here. This says they served chilled tomato bisque, salmon croquettes, and ice cream with fresh blueberry compote for lunch. Yummy. But not incriminating."

Kyle's hand landed on my shoulder. "I think this is your proverbial needle/haystack situation."

"I'm missing something, Kyle. The answer has to be here."

"The lab report will tell us what to look for. I'll call Bonnie today and check on the tox screen."

I followed him outside and begged for one more pass around the building. He shrugged and stayed on my heels. Still nothing.

Moving back toward the car, I turned when I didn't hear his footsteps behind me. "You coming?"

"Hang on." He sounded distracted as he half-jogged toward a falling-down storage shed on the northwest corner of the property.

I took off after him, huffing and cursing my block heels as I drew even. "I covered every inch of this place this weekend. That building is just waiting to be bulldozed," I said between breaths as he slowed to a walk just shy of the shed.

"Don't care about the building." Kyle knelt next to the split-rail fence, plucking the top off a plant. "But I do care about this."

I studied the round purple-black fruit, furrowing my brow. "I thought blueberries grew on bushes."

He nodded slowly. "This isn't a blueberry. This is phytolacca americana, commonly known as pokeweed. Highly toxic, especially the roots."

My eyes went wide. "And the berries?"

"Would definitely make a man sick. Too heavy a hand or too green a berry could cause death by respiratory failure."

Leaping Louboutins. I reached for my phone, snapping photos of the plants and the surrounding area before I flung my arms around Kyle. "You're a genius."

He laughed as he pulled away, tossing the plant to the ground. "We don't know anything for sure. Let me get the lab reports."

He started back for the car and I followed, practically dancing across the field. "I have a good feeling about this. How'd you spot it from way over there?"

He shook his head. "I didn't. I spotted the fence. We had to take this class on plant-based toxins last month, and this was one they talked a lot about because it grows wild around here. You said they served a blueberry something for lunch Thursday, and I saw the fence and remembered the instructor saying this stuff is dangerous for kids because they think it's a blueberry plant, and it likes to grow in the loose soil around fencerows. Just a hunch."

"An awesome hunch." I unlocked the car, feeling lighter than I had since Larry started pictures Friday night. "We're going to get it. And everyone who's been driving me nuts will have to apologize to Parker. How can Bob think he might have had a hand in this?"

Kyle shrugged, folding his long frame into the passenger seat. "I don't know your boss, but I know how much you love him, and my best guess is that...Well, the surface evidence is pretty damning. It takes either a pretty loyal friend," he winked, "or a brilliant law enforcement professional with a sixth sense about people," he laughed when I gently punched his upper arm, "to look past that without proof of anything else."

"Anything else you want to see, or shall we go by Jinkerson's place and call it a day?" I backed the car out of the space and turned for the road, checking the rearview.

"I heard the sheriff tell Landers he was staying in Richmond last night. You said the dispatcher is chatty, right?"

I barely heard the end of his question, my eyes locked on the mirror—and the black Lincoln parked near the barn we'd vacated not forty minutes ago. I turned around in the seat for a better view, pretending to be watching behind me as I backed up.

"Everything okay?" Kyle asked.

Nodding, I sped off the property.

I hoped it was, anyway. Thanks to my ridiculous propensity for total recall with things I read, I knew Joey's plate number.

What the ever-loving hell was he doing at Calais Vineyards?

* * *

I parked outside the sheriff's office and led Kyle into the building, focusing on Ella Jane. The only source that outdid the beauty parlor in a small town was the police dispatcher. They knew everything that went on. Literally.

She looked up from her laptop and smiled. "Good morning! Was the sheriff able to help you with what you needed Sunday? I'm afraid he's out of the county on an investigation this morning."

I let that go without comment one way or another, because I didn't want her to think her dad was suspicious of anything to do with me, since that might shut her up. "He was a big help, thanks." I kept my voice bright. "I just wanted to stop in and ask..." What? I needed a reason to be there. I panicked for three seconds, then shook my head and smiled. "Sorry. Not enough coffee this morning. Is the report on either incident out at Calais ready yet?"

She punched a few keys on her computer. "Doesn't look like the final versions have been filed," she said. "It's been insane here the past few days. I'll ask Evans if he's got anything ready when he gets here, but that won't be for another half-hour." She smiled apologetically and stood, punching the button next to her that unlocked the door to our left. "The coffee thing I can help with though. It's been pretty quiet this morning." She knocked on the wood trim lining the wall. "Why don't y'all come on back and I'll make a fresh pot?"

We walked through the door and I smiled a thank you. "I don't want to interfere with your work."

She waved a hand and pointed to her ear, where a little Bluetooth light flashed behind her perfectly teased blonde curls. "As long as I have my headset, I'm good."

We followed her to the station's teeny break room. She pointed us to seats at a white linoleum table while she puttered around putting on fresh coffee and getting everyone cups. I considered asking about Jolene Sammons for half a second and decided I'd hold that for if Kyle couldn't help with it. I didn't want to draw her suspicion with a left-field question when she seemed to want to talk.

"So things are back to normal after all the craziness of the weekend?" I kept my tone light.

She nodded. "Mostly. I mean, my dad is still running all over half the state trying to figure out what happened to Mitch. I've never seen him so frustrated."

"He doesn't have any leads?" Still just innocently curious.

"I think he had a new one yesterday, because he got a phone call really early and tore out of here for Richmond without a word to anyone."

I nodded, and she kept talking as the Mr. Coffee burbled. "He's just as afraid of finding out what happened as he is that he won't and someone will come take the case away from him."

I furrowed my brow and she smiled. "I've never understood why he went into law enforcement in the first place, really. He wants to see the good in everyone. And our family's been in this county a long time. Deep roots, and connections to most of the other folks out here. He doesn't want anyone to be capable of what happened to Mitch." She shook her head as she set two cups of coffee in front of us, then added containers of cream and sugar and a cup for herself before she sat down. "He's stuck. If he doesn't figure it out, he loses face with the department and the residents." She fell quiet.

We let it go until it verged on awkward, and I shot Kyle a do-something look.

"Thousands of murders go unsolved every year. The sheriff should do the best he can do, and that's enough."

Ella Jane kept her eyes on the table. "From what Mitch told me about his father, the Burke family will not just let it go," she said. "And the sheriff really doesn't want the feds or somebody crawling all over town."

Kyle didn't even blink at the quasi-insult. "Of course. Who would?"

"Me, for one," she said. "I want to know—really know—what happened to Mitch. And it's not like we get too many murders out here. Our guys, they don't know how to do this." She looked at me. "You're a reporter, right? Shouldn't we know something by now?"

I reached across the table and patted her hand. She was more hung up on Burke than I'd thought. "Not always. These things take time. Rabbit trails to chase. Truths to unravel. And that's after you find the people who know things and get them to talk."

She toyed with her coffee cup, nodding. "So many people hated Mitch, but they just didn't know him."

I tapped an index finger on the table. I'd tried so hard not to put her on guard by asking her a direct question about her relationship with Burke. But come on. I shot Kyle a look and he nodded ever so slightly.

I widened my eyes. "I didn't realize you two were close, Ella Jane. I'm so sorry."

"Can you keep a secret?" Her blue eyes were full of tears when she looked up.

"I'm decent at it."

She sucked in a deep breath and nodded as the tears spilled over. "I'm pregnant. We were going to get married next month."

26

I stared, my jaw going slack as Kyle pinched my knee under the table. I cut a look at him and saw in half a second that there was something he wanted to say, but didn't feel like he could.

I tightened my fingers around Ella Jane's hand. That might explain Burke's fancy secret dinner in Charlottesville Thursday, but left a dozen new questions in its place. Why didn't Burke want anyone to know he was taking her to dinner if he was going to marry her? Was she the last person to see him alive?

"I...I'm so sorry..." The words felt lame as they tripped through my lips, but with my brain spinning so fast, I had nothing else to offer. She clasped her other hand around mine and held on like she'd found a float in a sea of trouble. I covered that one with my free hand and patted. "Everything will work out." Lamer still. But I'd missed the charm-school lesson on consoling pregnant women whose would-be fiancés had met an untimely end, and improv was failing me.

I put pressure on both of her hands. No ring I could feel.

Ella Jane squeezed back and then pulled away, brushing at her eyes and glancing around. "I must look a mess." She tried to laugh. "Forgive me. I can't believe I just did that. Stupid crazy hormones—I swear, I cry at the drop of a hat, and I'm either not hungry at all or I want the strangest things to eat. This baby stuff ain't for sissies."

Kyle nodded and flashed a smile. "Think nothing of it," his best soothing Agent in crisis mode voice said. "It's often easier to talk to strangers about trouble than it is to talk to people you know. Less fear of judgement."

Ella Jane pulled in a shuddering breath and nodded. "Well. Thank y'all for listening. You really think this is still normal? That they're going to catch whoever did it?"

"I really do," I said, standing when she did. The coffee sat forgotten on the table.

She set her pink lips in a firm line. "All right then. Hopefully Daddy is finding out something in Richmond as we speak."

She walked us back to the door, pausing when she saw her computer screen. "The reports. Let me see if I can find Deputy Evans for you."

I smiled a thank you. It had slipped my thoughts in all the revelation, but I'd still like to have them.

She disappeared, and I drummed my fingers on my thigh. "Wow," I whispered.

"Just when I think I know where this train is going, we change tracks." Kyle shook his head.

"I'd say that was worth the drive out here all by itself," I hissed. "Though I seem to have traded two questions I walked in here with for a hundred new ones."

"The questions always come cheap. It's the answers that are pricey."

I smiled. "Only if you don't work hard enough."

"Takes a bit of luck too."

I opened my mouth to reply and closed it again when Ella Jane hurried back around the corner, talking a mile a minute into her headset. She kicked her chair out of the way and stepped to her computer, her fingers flying over the keys. "I have an ambulance on its way, Mrs. Toomey. I understand. Keep pressure on the wound, and they'll be there in four minutes. Yes ma'am, I know that feels like a long time. How is the bleeding now?"

Whoever Mrs. Toomey was, she was panicked such that we could hear her screaming in Ella Jane's ear from across the room. Ella's face stayed tight, but her voice was calm and even.

She didn't just have this job because her dad was the sheriff. She was good at it.

Kyle and I listened as Ella Jane consoled the woman until the paramedics arrived. When she pushed the button behind her ear to dismiss the call, she sank into her chair and let her head fall back. "Sorry about that. There's something else I've been lately—worn the heck out pretty easy."

I smiled. "Well, Mrs. Toomey would never have known it. You were great with her."

"Thanks. I like helping people."

She stared at us with a vacant look for a minute before she sat up. "Oh! Your reports. Evans isn't here, and they're not finished yet. I'll call you when they're ready and I can fax or email them if you don't want to drive all the way back out here."

Since the freedom of information act didn't require her to make that offer, I thanked her twice. "I appreciate your help," I said.

"I appreciate yours." She smiled, a little of the sadness in her eyes disappearing for the first time since I'd met her.

"Try not to worry," I said. "It's doubly bad for you these days."

I strode back to the car with Kyle on my heels, yet another new question floating up.

Mitch Burke was from an old-money family, and Kyle said his bank account was plenty healthy. If they were engaged, where was her ring? And why did her dad think they weren't serious?

* * *

"What do we know about the sheriff?" Kyle started talking before his door was shut, pulling his seatbelt around him as I started the car. "Besides that our murder vic knocked up his little girl?"

I picked up my phone and found Jinkerson's address in three clicks, tapping it up on my map. Twelve minutes. Pulling out of the parking lot, I returned my attention to Kyle. "I'm wondering if Sheriff Rutledge even knows about this baby." I bit my lip. Had I misunderstood him? "He said the other day he was glad Mitch wasn't the marrying sort, and mentioned shipping Ella Jane off to her aunt in Texas. I thought he meant he wanted them broken up. But what if he didn't?" I rolled my eyes. "Just when I thought we had an answer with your brilliant poison blueberry thing. Dammit."

Kyle patted my hand. "One thing at a time. I didn't get an I'm-hiding-things vibe from that guy."

"Me either. He seems like an open book. Country law enforcement, career, I'd bet on military service from the way he carries himself and speaks. Seems smart. Burke's social media feed does put him out here on Thursday evening though. He checked into a super nice restaurant—alone—at six thirty."

"So who was he eating with?" Kyle nodded, talking more to himself than to me. "I'm not technically assigned to this case, so I have to be careful how I ask, but I can check on security footage if you give me an address. See if a camera got something."

I sighed. "Thanks. I keep feeling like I'm missing something."

"I could tell by your face you didn't suspect she was pregnant. But I think she loved him. Don't you?"

"Maybe. Either way, I bet that chick has never even killed a spider."

"Plus, no rich playboy baby daddy, no child support. Engagement or no." Kyle raised his hands in mock surrender at my sideways glare. "Not trying to insult anyone. Just calling it like I see it. You can't get mad at me for agreeing with you."

I rolled my eyes, then focused them back on the blacktop in front of me as I made a left at the town's only stoplight. "Whatever. Anyway—it wasn't her. So who else do we got?"

"The sheriff."

I tipped my head side to side. "I dunno. I think he's too honorable to be a murderer."

"But especially if he did time on active duty, he's capable of it. And to protect his daughter? If I've learned one thing in all the years I've spent in police work, it's that lots of folks have a button or two that can push them to the unthinkable. So would this have pressed his?"

I held a breath for a three count, then blew it out slowly, a tickling in the back of my brain. "I wish I knew. There's too much to figure out, and..." The words choked off into a sob and I pinched my eyes shut and shook my head, snapping them open a half-second later. "I don't know what's wrong with me. I'm sorry."

He half-swiveled in the seat. "Stress. You have too much going on and it's making you emotional."

I nodded, Joey's car sitting outside Sammons's barn flashing through my thoughts and making it hard to breathe. Stress. Yeah. Just a smidge.

Slowing the car when the map indicated an upcoming turn, I raised a brow at Kyle as I drove under a rusted arch that probably used to read "Augusta Park," but now halfheartedly welcomed us to "Gust Ark."

Kyle's jaw loosened as he surveyed a trailer park that a swift wind would flatten in half a tick. "This..." He cleared his throat. "This is where Jinkerson lives?"

"According to the interwebs, the only Phillip Jinkerson in the county resides," I shifted into park in front of a rust-covered travel trailer that looked like it was once green, "right here."

Kyle shook his head. "Either Sammons can't afford to pay his people..."

"Or his people are spending their checks elsewhere."

There was that tickle again.

Hulk. *Even Mr. Jinkerson put money on us.*

"Leaping Louboutins, he has a gambling problem." Up flashed the photo of Burke with the similarly afflicted pitcher and Don Mario. And Sammons. "And didn't you say Burke was betting with the Cacciones?" My brows shot up, eyes widening as I turned to Kyle.

"Maybe this goose is the right one." He nodded to the door. "I don't have a warrant."

"He wanted to talk to me the other day. Let me see what I can get."

"Do your thing, Lois Lane."

I kicked the car door open and strode to the foot of the most dubious steps I'd ever seen. I've risked my life for a story before, though never at the hands of rickety construction.

I settled one heel into a groove on the bottom one and pushed up on that leg, keeping the other behind me for balance as I rapped on the metal door. Probably not attractive, but effective.

No answer.

I tried again, this time calling Jinkerson's name.

Nothing.

Turning to glance at Kyle, I slid two fingers under the lever latch and flicked them upward.

The door opened.

To a disaster area.

"Mr. Jinkerson?" Eyes wide, I gripped the edge of the door in one hand and the steps' makeshift railing in the other as I climbed into the upended space. It was warmer inside than out by a good ten degrees, thanks to a metal structure and little insulation. The air was thick, a familiar odor heavy in it.

Hell and damnation.

I turned a slow circle, the acrid rotting-meat stench making my stomach heave. Was Jinkerson hiding—or was he dead?

"God, please no." I've seen more than three people's fair share of corpses, but (thank Heaven) I've never actually discovered a fresh one.

I inched past a mustard gold booth, the vinyl seats cracked, the linoleum tabletop dulled by a layer of grime. "Mr. Jinkerson? It's Nichelle Clarke. We met on Friday night?"

Still no reply.

Shit.

Careful not to touch anything, I skirted open cabinets and a gaping mini-fridge, my eyes on the shoebox-sized bedroom and teenier bath straight ahead.

"Anyone home?" I fought the urge to take a deep breath, my stomach still churning from the stink, and plunged through the doorway.

Empty.

Whirling for the bathroom, I nudged the orange accordion curtain aside with the toe of one shoe.

In need of a bleach bomb, but no dead guy.

My eyes fell shut and I mouthed a silent "thank you."

Back in the little galley kitchen, I crouched in front of the open mini-fridge. One half-empty six pack of Keystone, plus the source of the stench: an open package of bologna and a ripped paper butcher's wrapper half-covering a lump of raw hamburger, both turning green in the warm May air. Standing, I pushed the little door shut with one foot and surveyed the rest of the tiny space.

The cabinets all hung open, and everything that looked like it belonged in them had been scattered around the room.

The place had been tossed.

"Nicey?" Kyle's voice came from outside. "You okay?"

"I'm fine." I stepped over a coffee mug and a saucepan and peeked outside. "There's no one here. But we're not the first people who've been here looking for someone—or something."

He climbed the steps and poked his head through the doorway, a low whistle escaping his lips. "What the hell is this guy into?"

"Who the hell knows? I'd say gambling is a safe assumption, but is it the only thing? Any evidence of whatever he's doing is probably long gone."

Kyle's head tipped to one side as he looked over the trailer's interior. "Probably. If they knew where to look."

"Huh?" I furrowed my brow.

"My folks had an old travel trailer like this for camping when I was a kid," he said. "And if I lived here and wanted to hide something, I know where I'd put it." His eyes drifted up. "I can't come inside without risking compromising a case, but since you're in there—go in the bathroom and check the ceiling. You should find a ventilation hatch above the toilet."

The toilet. In this place? I swallowed hard. "The things I won't do for a story."

"Or for a friend." Kyle winked.

I strode back to the bath closet and stepped past the accordion, gritting my teeth and picturing Parker and Mel, posing for photos Friday night.

He wasn't guilty. And if digging around in the most disgusting bath closet in Virginia was how I had to go about proving that, so be it.

The hatch was hard to spot if you didn't know to look for it, just a pattern of cracks in the dirty plastic ceiling. The cracks said it was good size too, and my heart stuttered as I eyed it. Just one little break. I rose up on tiptoe, but couldn't quite reach the catch.

"Fine," I grumbled, flipping the toilet lid down with my toe and testing with one foot to see if it'd hold me.

Satisfied that it would, I stepped onto the rounded plastic and reached for the latch.

Stuck.

A small scream of frustration escaped my throat.

"What?" Kyle sounded panicked.

"Nothing, just annoyed." I called. "The damned thing is stuck."

I worked a fingernail under the edge and pulled, and the door gave about a millisecond before my nail did. Clenching my jaw against the smarting in my hand and ignoring the drops of blood that fell to the floor, I reached into the recess in the ceiling.

And pulled out a manila folder.

Bingo.

I leapt off the toilet and ran back to Kyle, skidding to a stop in front of the door.

"You found something." His eyebrows went up.

"Something important enough to hide in the bathroom ceiling."

"Well? What is it?"

I shook my head. "Get the hell out of here now. Read later."

He nodded. "Solid plan. I'll drive."

I shut the trailer door before I followed him back to the car, clutching the folder tight against my chest and whispering a prayer that Jinkerson was okay, wherever he was.

Kyle steered us back toward I-64 as I shot Bob a quick *Think I'm onto something, will be in as soon as I can. Everything good there?*

Bing. *As good as an average Tuesday on Andrews's shit list can be. Charlie has a story coming at noon. He's waiting for it.*

Shit.

Thanks for the heads up. I put the phone in the cupholder and opened the folder, flipping through a two-inch stack of papers.

"Anything good there?" Kyle asked

"Maybe?" I turned past a photocopied article about the vineyard's growth and found a spreadsheet with a collection of numbers that made no sense, but had Burke's name handwritten in the upper corner of the page. I kept going and found a newspaper clipping—one of Parker's columns about the Generals' playoff run last season. Three paragraphs in the middle were highlighted, a couple of stars doodled in the margins. Next up: an article from a magazine about the Governor's Cup. Four pages of unlabeled numbers. Three letters from the sheriff about complaints from Leroy Fulton—interesting. Behind those was a letter from an attorney demanding return of Fulton's property and threatening legal action. So he did go to a lawyer. In the very back of the folder, I found the news clippings about Jolene's death.

All of them.

No notes, no highlights. They were just there.

"What the hell?" I mumbled, shaking my head as I slapped the folder closed and looked up.

"Now can I ask?" Kyle's tone was teasing.

"Several pages of random numbers, one with Burke's name on it. Some clippings about the vineyard and the baseball team. And all the news stories about Jolene Sammons's death. The more I think about that, the more convinced I get there's more to that story."

"You call the ME yet?"

"The file has been moved to storage. Eight to ten weeks. Oh, if it didn't burn up a few months ago." I rolled my eyes. "On one hand, it's been forever and I get it. On the other, knowing what happened to her might help Parker and I don't have that much time. Not that I have a lot of choice."

Kyle nodded. "We weren't involved in the case, which means coming up with a reason to ask for a report that old could be tricky, but let me see if I can work some magic. Damned shame for people who loved her to think she took her own life if she didn't."

"Agreed. DonnaJo is trying too. She knows everyone over there."

My stomach burbled and I spotted a Sonic sign at the next exit. "You hungry?"

"I can always eat," Kyle said. "And good for you, taking better care of yourself."

I let my thoughts wander back to Ella Jane as Kyle steered the car into the restaurant parking lot. She must be terrified, feeling so bad and being alone. When my eyes pricked again I let it go.

It wasn't until I'd inhaled a burger and a large order of tater tots and stolen three onion rings from Kyle that it hit me.

I dropped the napkin I'd been wiping my hands on into the empty brown paper sack and dove for a pen and pad.

"What?" Kyle sat up straight, putting his half-eaten burger on the dash.

"Celia. She was supposed to have just broken up with Burke. And now Ella Jane is pregnant and Burke is dead," I jabbered as I scribbled it down.

"And Celia is skulking around talking about making people sick and looking like hell." Kyle stuffed the burger back into its wrapper and dug his phone out of his pocket. "Holy shit."

"Take the sheriff for a beer and see how much he knows about her."

Looking up from his screen, he started the car and threw it in reverse. "On it. And you?"

I nodded to the folder.

"I'm going to poke around this gambling thing."

27

I dropped Kyle in front of his building and he offered a reassuring smile as he shut the door and leaned in the open window. "We'll get there. I'll call you in a little while."

"Good luck," I said. "And thanks again."

"You behave yourself, and for the love of God, be careful."

"I won't do anything that would put me in danger." I smiled. "Trust me."

His ice blue eyes rolled back. "No comment."

I laughed and waved as he turned for the front of the building.

Snatching my phone out of my bag, I dialed Joey's number.

Before he could get the "hey" all the way out of his mouth, I started talking.

"You said you couldn't go to Calais when we talked on Saturday," I blurted. "But I saw your car there this morning. Are you still there? Please tell me you don't have anything to do with Burke."

I gripped the steering wheel tighter as I turned on Grace Street, a heaviness in my chest as I waited for the answer. But I had asked. Not long ago, I would've been too afraid of the answer to force the question out.

"Of course I don't. I meant it when I told you I didn't know the guy," he said. "What I do know is it doesn't seem to matter what's a good idea and what's a bad one where you're concerned."

I let the subtext go for the moment, blowing out a breath I hadn't realized I was holding. Of course he didn't. Because he was really telling me the truth—the whole truth, this time.

"I did some digging on Jolene Sammons," I said. "Old news articles was all I could find, but it's a start."

"Let me guess: Her death was wrapped up really quickly."

"I haven't been able to get hold of the coroner's report, but the paper said the sheriff closed the case in ten days. Though Sammons has some new partners at the top of my suspect list."

Deep breath in.

Heavy sigh out.

"One of those wouldn't be a guy named Phil Jinkerson, would it?"

I parked the car in the *Telegraph* garage and shut off the engine, letting my head fall back.

"It would indeed. Why do you know that?"

I could almost see his long fingers touch his temple, his tell for frustration or indecision. "He owes some dangerous people a whole lot of money, Nichelle. I started asking about Sammons the other day, and I came across someone who knew this Jinkerson guy because Dale introduced them. He was heavy into sports betting, and lousy at picking winners. Two days was as long as I could stand not stepping between you and this kind of trouble. I drove down this morning to make sure Sammons knows I wouldn't be happy if you got hurt trying to chase down whatever's going on out there. And to sit down with this Jinkerson myself. I'm pretty good at reading people."

He was trying to protect me. Better still: He was talking to me. Honestly. Not hinting and issuing vague ominous warnings. A smile played around my lips despite the spiraling insanity of this story.

"You didn't find him, did you?"

"I'm sorry to say I did not. Dale hasn't seen him since Saturday."

My fingers curled tighter around the phone.

"I went to his house. Someone had tossed it pretty good already."

"Wasn't me." Joey chuckled.

Damn. "Someone you know?"

"Let me see what I can find out without raising any eyebrows."

"Thank you." The words came out throaty and raw. "Really."

"Anytime, princess." His voice was soft. "Still on for dinner?"

"My place at five thirty? We can cook something if you want to stay in."

"I'll see you tonight." He clicked off the call.

I kicked my door open, my brain spinning in at least thirty directions—the most tempting of which was planning my evening.

Focus, Nichelle.

Sports betting, huh? Just exactly how deep was Jinkerson in?

* * *

I strode straight off the elevator to Parker's office, where I found him staring at his computer. His fingers rested on the keys, but the screen was blank.

I shut the door behind me and moved to the desk. "How you holding up?"

He shook his head before he turned around. "Half the people I know, not to mention a few cops, think I might be a murderer, and I'm supposed to get married this weekend at the scene of the crime. I feel like I'm losing my mind." He rested his elbows on the desk and dropped his head into his hands. "How did my life go from perfect to completely screwed in less than a week?"

I plopped into the chair behind me and pasted on my sunniest smile. "Sounds like you need a nosy crime reporter. Lucky for you, we happen to know one."

He raised his head and tried to smile. "We do, huh?"

I nodded, letting the smile fade as I caught his gaze. "Sports betting. I'm not asking for the cops or for the crime desk, and you can't bullshit me, Parker. I need some questions answered. Right now."

"What the hell does gambling have to do with my wedding?"

"Kyle thinks Burke was into it. 'Special guest of guys who do things like kill a man and stuff him in a barrel and then go have dinner without washing their hands' into it. And now I've got a missing vineyard manager and a good lead that says he was playing with those same folks. Plus, what we can find says Burke was winning—and Jinkerson wasn't."

Parker's eyebrows disappeared into his unruly blond hair. "One thing

Mitch always had over everyone was money. Why would he get mixed up in that?"

"The same reason the two richest guys in my high school stole car stereos on the weekends. It's a rush." I bent to retrieve a pad and pen from my bag and blinked when the room spun as I sat back up.

"You okay?" Parker asked.

I nodded. "Pulling all-nighters isn't the fun it was ten years ago. It apparently takes days of solid sleep to get back on my feet now."

He reached across the desk and squeezed my hand. "Thank you, Nicey."

I smiled. "Of course." I flipped the pad open as he leaned back and laced his fingers together behind his neck. "Who do you trust?" I asked.

He smiled. "That's not the easy answer it would've been this time last week, huh?"

"I'm so sorry, Parker."

He shook his head. "It's okay. Good to know who your friends are, right?"

He barely got the last word out before we both sat up straight. "Tony!" we blurted in unison.

Parker chuckled and sat back in his chair. "Great minds blah blah something something." He winked.

I bit the end of my pen. "I asked Ashton once if Tony was ever involved with anything shady and she swore he wasn't."

"He would never. But he knows everyone. I mean...every. One." Parker pulled his phone out and tapped the screen a few times while I scribbled notes. If Tony knew anyone who could tell us what Mitch might've been betting on, it could be the piece I needed to get to who put him in that barrel.

Parker stood. "You up for a little drive? Tony's in Williamsburg. Says he can meet us in New Kent in half an hour."

"Let's go." I followed him back to the elevator hoping Kyle was having some luck with the sheriff and the lab. There was a way out of this mess—one with a happy ending. Maybe the path to it was through New Kent.

* * *

Tony Okerson stirred sugar into his coffee, his hand moving at slow-turtle speed as his brow furrowed before he looked back up at us.

"Damn, man." He shook his head at Parker. "This is a clusterfuck if I've ever seen one."

Parker's laugh was dry. "You don't have to tell me twice."

I tapped my pen on the table. "A more accurate word hasn't been invented," I said, flipping my notebook open. "I know this is a lot to take in, but we have about four clocks running against us here, Tony. Is there anyone you can think of who might talk to us about this? Anyone Burke knew, maybe?"

"I didn't really know Mitch Burke, but what I've heard about him made me okay with that." Tony sat back in the booth and spread his arms down both sides of the bench. "I'm sure I know some guys who did though, if he was that into betting." He drummed his fingers on the laminate bench top. "The question is whether they'll talk to you or not. People tend to get antsy around reporters asking about illegal activity."

"I'm not looking to indict anyone on a gambling charge. All I want to know is if this can lead us to who killed Burke."

"Right. And how do I go 'Hey Rob, come talk to this reporter about your bookie, and oh by the way—know anything about this recent murder?'"

Any sane person would tell us to go straight to Hell.

Ugh. I tapped one foot.

"So, we'll go undercover. Just say I want to place a bet on Thursday night's Generals game."

Tony's head bobbed slowly as he reached for his phone. "Let me make a couple of calls."

He stepped out into the sunlight, scrolling through his contacts as he walked. I watched through the grimy plate-glass window at the little roadside diner where nobody cared who any of us were and cared even less what we were discussing.

"He's a good friend," I said.

"They're the best." Parker sipped his soda and smiled. "You're not too shabby yourself."

I didn't get another word out before Tony slammed back through the front door, reaching the end of the table in three long strides. "Y'all are never going to believe this."

I sat up straight, taking in the extra-wide of Tony's famous baby blues and the tight set of his jaw. "What?"

"Former teammate of mine likes to place occasional large bets. Never on football, even these days. But horses, baseball, boxing. Probably other stuff I don't know about." Tony's words were clipped, a marked departure from his easy drawl.

"I told him I had a friend who wanted to put a chunk of cash on Thursday's Generals game." He shook his head, and a light went on in mine.

"Oh, shit."

Parker's head whipped back and forth between the two of us. "What?"

Tony held my gaze for a second and nodded. "Yeah. He told me if I want to bet on baseball in Richmond, there's only one bookie to talk to—Mitch Burke."

Leaping. Louboutins.

28

I couldn't have told a judge how I steered the car back to the *Telegraph* building if Virginia's sentence for distracted driving was a whole summer wearing clogs.

Parker and I spent the entire drive lost in our own thoughts. I was desperate to get ahold of Kyle, but afraid to interrupt whatever he might be doing. If Burke wasn't betting, that explained why his financials didn't show evidence of gambling. But how the hell did a pretty-boy pitcher from a wealthy family end up running a bookmaking operation? He worked for the baseball club, for crying out loud. And Jinkerson—if he was betting through Burke and losing, and now Burke was dead, no cop would give Parker a second thought until they found him. Puzzle pieces crashed together in my head, and I tried to shake it clear, noticing as I did that we were parked in the paper's garage.

"Wow." Parker let his head drop back against the seat.

"Yeah."

"So what now?"

"I don't think I've ever seen a murder victim with more enemies." I shot him a sideways glance. "I went back out to Augusta this morning and talked to the dispatcher, who also happens to be the sheriff's daughter."

He turned his head without lifting it. "And?"

"And she's carrying Burke's child. Says they were planning to get married."

Parker's emerald eyes popped so wide I could see white all around the green. "Holy...He was into a little bit of everything, huh?"

I snorted. "And everyone. The girl at the vineyard, Sammons's niece? She thought they were getting married until recently."

Parker whistled, punching the button to release his seatbelt. "I'm really sorry for what happened here, but does it seem to you that he just kind of went through life discarding or upsetting people as he pleased? There are consequences for that kind of behavior."

"It appears he learned that the hard way." I shook my head. "The rules are different for the rich a lot of the time, you know? When daddy's money can always bail you out of trouble, and you don't have to treat anyone with respect, I guess this is what it turns you into."

"A monster." Parker shook his head as he kicked the door open. "Makes me suddenly grateful for my solidly middle-class upbringing."

I laughed and followed him to the elevator. "Amen to that."

I checked the time on my phone when we stepped into the newsroom. Just past three. Bob would be in with the section editors finalizing tomorrow's edition for at least another twenty minutes, so I hurried to my desk and flipped my laptop open, logging onto Channel Four's site to stalk Charlie and pulling out my notes for the day.

Her piece on Burke was the fifth story down, and my fingers shook as I clicked the trackpad to bring it up. I scrolled, my eyes scanning for Parker's name.

Not there. I went back up and read it from the top.

Nothing. Nothing she couldn't have gotten from the obit or my story anyway. She'd talked to two people in the Generals' front office and had a line about an ongoing police investigation.

That was it.

I pulled a pen from the cup on my desk and clicked it in and out as I stared at the screen. Just because she hadn't run it yet didn't mean she didn't have anything. But why would she sit on it?

I couldn't come up with a good reason, and certainly had more pressing questions to spend my time on than whether or not I was beating Charlie this week. Andrews could take his bitching straight out to the beach for a flying leap off the first pier he saw. We'd had three shark attacks over spring break too.

I clicked over to the police reports database and opened my email, hoping there was nothing too involved that required my attention.

An armed robbery at a convenience store in Short Pump, and the final report on a meth trailer in Goochland that went up in flames as the drug unit was getting ready to bust the operation. Four arrests, though three of those people were still in the burn unit at St. Vincent's.

Easy enough. I pulled my two earlier stories on the fire and wrote a new lead about the arrests, added the background about the six-month investigation into the manufacturing operation, and a few quotes from the fire marshal about the dangers of cooking drugs—both in general and in an enclosed space.

I got lucky and managed to catch the convenience store's owner by phone, but not so lucky in that he screamed for twenty minutes about high rent and safe parts of town and how he was just going to buy a gun of his own. I thanked him and replaced the receiver, shaking my head.

People who don't understand that criminals have cars always astound me, and then there's the statistical likelihood that him having his own weapon would just end with him or one of his employees getting shot. Ugh. Kyle'd even conceded that one after months of trying to get me to buy a gun over my loud assertions that I've met folks capable of shooting other people enough times to know I'm not one of them, and it was a dumb idea. Mace, I can handle all day. Especially with the nearly lifetime supply Kyle sent over when he heard that.

That only left Aaron, who didn't answer his desk phone or his cell. I left messages on both before I opened a file and wrote the rest of the story, leaving a hole for his comment and tacking the Crimestoppers hotline number onto the end.

Clicking back to the first window, I read through the copy on the fire once more before I attached it to an email to Bob, adding a note that we had file photos from when Lindsay went to shoot the charred remains of the trailer a month back.

I glanced at the clock and smiled. Four cups of coffee and a little motivation, and I had done all that in just over an hour. I'd take any small victory I could get.

Turning back to my notes on Mitch Burke, I opened the file I'd started on him over the weekend and started typing all the new information. I'd just added an all caps "BOOKMAKING? REALLY? WTF?" when the Channel Four Twitter feed popped up in the corner of my screen with *Happening Now: Richard Burke to hold press conference Wednesday morning RE: death of son Mitch. Watch News4 for up-to-the-minute coverage.*

I closed my eyes and rubbed my forehead, Aaron's voice ringing in my ears. "Richard Burke wants Grant Parker in a jail cell."

The cops failed him, so he was taking his crusade to the media. I felt for the man, but he was testing my patience.

I didn't need to beat Charlie. But I did need to know what the hell she thought she had on Parker and where she was getting her information—though I suddenly had an interesting theory on the latter.

I popped to my feet and grabbed the notebook and pen off my desk, half-running to the elevators. Andrews wasn't the only person in this building who could be determined when he wanted something.

* * *

"The one time in like, ever, that I want to talk to that little weasel. Of course he's not in." I muttered the words too softly for Shonda to hear, gritting my teeth as I returned her half-vacant smile, my eyes on the closed door to Andrews' office behind her.

"Is there something else I can do for you?" she asked.

I shook my head, feeling a bit sorry for her. She was pretty. Super sweet. Not terribly bright. Everyone assumed Andrews kept her around because their long lunch meetings more often involved a bed than any actual food, which made her the butt of constant jokes.

"I'll let him know you're looking for him," she said, jotting a note on a pink message slip. "I'm not sure if he'll be back today though."

I nodded a thank you and turned back for the elevator as she stood. "I think I need more coffee." She smiled. "Compiling these reports for Mr. Andrews is making me sleepy. So many numbers, they all run together."

She turned for the break room, and my feet rooted to the tonal gray striped carpet that was far chicer than the newsroom's mottled disco-era brown.

I glanced over my right shoulder. Shonda was gone. My left. The door had to be locked. Right? I put on my best nonchalant face, glad for once that Andrews was so pompous he kept this floor to himself and three overpaid bean counters who were never in the building.

I twisted the knob and let out a gasp when it gave. Spinning a circle, I shot glances to every corner of the floor.

"I don't know if he'll be back today," she'd said.

Let's hope not.

I ducked into the office and shut the door behind me, plunging the room into cavern-worthy darkness. Andrews had to be the only executive in the world with no windows. A view is distracting, he said. Personally, I took it as evidence that he wasn't human.

I dug out my phone and clicked the flashlight on. What the hell was I doing?

Probably being dumb. I paused and bit my lip, looking back at the door. He'd fire me in a hot minute if he caught me. But I needed a better idea of what Charlie knew, and Andrews was the only person who'd spoken to her. I spun back to the desk.

That tweet coming up on my screen made me want to shake Richard Burke, even as sorry as I felt for him. But it also made me realize that Andrews had blown an awful lot of hot air at Bob and me yesterday morning, and given us very little information about what had caused him to do so in the process. And we were both so afraid of our resident asshat, we didn't notice.

I disliked feeling afraid.

I surveyed the desk. Neat as a pin (seriously, what did he *do* all day?). I flipped through his inbox: mail, phone message slips sporting Shonda's big loopy handwriting, a file folder with a lot of numbers on the papers inside. No legal pad, no post its, no notebook.

Scurrying around to the other side, I slid the top drawer open. Paper clips, staples, Tic Tacs, and a condom. Ew. I slammed the drawer and moved on to the cabinet in the credenza before my brain could get too far into why he needed prophylactics in his desk.

A yellow legal pad sat atop a stack of fat manila envelopes. I pulled in a deep breath and said a silent prayer as I picked it up, my pulse taking off like I was preparing to jump a wormhole to another galaxy.

"Come on," I whispered as I flipped pages looking for Charlie or Parker's names.

Nothing.

Just jumbles of figures, doodles, and names of a few people I vaguely recognized as being either on our board or somehow involved in local politics.

I was ready to chuck the pad across the room and head back downstairs when the second-to-last page caught my eye.

Because it had Sammons's name in block letters across the top.

And Burke's right underneath it.

What the ever-loving hell?

I moved the flashlight across the page, my thoughts spinning in sixteen different directions as I tried to decipher Andrews's personal brand of shorthand.

Focus, Nichelle. I had time to figure out why our rat fink boss hadn't copped to knowing the murder victim later. Right now, I needed to make out why he knew him. And what he wanted with Dale Sammons.

None of Andrews's scribbles, beyond the names, made much sense. There was a star next to an all-capped LAT. Like your shoulder muscles? Were they working out together? I almost choked on the mental picture, shaking my head. I flipped three more pages, two of them blank. Rewound to the lists. Members of our board of directors. Politicians. Numbers.

And in the left margin of the last page: Bob.

I blinked, forgetting to breathe.

Was Andrews pushing so hard to get rid of Bob because of something to do with Dale Sammons and Mitch Burke? I'd walked into the mother of all coincidences if not, and almost nine years covering cops and courts would convince anyone that true coincidences were rarer than comfortable stilettos.

I tapped my phone to life and snapped pictures of the pages, setting the pad down and pulling the top envelope off the stack. My fingers shook so much when I went to open it I cut two of them on the paper.

Sticking my bleeding fingertips in my mouth, I nearly jumped out of my skin when I heard Andrews's voice from the other side of the closed door. Shoving the envelope back in the desk, I scrambled to the closet in the far corner, flinging his wool coat to one side and yanking the door shut behind me just as the lights came on.

Now what?

29

My shallow breathing was louder than a Pantera concert—between it and the blood pounding in my ears I wouldn't have heard Rick Andrews if he walked straight to the opposite side of the closet door and screamed like Freddy Kruger was under his desk.

I closed my eyes and said a fast, fevered prayer. Snooping had gotten me in trouble before, but I'd never actually been afraid it would cost me my job.

Holding my breath for a ten count, I followed that with a couple of slow ones. I could stay still for a while. Hopefully Andrews just forgot something and was on his way back out.

Please.

Closing my eyes, I listened. The chair squeaked like someone had flopped into it. Someone small and weaselly. Damn. Don't sit. Get out.

"I wonder what Clarke wants with me," Andrews said, sending my pulse speeding off to the races again. Deep breath. Focus. I hadn't told Shonda what I wanted. I waited for her to tell him that.

"I'd bet she wants to know something about your talk with Charlie Lewis." The nasally twang popped my eyes wide, my stomach plummeting to my toes.

No.

Freaking.

Way.

Andrews snickered. "You'd win that bet, wouldn't you? I wish you could've seen her face. She always tries her hardest to stay calm for Jeffers's sake, but she was pissed. I daresay I don't think she likes me very much."

Shelby laughed, and I tamped down a nearly untampable urge to slam the door open and punch her in the throat.

Footsteps. Slow, deliberate ones. Shelby's voice was an octave lower. "Being liked by Nichelle Clarke is overrated, baby. Handy. But overrated. Now back to this bet. Just what would I win?" I got a mental image of her running a manicured hand along Andrews's...anything...and needed a barf bag.

Jesus. Not only was she a lying, conniving, self-serving...I couldn't think of a word foul enough...but—Rick Andrews? Have at least a little self-respect, Shelby. I actually shuddered. Not that they'd notice if I decided to do the Macarena at that point.

He chuckled and I clapped my hands over my ears. Bad enough, walking in on Celia and Bubba in the barn out at Calais. If I had to listen to Shelby do the wild thing with Rick Andrews, my brain might explode.

Three hours (maybe ten minutes. Long ones) later, I loosened one hand. Nothing. I peeled the other away and leaned closer to the door. Wood squeaked against wood and someone made a low, throaty sound. Sweet mother of...They were on the desk. Ew, ew, ew, ew, ick. I pinched my eyes shut and shook my head. Not that anything could bleach that image out.

"We should go before someone sees us," Shelby breathed.

Yes. Do that.

Please, for the love of all that might've ever been holy, go.

Andrews whined. Whined. In the middle of making out.

Yuck.

"We have to be smart just a little longer." Shelby's tone took on a wheedling edge. "Come on. I'll meet you at your place and I'll—"

My hands flew back up. Nope. Don't want to know.

I waited three beats before I eased one palm away. "Fine. I'll be a good boy." Andrews sounded pouty, and I felt vomity for the second time in fifteen minutes.

The chair rolled across the floor, the sliver of light disappearing from under the door a few seconds later. When I heard the latch click, I stayed put for a few more minutes in case they were leaving separately, then cracked the closet door open.

All clear. My breath escaped in a *whoosh*, the room spinning around me. I cast another look at the cabinet with the stack of papers. I wanted to know what was in them, but what if someone came back?

Smarter to avoid tempting fate twice, right?

Right. I might not know what I didn't know, but I knew more than I had an hour ago. All I wanted right then was to get to Bob.

I crept on tiptoe to the door. Shonda's phone rang. "Rick Andrews's office, how may I help you?" she chirped, and I wanted to hug her. Everyone thought she was sleeping with Andrews, and it turned out to be Shelby. Shelby, who'd put on a great front of pretending to be an actual human—and friend—for a year. I'd trusted her. I'd made Mel invite her to the wedding, and then let her wheedle me into an invite to the rehearsal too!

I didn't think she knew about Burke before my story ran on Monday, but for all I knew, she was the one who'd tipped off Charlie. Hell, she might be where my little friend Girl Friday had gotten half the information she'd driven me batshit with for months before she got bored with her blog and stopped posting on it. I tried to push down the hollow "trust no one" feeling, but it oozed around the edges of the drawer I tried to shut over it.

I detested feeling stupid. I leaned my forehead against the back of the door, every single time I'd talked to Shelby right up through Monday morning flooding my thoughts. She'd hated me for so many years. Why had I believed she suddenly flipped a switch and wanted to play nice?

Because I wanted to. That's what Emily would say. My mom too. Too trusting—on a list of my faults, it had to hover near the top, which was pretty funny for a crime reporter when you thought about it.

I liked to believe there was good in everyone, and drawing it out was rewarding. Objectively, Shelby had become a kind of project for me at some point in the past year. Not only was I trying to like her, I wanted my friends in the newsroom to like and accept her. I thought being part of the group would make her feel secure.

Shonda's chair skated backward, and I put a hand on the knob. Give her a minute. I listened to her retreating footsteps, still fuming.

Maybe it hadn't been smart to trust Shelby. Hindsight and all that.

But self-flagellation had never been my favorite pastime. Stupid notwithstanding, I was also angry.

And thrilled that she and Andrews had no idea I was onto their game.

* * *

Shonda's still-lit computer screen showed row after row of numbers. I wanted to stop for a closer look, but I wanted to avoid getting caught more. Let Andrews keep thinking he was clever.

I made it all the way to the elevator without breaking into a run, but the newsroom wasn't so lucky. I nearly mowed down three photographers, a sports writer, and two interns between the elevator and Bob's office, which I barreled into without knocking, slamming the door behind me for good measure.

My editor flinched, sitting up straight and turning to face me when I flopped into my usual burnt-orange velour armchair, gulping deep breaths.

"You going to make it?" Bob's eyebrows lifted.

"I—" More air. Why couldn't I breathe? Was this what an anxiety attack felt like? I closed my fingers around the ends of the armrests on the chair and nodded. "Jesus, Bob," I huffed. "I can't—you won't—" I shot a glance at the closed door and wished it had a lock.

"Nichelle?" Bob leaned forward, his bushy white eyebrows drawing down. "What? The old man has a heart condition, remember?"

"Shelby," I choked out.

His face brightened. "Did she find something on Burke? I'm so glad the two of you are getting along better these days. She'd be a good reporter if she just—" He bit the word off when I raised one hand.

"She's sleeping with Andrews." I managed to keep my voice relatively low, given that my blood pressure must've been high enough to force the words out in a scream.

Bob froze for a second, then sat back, his shoulders slumping into the chair, eyes locked on mine. "You're not kidding."

"What kind of sicko would joke about Rick Andrews having sex?"

Bob snorted. "I'd tell you to be nice, but my fatherly need for admonishment seems to have abandoned me on this point."

"I wish my ability to conjure mental images would follow suit," I said.

Bob's eyes fell shut and he shook his head. "Start at the beginning."

I did. Bob stayed quiet through the whole story, his eyes going wide when I told him I'd gone snooping in Andrews's office, and wider when I told him what I'd overheard.

When I stopped talking, he leaned forward and rested his elbows on his knees. "I don't have to ask if you're certain it was her." It wasn't a question.

"It was her," I practically spat. "I can't believe I was stupid enough to think she was my friend."

"Now don't be too hard—" Bob began, and I shook my head.

"Already over it. Her fault, not mine. Check. But here's the thing: They don't know we know. And Andrews is up to something."

"When has he not been? Sniveling little...Well. Let's go back to these papers. You said you saw Burke's name?"

I nodded, pulling out my phone. "You don't think Mitch was back to angling for a job here, do you? Andrews has been awfully hot for me to smear Parker in the paper this week..." I trailed off, my eyes going wide. "I thought he was just being an ass, but what if there's more there?"

Bob's mouth popped into a little O.

"Damn. I saw them together a couple of months ago. Andrews and Mitch. Thought nothing of that until just now."

"You what? Where?"

"They were having coffee at a little shop I like over in Shockoe Slip. Looked like they were pretty deep in conversation. Andrews likes to feel important, and I just assumed he knew Richard Burke, and Mitch by extension, because of that."

What? Andrews had been trying to get rid of Bob for months, and now he was after Parker—and he'd neglected to mention he knew the murder victim?

"Bob, what if Mitch Burke was after your job?"

Bob shook his head. "That would sink the paper inside three months. Andrews is a social climber, but he doesn't care about anything as much as he cares about the bottom line and looking good in front of the board." He held out a hand. "Let me see what you found."

I clicked to the photo and handed the phone over.

He zoomed in on the image and moved his finger across the screen a few times.

"I didn't recognize all the names, but I know some of those folks are in local politics," I babbled. "And why wouldn't he say he knew Burke?"

He zoomed out and swiped to the next image, then tapped in, his face going as white as his hair. "Oh, dear God."

I popped out of the chair, trying to read upside down as I leaned over the screen. "What? What did I miss?"

Bob moved one finger across the photo, his head shaking slowly back and forth. "The bottom line." He slumped back in the chair and put my phone on his desk. "Jesus. I suppose at least I have him pegged right."

"Bob," I half-shouted, sucking in a deep breath and snatching up my phone. The jumble of letters and numbers, save the names of two of the people currently tied up in a murder case Andrews seemed keen to let Parker hang for, still didn't click together for me like they obviously had for my editor.

Bob leaned back in his chair, raising his eyes to mine. "Andrews only cares about the money. I'd bet those papers you saw are reports and proposals he has all ready to take to the board as soon as he can get rid of me."

I waved like a lunatic trying to guide a plane home. "Why? Care to share?"

"His notes here: He's got a majority of board members on his side, according to this list, and I'd bet my house these numbers are profit margins from the *LA Times*. He wants to sell the front." Bob shook his head, disgust practically running down his chin. "Ads on the fucking front page. He knows I'd never let him get away with that."

30

My eyes locked on Bob's Pulitzer and stayed there for a good ninety seconds.

In nearly a year of killing myself trying to keep Andrews in his cave, I'd come up with some pretty crazy reasons for his behavior, though I honestly thought it was just plain old-fashioned jealousy. But this...the front page was sacred space. I knew from long-ago history of media classes that it wasn't always that way, but it had been for more than a century, and with good reason.

Ads had their place and their function, but most people subscribed to the paper for news. A good front page told readers at a glance what was most important in their world today. Car prices or airline fare sales hardly kept with the theme. Moreover, the kind of money people paid for front-page ad placement often translated to not-so-subtle control of a paper's editorial content.

It wasn't just selling space. Andrews wanted to sell the *Telegraph*'s principles. The paper's soul.

No. Bob would never go for that. None of us would.

"I—" I swiveled my head back to my boss. "Wow. Just...wow. Can he do that?"

Bob waved a hand toward my phone. "The *Times* is. And it looks like they're making money with it."

I resumed my seat. "Are we hurting for money that badly?"

Bob shook his head. "We are not. Not lately, anyway. We've even seen an uptick in paid online subs, which is unheard of for a paper our size. You're doing good work, kiddo. I can't prove it, but I strongly suspect that people are willing to pay for access to our crime reporting because they get the whole truth, and they get it first, from us. Your work and Grant's column are keeping the lights on around here these days."

I smiled. "Well, thank you. Nice to know I'm doing my part."

Bob shook his head, his color returning and his volume increasing. "We don't need this. It might be different, even for a dinosaur like me, if we did. But we don't. In an era when papers all over the country are closing their doors and laying off more people every year, we're holding a steady page count, increasing revenue from sources everyone else thinks are non-starters, and managing to stay relevant even with the internet and social media breathing down our necks twenty-four hours a day." Bob thumped one fist on his desk. "We work ourselves to death because some of us still see what we do as honorable and important to the community, and the ship is being run aground by a man who cares about nothing but his bonus structure, which would certainly benefit from this bullshit."

My eyes popped wide, and I reached for Bob's hand. "Easy there, chief. Your blood pressure."

He closed his eyes and pulled in a couple of deep breaths, squeezing my fingers. "I know."

Letting go, I tapped a finger on my knee, uncrossing my legs and recrossing them the other way. "So what do we do about it?" I asked.

Bob raised his eyes to mine. "Pardon?"

"We now have the advantage, chief. He doesn't know we know what he's up to. For months, I've run my ass off to impress him, and you've been afraid of him, but I'm not scared anymore. I'm pissed the hell off. So what's our smartest move?"

Bob's lips disappeared into a thin line. "That's a good question. Almost like you ask them for a living or something." He winked and I grinned, glad I'd pulled him out of his panic so easily.

"Or something."

He ran one hand through his thinning white hair. "Let me think on it a while. What've you got for me today?"

"I sent you one already, I'll have the other finished as soon as I find Aaron, and Richard Burke has called a damned media circus show he's billing as a press conference for tomorrow morning that I should probably advance, since Charlie has it."

"We still don't know what she's got on Grant?"

I bit my lip. I didn't want to argue with Bob about Parker anymore. I just wanted to prove him wrong and put the whole damned thing behind us.

"Nope. I went looking in Andrews's office for it, but found nothing."

"Oh, you found something. On balance, something better."

I nodded and stood. "Glad that mess is figured out. On to the next one."

"Keep me posted."

I stepped back into the newsroom and dialed Aaron again from my cell. No answer. I opened a text.

Need forty seconds of your time for something unrelated to Burke. Want to go home. Call when you can please.

I didn't make it back to my desk before the handset started buzzing. I slid a finger across the screen and raised it to my ear. "That was fast."

"Not sure what you're talking about, but I have a feeling you've got the wrong guy," Kyle said. "Fast isn't my style."

I rolled my eyes, then focused on the big silver and glass clock on the wall over the elevators. Four fifteen. I was too tired to tell if the day was flying or crawling. "Wrong cop. But boy do I need to talk to you," I said. "Can you give me a few to finish something up and then meet me at Byrd Park? I feel like walking."

"Of course. Half hour?"

"Perfect."

* * *

Aaron texted me a reply for my robbery story, but I didn't miss that he refused to say why he couldn't talk. And I knew him well enough to know that wasn't good. Adding that to what he'd said about Richard Burke and the press conference Burke had planned for morning, I came up somewhere between intense worry and outright panic.

Tick tock, Nichelle.

I opened a blank file and stared at the cursor for a half-second, letting all the worry of the day wash through me before I shoved it aside and started typing.

Richmond real-estate developer and Virginia History League President Richard Burke will speak to reporters on behalf of his family Wednesday morning, a representative of BurCo announced Tuesday afternoon.

"We appreciate the respect of our clients and friends as the Burke family deals with the tragic loss of Mitchell," a press release announcing the event states. "Richard and Annabeth Burke wish to thank the community for the outpouring of love and support that has helped comfort them at this difficult time."

Scrolling back to the top, I scanned the lines from the press release three times, something dancing around the edges of my thoughts. I didn't like Richard, but recognized that his abject hatred of Parker probably contributed to that.

Emailing the story to Bob and packing up my computer, something kept bugging me. I was halfway to the elevator before I got it.

Throwing my bag into the passenger seat, I slid into the car and dug my phone out, clicking my web favorite for Channel Four. Not the first lines, but the third paragraph of the press release was nearly verbatim in Charlie's report. From yesterday.

She had the inside track with the family.

At least she wasn't getting her information from someone closer to Parker. I'd take any little win this week.

Having an answer to at least one question numbed the sting of losing to Charlie a bit as I turned out of the garage. And Richard Burke couldn't avoid me in front of TV cameras tomorrow morning.

Parking the car near the boathouse, I strolled to the concession window on the back side of the octagonal brick building, asking for a diet Coke.

No Kyle yet.

I perched on a bench where I could watch the paddleboats and geese circling the little lake, keeping an eye out for Kyle. Straggling cherry and pear blossoms drifted off the trees with every flutter of the breeze, pale petals blanketing everything from the water to my hair.

Five minutes of sunshine and flowers did wonders for my mood—by the time Kyle's Explorer turned into the lot, I was even smiling. I hopped up and met him on the sidewalk.

"You won't believe what—" I began.

"Guess what Bonnie—" he blurted.

We both stopped.

"After you," I said as he offered a small bow and said, "Ladies first."

I rolled my eyes. "Rock paper scissors?"

My scissors cut his paper, and he fell into step beside me as I recounted Tony's bombshell about Burke, plus what I'd dug up (not that I said where) on Jinkerson, and what I'd noticed in the press release and Charlie's story.

"Damn." Kyle blew air out in a low whistle. "A bookie? Why the hell would a guy like that..." He shook his head. "Never mind. I learned a long time ago that criminals think differently than other people. But that explains the photos I found and the financials. I can do a little more digging from that angle and see if he'd pissed anyone off lately. Particularly Jinkerson."

"Perfect. And thanks. Okay, now you." I shot him an expectant look as we rounded the end of the lake and started a second lap, breathing in the magnolia and fresh-cut grass that meant summer was coming.

"First, I got a hit on your fingerprints."

I stopped walking. "We actually got one that wasn't mine?"

"And she had a public intoxication arrest last year, so it was easy to find." He smiled.

"She?"

"Maisy Sue Westlake? Ring a bell?"

"I—" I opened my mouth, then stopped. Maisy? What the hell?

Kyle watched my face expectantly. I shook my head. "Sorry. She's one of Mel's bridesmaids."

"Was she in your room at any point when she might have touched your computer?"

"Not with my permission. But what was she doing?"

"Sounds like we ought to find out. I'll get more background, associations, et cetera. Why is she a bridesmaid?"

"Childhood pal of Mel's."

"No connection to Burke?"

"Not that I know of. But I believe we should check that out."

"Shouldn't be too hard." He nodded. "Thing two: Bonnie wasn't as hurt by our breakup as I thought, and she agreed to meet me for coffee this afternoon."

"More coffee? You won't get a bit of sleep."

"Worth it. Get this: You know how I said before that the sugar in the wine accelerated the decomp such that they couldn't tell how or when Burke died without some fancy-pants science work?"

I nodded. "Because why should anything be easy?"

"The tox screens all came back worthless because of the wine, so no telling on the poison thing," he said.

Damn. I sighed, and he patted my shoulder. "But. Big but. Some of the fancy pants, thanks to Bonnie, says it's likely Mitch Burke was killed last Thursday morning."

I shot a silent thank you to the heavens as I grabbed Kyle's hand and squeezed. "Before Parker saw the emails?"

Kyle nodded. "Likely. Not for sure. So we're still not in the clear, but I like this. The bigger thing is that she was able to examine the bones today. There's a nick on his collarbone that suggests he was stabbed."

I stopped walking. "Stabbing isn't generally a premeditated crime," I said.

"Nope." He shook his head.

"Which might be good for Parker because if he went all the way out to Calais intending to kill Burke, surely he'd have gotten hold of a gun."

Kyle nodded. "Bonnie's trying to narrow down a weapon and confirm cause of death."

"What would I do without you?" I asked. "I can't possibly thank you enough. We may pull this off yet."

Kyle nodded, putting one hand on my elbow and starting for the parking lot.

"Where are we going?"

"You are going to do something fun. Blow off some steam before you make yourself sick from the stress," he said. I blinked, my thoughts wandering to my dinner plans. Was Kyle psychic? "I am going to haul ass over to the courthouse and see if I can catch a lingering judge. I want a warrant for Jinkerson's financial records."

My face could've split from the force of the smile as I threw my arms around Kyle when we got close to my car. This rabbit trail felt like it might be the right one. Just in the nick of time.

"We're not in the clear yet, but we'll get it," Kyle whispered into my hair, tightening his arms around me. "Go on home. Take a night off."

I smiled as I stepped back. "Bonnie should be more upset. You're a pretty great catch. Thank you."

He nodded, his lips disappearing into a thin line, before he turned and strode to his car. "I'll call you if I get lucky," he said. "Um. With the warrant."

I waved and slid into the car, hoping the universe could spare enough luck to save the wedding too.

31

Checking the mirror, I slicked on some lip gloss before I half-ran to the door. It hadn't actually been a hundred years since I last saw Joey, but it damned sure felt like it. And while he'd seemed fine on the phone, I was determined to put a rest to his insecurity about Kyle—no matter what that required.

I found him in his favorite corner of my sofa, Darcy curled in his lap like she owned him.

The dark eyes that met mine were more open than I'd ever seen them, the depth of emotion so vast I might fall in if I looked too hard.

Every word I'd planned to say flew right out of my head.

I crossed to the sofa in four strides, moved Darcy to the floor, grabbed the butter-soft Italian lapels of Joey's jacket, and fell into his lap as I covered his lips with mine. His eyes popped wide for a half-second, his mouth stiff with shock.

I shut my eyes and tightened my grip, pouring everything I felt for him into the kiss.

His arms went around me, squeezing when I flicked the crease of his upper lip with the tip of my tongue. I ran my hands up his chest to his shoulders, then buried them in his hair as I slid my tongue over his, electricity skating across every nerve. I'd never minded letting Joey lead when things got physical, but being the one in charge was a whole different kind of thrill. I curled my fingers around his thick dark hair and pulled him closer, letting my lips brush over his jaw.

"Hello there to you too," he choked out, his voice hoarse.

"You trusted me," I mumbled against his lips, my fingers moving to loosen his tie. "Things have been good between us for a while now, but this week—this story." I pulled back a half-inch and locked eyes with him as the tie came free and fell to the floor. "You trust me. I'm not often short for words, but I don't think I can find the right ones to tell you how big a deal that is to me."

He put his hands under my arms and lifted, turning me to face him. My skirt sliding up, I moved one knee to each side of his hips.

Brushing my hair back, he nodded slowly. "I'm glad. I want you to trust me. I want…I want so much more than I could tell you, Nichelle." The words were almost a whisper, his eyes dissolving into chocolate pools.

I framed his face with my hands and kissed him again, then trailed my lips across his jaw to his earlobe, grazing the soft skin with my teeth and smiling at his sharp intake of breath and the way his fingers flexed into my hips. "Like what?" I whispered.

He slid his arms around my waist and squeezed, dropping soft kisses along my collarbone. "Like things I have no right to wish for. What kind of future—"

I put one finger under his chin, raising his face back to mine. "This kind." I punctuated the words with slow, simmering kisses.

"Nichelle," he practically growled, pushing at my shoulders, "I'm serious. There's more to life than this."

Sitting back, I let my fingers graze the stubble on his jaw. "I know that. But since I've misplaced my crystal ball, I have to follow my heart. We have something good. Something special. That's all that matters." I flicked the top three buttons on his shirt open, slipping my hands under the starched cotton. "Absolutely all that matters." I meant every word.

His head fell back, his hands moving up and down my spine as I rained kisses on his throat. Letting out a low groan, he sat up and pulled me close, burying his face in my hair.

"God, I love you."

The words ricocheted off the walls like AK fire, my whole universe narrowing to a foot and a half of space on my sofa.

I listened to people talk for a living. In nine years working cops and courts, I'd heard dozens of murder confessions and thousands of hours of sob-punctuated testimony from victims and grieving loved ones alike.

Never—not ever, not once—had my ears pricked to more emotion loaded into three simple syllables.

And I couldn't move. Not a breath, not a muscle. Even the ones that make my mouth work.

My tear ducts, however, flipped into overdrive.

He let out a shuddering breath, easing me back until he could see my face. A smile played at the corners of his mouth when he saw the welling in my eyes. "I'm not sure I meant to say that out loud, but I'm damned sure I mean it." He closed his eyes, resting his forehead against mine, and something in my heart shifted.

For better or worse, it wouldn't be the same again.

I bit my lip, tears spilling over as I burrowed into his arms, my words muffled against his jacket. "Me too." Turning my head, I cleared my throat and let the next words fall one by one. "I love you. So much."

He traced his fingers lightly up and down my arms and across my shoulders. "That's the best news I've heard in...maybe ever."

I sat up, wiping at the mess of mascara running down my face. "Not quite the sexy look I'd pictured for this moment, but at least you know I mean it."

He moved his hands to my hair and used his thumbs to brush away the last of the tears. "You are stunning. Always." His full lips tipped up at the corners, his dark eyes holding my gaze. "Stunning, and smart, and stubborn."

"And all yours." I brushed my fingers over his cheek. "Good, bad, and indifferent."

"All mine." He raised his face to plant soft kisses on my cheeks. "I like that."

He stood, lifting me like Darcy would be more burdensome. I smiled. "And don't you forget it."

A half-dozen more breathless kisses later, he laid me on the bed and shrugged out of his jacket.

"No danger of that," he said as he tossed the jacket aside and went to work on his shirt. "I am seriously inept at forgetting anything to do with you."

* * *

It was dark when I climbed out of bed, leaving Joey sleeping as I tiptoed to the shower. I turned the hot water on and slipped my arms into a robe before I went to the living room to check my phone, hoping Kyle had gotten his warrant.

No Kyle.

I had one text from Parker (*call me when you can*), and six missed calls from Jenna. Weird.

I clicked the return button and raised the phone to my ear, leaving the water running as I stepped onto the front porch.

"I was just putting together the search party," Jenna said in place of hello.

"Sorry. I was...tied up."

"If that has something to do with Pretty Boy, I don't want to hear it." I could practically see Jenna's nose wrinkle, and I sucked in a breath so sharp I choked myself.

"Poor word choice," I said when I stopped coughing. "What's so urgent?"

I heard a deep breath go in, followed by a pause and a long sigh. "I just —you've been busy with your other friends and their wedding and your boyfriend, and I miss you. You know? Things here are kind of a mess, and... what're you doing tomorrow night? Can I crash for a mid-week girls' night?"

The "of course" stuck in my throat, partly because of the softball-sized lump the sadness in my best friend's voice called up, but also because I was buried in this Burke investigation, and with Charlie half a step behind me and the Andrews/Shelby mess, I wasn't sure I could handle one more thing.

But I'd figure it out. I fluffed the cushions on my porch swing and perched on it, watching lightning crackle across the western sky. "Jen, I'm so sorry. I didn't mean to make you feel forgotten. I don't even know how to begin to explain how smothered I am this week."

"Oh. Of course. I get it." She couldn't have sounded more bereft if someone had run over her dog. If she had one.

"No! You don't—of course you can come by. Seven work for you? I miss you too." I really did. And I felt like a terrible friend. "I need more hours in the day. Can we get someone on that?"

Jenna laughed. "I really do get it. I've just had about all I can take this week, and I need some Nichelle time. Thought I should speak up."

"I'm so glad you did. See you tomorrow night."

"Don't get tied up again." She giggled.

"Not what I meant!" I clicked the end button, opening my texts and shooting Kyle an *any luck?*. Thunder rumbled in the distance as I hustled back to the shower.

I nearly choked again when Joey grinned his sexy grin as I pulled the curtain back. "I thought you'd never come back in the house," he said. "Care to join me?"

I did indeed. I let my eyes roam over his damp skin, taut over the layer of muscle beneath. Damn, but he was hot. I dropped my robe and stepped under the spray. "I cannot tell you how much I hate to say this, but I may yet have work to do tonight."

Joey tipped his head to one side, then grabbed my wrist and pulled me close to him, locking his arms around my waist and dropping a kiss on the tip of my nose. "You're cute when you're ridiculous. Have I told you that?"

I pushed up on tiptoe and landed a chaste peck on his lips. "You're sexy when you're trying to be tempting. But I'm serious. Mitch Burke was a bookmaker. Sports betting specifically, I'm told."

Joey froze, his eyes going wide as a clap of thunder rattled the windows and the sky opened up over my house.

I waited three beats before he shook his head. "That's who they were protecting."

"Huh?" I furrowed my brow.

"This Jinkerson guy. Shouldn't have been hard to find out who he owed money to, but I got three vague replies and one direct 'it's none of your damn business.' They're protecting someone. Odds are, it's your murder vic."

I picked up the shampoo and poured some into my hand, trying to keep my voice even as my heart took off for the races. "Why would your... associates...do that?"

"Two reasons I can think of: because they know why he's dead, or because he's more important than anyone thought." His hand drifted to his temple. "I don't like this, Princess."

I lathered my head, fighting panic. "I don't exactly love it. But I can't just walk away."

His fingers covered mine, his bigger hands taking over scrubbing my scalp. "I'm not a hundred percent sure I can keep you out of trouble."

"And I don't want you getting yourself in any trying to look out for me." I stepped under the water and rinsed my hair, trying desperately to come up with something that would convince him to back off. Celia. Alexei. I opened my eyes and raised them to his. "There are so many stories around this murder it gives me a headache when I think about it too hard—you still have that friend at the INS?"

"I do. Was Mitch Burke an international bookie?"

I laughed, shaking my head as I motioned for him to turn and let me scrub his back. By the time I was done, he had all the specifics on Chef Alexei.

"You're not kidding about the wide variety of possibilities. But I like a chef who knows his poison better than the gamblers, for sure. I'll see what I can get."

"Thank you." I rinsed the sponge. "Please be careful. I don't want you to get hurt."

Lightning crackled, lighting the sky outside the teeny porthole window an electric blue, thunder crashing before the glow had faded. I shut off the water.

Joey nodded, wrapping me in a towel and pulling me close.

"Back at you, baby." His chin rested on top of my wet hair as another crash outside took out the lights. "I may not have the key to your puzzle, but I can keep you safe tonight."

32

The power came back on with a bleep of the microwave a little after midnight, and I let Joey out the kitchen door at five thirty with a long kiss and a promise to call later. By six, I was on my second cup of coffee, pacing the house as I waited for it to be something resembling a respectable telephone hour.

"I need a list, Darce."

She raised her head and looked around when I said her name, then returned her chin to her paw when she didn't sense any food nearby.

Poor Darcy. If it was possible for a dog to think their human is crazy, mine had plenty of reason to.

I grabbed a pen and pad from the basket on my end table and perched on the edge of the sofa.

BURKE

—Bookmaking: How did this start? Clients? Caccione ties?

—Wealthy family

—History with Parker

—Threatening e

. . .

My mouth popped into an O. The pen fell to the floor.

Kyle's voice floated through my head. "Likely he died early Thursday morning."

Early. Thursday morning.

Not just before Parker saw the emails.

Before Bob got the emails.

I was a thousand percent sure that they'd arrived just before lunch. Splitting hairs? Maybe.

But maybe not.

"Holy. Freaking. Manolos," I whispered.

What if Burke hadn't sent those horrifying letters at all?

I picked up my pen and chewed the end of it. Who could write something like that?

The kind of person who could stuff a guy in a wine barrel, maybe? I jumped up and paced.

"This is crazy, Darce," I said when she lifted her head. "Why would anybody bother with such an elaborate cover?"

She raised her nose and sniffed for food before she huffed and resettled her chin on her paws.

Why? Because they wanted to give Parker a motive.

My pace quickened.

Early Thursday morning. "What am I missing, Darcy?"

She didn't move that time. My dog is only social when there's food to be had.

Social. I paused.

Food.

The mystery solo dinner on Facebook was Thursday evening.

Damn. I sprinted for my laptop, nearly dropping it before I got it open thanks to my shaking hands.

I clicked to Mitch's page and scrolled past more than a hundred sympathy messages before I found it. Clicking it up, I read the fine print.

Scrolled down more and checked other posts, then went back up to the sore thumb—not only was nobody tagged, but it was the only check-in for months—maybe forever—that wasn't geotagged from the iPhone app. Which meant this last one likely came from a computer.

I scurried back to the living room and grabbed my phone. Jenna was always up with the sun.

"You're not canceling, are you?" Her voice was wary.

"Nope. Need to pick your husband's computer geek brain."

"Good luck with that. Some sort of security breach at the bank has had him working around the clock all week. I'm taking the kids to his mother before I come to your place tonight."

I pinched my lips together to keep a scream in, then thanked her and promised to be home at a decent hour before I hung up and clicked my messages. Finding Chad's name, I opened a new one. *Major urgent Nancy Drew question: Can you find an IP address from a Facebook post?*

Send. I crossed my fingers and stared at the screen.

Delivered. Read. Gray dot bubble.

Bing. *I'm kinda busy trying not to lose my job.*

So sorry to interrupt, wouldn't ask if it wasn't life or death.

Whatever. What do you need?

He was stressed. I could relate.

It's a public profile, Mitch Burke. There's a check-in from last Thursday night at a restaurant in Charlottesville. But it looks like it came from a computer, since all the others have his location services on through his phone. Need to know where the computer is.

Bing. *I'll get to it as soon as I can.*

I added a half-dozen smileys to my thank you, hitting the back button and noticing Parker's text from the night before. I touched his name. *Have a thing this morning, catch up in a bit?*

I sent the text and went to finish getting dressed. Richard Burke's media circus pre-empted the staff meeting, and I wanted a front-row seat.

I parked on Fifth Street, about a half-block down the canal from the ironworks, and walked down the steps and along the water, my thoughts trailing to Joey and how much I'd like to bring him here. His words, the raw truth in his voice the night before—my skin tingled all over at the memory. Maybe my happily ever after wasn't as far out of reach as I'd thought.

I found a custodian setting up a podium in front of the old waterwheel that once powered the factory, and a few guys unfolding rows of chairs. Grabbing a seat at the left end of the front row, I let my thoughts roam, the quiet of the morning and warmth of the sun lifting my spirits. It was only eight fifteen. Burke wasn't due here until nine, and the museum didn't open until ten.

Charlie, however, apparently had the same idea I did about early arrival.

"Is there anything you don't have to beat me to?" she huffed, plopping into the seat next to me while her cameraman set up in the center aisle.

"I wasn't trying to beat you, Charlie." My voice sounded tired. "I just wanted to make sure I didn't miss anything."

She lifted her sunglasses and gave me a onceover. "The way I hear it, you're missing half this story. Or refusing to tell it. I'd rather believe the former, because I respect you. But since it's just us girls this morning—are you protecting Grant Parker?"

"Where the hell are you getting your information?" I didn't mean for the words to sound so sharp, and I pulled in a deep breath when she flinched, her blue eyes going wide before the shades dropped back over them. "Sorry. I'm under too much stress, and that's not your fault." Any more than usual anyway.

"Sore spot?" she asked.

I shrugged, holding my tone carefully even. "He's my friend, and you're insinuating that he murdered someone. So yeah, maybe a little."

"I'm not insinuating anything. Just warning you that this could get very complicated very quickly."

I turned to face her. "What are you up to?"

"Wouldn't you love it if I were stupid enough to share that." She smiled. "For months now, I've taken second to you on every important story to come through town. Not this time." She strolled to the podium to direct mic placement, and I stood, draping my lavender sweater over a chair at the opposite end of the row on my way to the water's edge. Charlie was getting under my skin more than she should, and the last thing I wanted was a big scene in the middle of an event.

When other reporters started to filter in about a quarter 'til, I went back to my seat and fished out a notebook and pen.

Richard and Annabeth Burke arrived at five after nine and took another ten minutes to huddle with a couple of powerbroker attorneys I recognized from the courthouse before they stepped to the podium, at ease in front of the cameras from years of TV appearances.

Richard cleared his throat and thanked everyone for coming. His voice had the unaccented precision of old money and an Ivy-League education.

My eyes skipped to his wife.

And locked there. On her earrings, in particular.

I wasn't sure where else I might've seen Annabeth Burke, but I'd seen those earrings at dinner last Friday night, the face attached to them twisted into a glare.

Holy Manolos.

She really was looking at Parker. And before Sheriff Rutledge could've possibly notified them about Mitch.

If Mitch didn't still blame Parker for his sister's death, his mother sure as hell did.

No wonder Richard was pressing Aaron to haul my friend in.

I wanted to shoot a glare straight back at her, but couldn't because I felt so sorry for her. I couldn't imagine Jenna losing even one of her babies. Both? Horrifying.

My eyes skipped to Richard, who was thanking the RPD and Sheriff Rutledge for their hard work.

"I also want to thank the communities my family and I are so blessed to be part of. From Virginia Tech and Blacksburg through the valley and to the historical community here in Richmond—we've felt your love and support this week, and appreciate it more than I can say."

I scribbled.

He paused, and hands went flying all around me. I kept mine at my side. "Charlie." Burke nodded to her.

Yep. Credible source she'd found for herself, the victim's angry, grudge-toting parents. Nice.

"What's your favorite memory of your son, Mr. Burke?" Charlie asked.

Richard Burke smiled and shook his head. "There are so many good ones. My favorites all involve a baseball diamond though. He loved the game. He loved the Generals. And while he and I may not have seen eye to eye on this new ballpark everyone is talking about, I'm here today to tell you all that it will have the full support of BurCo going forward."

A collective gasp went through the crowd. Sammons wanted to stomp all over a historic part of the city to build his massive new stadium, and hadn't even bothered using classical architecture that might make it sort of kind of blend in, according to the story Mel had been so worried over Monday.

Richard Burke was the voice of Virginia History. He'd restructured his grandfather's company to preserve it.

With him behind this stadium, there'd be little stopping it.

I jotted notes, mostly for Melanie, since this was her baby. Everyone around me dove for their iPhones.

Journalism in the age of the Internet 103: Nothing lights up Twitter like a big announcement. I fished out my phone and tapped the little white bird icon, typing *BREAKING: Richard Burke says he'll back new ballpark in son's memory. #RVA #news @Telegraphnews*

I posted it, knowing our web editor would see the tag, retweet it, and tease it on our site.

I put my phone down just as Burke pointed to Dan Kessler from WRVA.

"Mitch was a healthy young man, and the police departments involved have said little outside that they're looking into his death. What happened to him?"

I closed my eyes as every reporter around me leaned forward a hair.

"I understand their caution and respect the work the police are doing," Burke said, glancing at his wife from the corner of his eye. She pinched her lips into a thin line. "But I also can't keep quiet about this any longer. Mitchell was murdered. And while everyone is asking questions, I have a few I'd like Grant Parker to answer."

33

Boom.

Burke's bombshell left everyone still for a full thirty seconds before the patio erupted, people digging for their phones and screaming questions all at once. "Can you clarify that statement?" and "Are you accusing Grant Parker of murder?" zinged past me a hundred times in twelve seconds. Burke took a step back, putting an arm around his wife, who hid her face in his shoulder. One of the attorneys moved to shield the two of them, and the other stepped to the podium and raised both hands.

"That's all for today, folks. Mr. and Mrs. Burke thank you for being here and for your understanding."

I jumped to my feet and grabbed my bag, striding for the steps.

"Nichelle! Nichelle, wait up!"

I sucked in a deep breath, one foot on the bottom stair. So close.

Pasting on a smile, I turned to face Kessler. "What can I do for you, Dan?"

"You and Parker are tight. What gives?"

I kept the smile in place. "I have no idea what you're talking about."

"Come on. The man just said his son was murdered and dropped Parker's name a half-sentence later. You know more than you're letting on. Are you protecting him?" He glanced over his shoulder at Charlie. Not surprisingly, she'd penetrated the wall of attorney and was deep in conversation with the Burkes. Everyone outside their little circle looked irritated. "Charlie will have your ass, and you know it. She's tired of you beating her to every punch, and hungrier than I've ever seen her. What's going on?"

"If Parker was a murder suspect, wouldn't the best people to ask about that be…oh, say, the police?" I put on my best innocent tone, not that it fooled Dan.

"Give me a break. They're not talking, and you know it. I just can't tell if you're the reason for it. Did you ask White to keep this quiet? Everyone knows you're the detective's pet."

"Sorry, Dan. Can't help you." I jogged up the steps. "Have a good day."

By the time I made it back to my car, my heart was pounding like I'd run a 10K. I dialed Aaron's cell for the fifth time. "Pick up, dammit."

Voicemail.

I stowed the phone in my bag, trying to even my breathing. Nobody would run an accusation like that without comment from the PD. It's a direct route to a lawsuit. I needed Aaron to buy me just a bit more time.

"If he's not answering me, he won't answer them either," I muttered to myself as I started the car. Surely I was right. I hoped.

* * *

I plopped down at my desk a few minutes later, snatching up the phone and dialing Sheriff Rutledge's office. Ella Jane's sweet voice came on the line and I tried to control my tone as I asked to speak to her dad.

"He's still up in Richmond," she said. "I have those reports you wanted the other day though. I can fax them if you'll give me your number."

I rolled it off and thanked her.

"Sure thing. Anything else I can help with?"

I bit my lip. Worth a shot. "I wanted to ask the sheriff if anyone's filed a missing person's report this week," I said. "I heard something I'm looking to confirm. On the record."

"You heard right. Phillip Jinkerson was reported missing yesterday afternoon. Nobody's seen him since Saturday."

"Are y'all thinking he left town?" I asked.

"His car is gone, but none of his things seemed to be missing when they searched his home." Her voice dropped to a conspiratorial whisper. "There was blood on the bathroom floor. Not a lot, but enough to notice. That's probably more than I should tell you without permission though."

Oh, Lord. My fingernail. Not that I could blurt out that I'd (technically) trespassed and (technically) stolen some documents from their crime scene before it was a crime scene. I clicked off the call with a thank you, dialing Kyle next.

"Morning," he said. "I'm waiting to see a judge about the vineyard manager's bank records as I speak."

"That vineyard manager is now officially missing. Like, report filed, not showing up for work missing. Ella Jane said his car is gone too," I blurted without a hello. "And Richard Burke dropped Parker's name at his presser this morning, and it's possible I'm actually losing my mind, Kyle."

"Shit." His voice was tight. "It'll be okay. They're ready for me. I'll call you when I can."

"Thank you."

I dropped the phone into the cradle and opened my laptop, staring at the blank screen. What on Earth could I say about Richard's little show that wouldn't cast Parker in the worst possible light?

* * *

It took me an hour to tiptoe across the minefield that was the Burke story, shading it with every bit of benign information I could find. I quoted Richard as saying Mitch was murdered, but left Parker out for the time being. If Aaron suddenly started returning calls, I'd have to add it. But no one else could use it without talking to the cops. Not credibly, anyhow.

I checked Parker's office, but it was dark. I wanted to ask Melanie if Maisy had been one of those notches on Mitch Burke's bedpost, but her cube stayed empty all morning too, and by lunchtime I was due back at the courthouse for DonnaJo's closing argument in the assault case.

She nailed it again. An hour in, I had a whole notebook full of great quotes, and the defense couldn't touch her case. It would make a nice metro front for tomorrow.

The judge called a recess at two thirty and DonnaJo handed me a thick file folder as I walked up the aisle toward the doors.

She smiled at my wide eyes and open jaw.

"Thank God for summer interns," she said. "One of them spent six hours in a warehouse the ME's office uses for storage yesterday tracking this down. Not sure what you want with an old suicide, but I hope it helps you."

I squeezed her shoulder and hugged the file to my chest, batting away the urge to open it with Charlie twelve feet away. "You are amazing," I said. "Thank you, doll."

I stepped outside to return a call from Kyle.

"There you are," he said when he picked up.

"Sorry. Trial. Please tell me you have something."

"I have a couple of somethings. The first being that Phillip Jinkerson—surprise, surprise—was in pretty rough financial shape. Until about four days ago."

"Huh? Did he win big or something?" Because...murdered bookie in the wine barrel.

"Not sure of the source yet, but there's a big deposit to his checking from an offshore account."

"When?" I held my breath.

"Friday."

Hot damn. "Murder for hire? Mr. Fulton had an alibi all ready, and that would be pretty smart of him. What if Celia was telling the truth when she said she saw Jinkerson out by the barns Friday afternoon? Could Fulton have paid Jinkerson to do away with Mitch?"

"I feel good about this one, Nicey." I could hear the smile in Kyle's voice.

"Any chance you can pull rank and find out how hard they're searching for him?"

"I'll do you one better and send some agents out to assist."

"You're the best, Kyle."

"And I'm not even done yet. Bonnie found something this morning."

I glanced heavenward and curled my fingers tighter around the phone. "What kind of something?"

"Remember I said she thought Burke was stabbed? The nick she noticed on his collarbone had no remodeling, and there's one on his C-4 vertebrae that lines up with it on an upward angle."

"Could one stab wound really kill a big guy like Mitch?" I furrowed my brow, catching sight of one of the Armani twins who'd been with Richard Burke that morning. He was talking to Jonathan Corry, the Commonwealth's Attorney. Quite animatedly.

Shit.

I refocused on Kyle. "I'm sorry, can you say that again? My brain is firing in too many directions today."

"I said, the subclavian artery is between the two. Here's the big thing: we're looking for a double-edged blade. Some sort of dagger. Not a knife. Nicked the top of the collarbone and the bottom of the C4, and severed the artery in between."

"On an upward angle?" I asked, my brain shaping a puzzle piece.

"Yep."

"So he was stabbed by someone shorter than him?"

"Or someone who was sitting down while he stood."

I nodded, my eyes still on Corry and Burke's lawyer. Corry's face had gone from annoyed to interested. I'd bet my shoe closet I knew why, and I didn't like it.

"One more favor? Can I beg?" I asked Kyle.

"Almost never necessary, but appreciated anyway."

"Stop it. Speaking of Bonnie, I have the ME's file on Jolene Sammons. I don't suppose she might peek through it? I can take it home, but I have no idea what I'm looking for."

"DonnaJo came through, huh? I'll sure ask her. You going to be at the courthouse for a bit?"

"At least another couple hours."

"Which court? I have to come down there anyway."

I told him the judge's name and he promised to be there within the hour.

Twenty minutes later, I slid over to let him into the back row next to me and passed him the folder. "I had another crazy idea this morning." I whispered.

"What?"

"The emails didn't hit Bob's computer until lunchtime Thursday. They aren't signed. We all assumed they were from Burke because of the return address being the same as the others. Now I know you said Bonnie wasn't positive about the time of death, but—"

"I'm with you. Clever killer we're dealing with, if you're right."

"Chad is tracing the IP for the mystery dinner check-in too. It came from a computer, and Burke usually used his phone."

"Nice. Keep me in the loop. I have a meeting that may run late, but I'll have my phone on vibrate if you need me."

"Thank you, Kyle. Call me if you find anything."

"Absolutely."

He slipped out and I turned back to the trial, watching the defense lawyer try to pick apart the police report.

Police report. I'd stuffed the ones Ella Jane faxed over into my bag as I flew out the door to the courthouse.

I pulled them out, squinting at the tiny letters of the officer's narrative on the body discovery. A bunch of stuff I already knew.

Except the part where it showed a diagram of the tool Hulk used to taste the wine and how the end had come into contact with the body.

If I took that shape, made it silver and turned it upwards....

I had the thing Celia swiped from the barn Sunday morning.

34

A thousand and one reasons for Celia to take the siphon flashed through my thoughts, some of them way grosser than others. By the time court recessed for the day, I had flipped back to near-certainty that she was our murderess.

I sped back to the office, sifting through every second of the past few days for whatever I'd missed. I texted Aaron that Sheriff Rutledge needed a search warrant for Celia's house.

He didn't answer.

But Joey did: Chef Alexei had entered the US through Raleigh Durham airport. I dropped my bag at my desk and fished out my notes, checking them against the text.

Alexei came to America on a student visa two months after the reality TV scandal. I went back to Google.

Three international food TV (that's a real thing, apparently) bloggers told me the Russian Gordon Ramsay got sick from the redhead's stew, and it was later discovered that Alexei, upon figuring out he'd borked the recipe and ruined his own, slipped an extra ingredient into hers. Though the show makes it look like every recipe is made and tasted at once, that's thanks to crafty editing: Once it's down to three chefs, they're judged hours apart (all the better to stress everyone out and have short fuses ready for the cameras). So when the judge started puking a couple hours after he sampled the first dish of the day, she got cut.

Fascinating stuff. But my eyes kept going back to the poison. Which one blogger said Alexei grew in his father's greenhouse for the gorgeous bell-shaped violet flowers.

American pokeweed.

Jiminy Choos.

I paced, texted Aaron twice more and then tried Kyle before I shook it off and sat down to get my copy for the day finished.

By the time I'd filed both stories and driven home, I was ready to crawl under the covers and stay there for a month.

If only I didn't still have six million and two things to do.

I fed Darcy, turning the day over in my head as I rinsed and refilled her water bowl.

My social media feeds were full of every reporter in town waxing on about the new ballpark, and how Richard Burke was setting aside his own ideals to see his late son's wish come true. Dale Sammons's office had issued a statement an hour after the press conference saying they'd worked through a few obstacles at City Hall and were suddenly on the planning and zoning agenda. Next week.

How convenient.

Something skated around the edge of my thoughts, and I put Darcy's water on the floor and wandered to the bedroom, rearranging my shoe rack and gathering laundry. My brain felt foggy. Almost like I'd had too much to drink. Not possible, unless I counted coffee.

I dumped a load into the washer, Andrews's notes flashing through my head.

Ballpark.

Burke.

Sammons.

Parker.

Mel wasn't thrilled about this ballpark thing, and she said her opinion was influenced by Parker.

Andrews was pushing me to cast suspicion on Parker—and talking to Sammons about selling our front page. The kind of money he'd be asking would give Sammons some major power over the *Telegraph*.

Dale Sammons had to know why Mitch Burke hated Parker. And might very well be able to get into Burke's email and social media via saved passwords on a work computer.

Aw, hell. I'd have given anything to know which of these geese deserved chasing.

I snatched up my phone and dialed.

Voicemail.

"Of course," I grumbled as I listened to the smooth tenor say "You've reached Grant Parker at the *Richmond Telegraph*. I can't talk right now, but please leave me a message or email me at Parker knows baseball at telegraph dot com, and I'll get back to you as soon as I can. Go Generals."

"Parker, I think I might've figured part of this out." I tried to keep my voice even. Didn't really succeed. "Call me as soon as you get this."

I clicked off the call and flung the phone, shuffling to the wine rack as the doorbell rang.

"You have the most perfect timing." I opened the door and pulled Jenna into a hug. "Has it really been a hundred years? Because it feels that way."

She squeezed back, laughing. "You've been a busy lady."

"I'm so sorry if I made you feel like I've been too busy for you." I turned for the kitchen and waved for her to follow.

"Eh. I'm overly sensitive these days. Just ask my husband." She laid a box of chocolate on the kitchen table and nodded when I held up a bottle of wine and raised one eyebrow.

"Elaborate, please," I said.

She shrugged. "I don't know. It's like I have PMS all the time. I think my hormones are shifting, but I wish they'd hurry up about it. Chad has taken to being moody and snippy, and I'm so tied up with the kids and the shop, I don't have the energy to ask why."

I poured two glasses of wine and set them on the table, opening the chocolates and pulling out Jenna's chair before taking the other myself. "Sounds like a rough week, doll. For what it's worth, Chad was pretty short with me this morning, and I haven't heard back from him on the question I asked either. So it's not just you."

Jenna sighed and sipped her wine. I covered her free hand with mine and frowned. "That face says this is more than a little problem."

She raised teary eyes to mine as my doorbell rang. "Fabulous time for a drop-by." I rolled my eyes and stood. "Give me thirty seconds to get rid of whoever that is."

The words didn't get all the way out before four rapid, pounding blows hit the other side of the door. "Nicey, please, you have to be here," Melanie sobbed. "Please open the door."

Jenna's eyes popped wide as I ran to the door and flung it open. A teary, snotty mess of a bride-to-be fell into my arms. "Melanie, what in Heaven's name?" I stroked her hair and turned back to Jenna, who was already on her feet getting a third wineglass.

One friend in crisis at a time would be way easier to manage.

I tried to pull back and make eye contact with Mel, but she clung to my shoulders, still bawling.

"Melanie, honey, I need you to talk to me." I kept my tone soothing. Impressive, considering I was on the verge of a nervous breakdown. What now?

"Grant. He never came home and he's not answering his phone, and now there's a police detective at my house. I'm scared, Nicey. I didn't know where else to go."

I froze, my arms tightening around Mel, my brain flat refusing to process anything for a few blinks.

Glass shattered in my kitchen as Jenna gasped, and my legs remembered how to work. I half-carried Melanie to the sofa, looking around for my phone. No dice.

Not Parker.

Please, God, no.

I swallowed a frustrated scream and pulled in a deep breath, keeping my voice even and clear. "Hey Siri, text Kyle."

The magic of technology.

I settled Mel into the pillows as the phone binged and my Australian man-voiced robot friend asked, "What would you like to say to Kyle?"

Lifting Mel's foot, I snatched up the phone, putting the microphone close to my face as I handed Mel a box of tissues.

"Hope your meeting is over. We just hit Defcon 1. Call me."

35

The twenty-five seconds it took Kyle to ring my phone were just about enough time for me to totally lose my shit.

I balled my free hand into a fist, nails digging into my palm as I gulped air, trying to hold it together. I couldn't flip out in front of Melanie.

Jenna rushed to the couch with a brim-full glass of red, perching next to Mel and pressing it into her hand.

"Small sips and deep breaths, honey. It will all be okay," she said.

I shot Jen a grateful smile and hustled out onto the porch when the phone buzzed, putting it to my ear as I shut the door behind me.

"Jesus, Kyle, Parker's missing." My voice cracked halfway through the last word. Saying it out loud made it more real.

"What?" I heard rustling in the background, like he'd dropped a stack of papers. "Start at the beginning."

"I don't really know where that is. Mel showed up here a few minutes ago, a hot mess because he never came home, won't answer his phone, and there're cops at her house."

"What did the cops say?"

"I haven't talked to them. I called you."

"No, what did they say to Melanie?" His strained patience came through loud and clear.

"Oh. I haven't had a chance to ask. Kyle..." I bit down on panic before I spoke again. "I have a really bad feeling. We have to find him. Now."

"Okay." I could practically see his hand moving to his hair. "Okay. I'll be there in ten minutes. See if you can calm her down, and find out what she knows."

"Thank you."

I clicked off the call and turned back for the door, flinching when the phone buzzed in my hand. I lifted it and glanced at the screen. Aaron.

Shit.

"Hey," I said, putting it to my ear.

"Do you know where Grant Parker is?" His voice was tight.

"Nope."

"Nichelle, I need you to tell me the truth," he snapped.

"Detective White, I'm not known for lying." I put more frost into my voice than the snow queen could've mustered.

He blew out a long sigh. "I'm sorry. This is bad. Really bad. Sheriff Rutledge has a warrant for Parker's arrest. Richard Burke is screaming for someone's head—preferably mine and Landers's, because he knows we had Parker in here the other day and let him leave."

Shit, double shit.

"Warrant?" I asked.

"The lab is pretty sure Burke was stabbed. We found a pocket knife at Burke's place with Parker's prints on it today."

My eyes fell shut. A hundred years later, I pulled in a shuddering breath. "He didn't do this, Aaron."

"I know he's your friend, Nichelle, but the evidence—"

"The lab also told Kyle today that Burke was probably killed Thursday morning," I cut him off. "Bob didn't even get the email threatening Mel until like noon. So where's your motive?"

"The official lab report says time of death is difficult to pinpoint because of the sugars in the wine." Aaron sighed. "I know you don't want to believe this, and I don't even blame you, but if you know where he is, you have to tell me."

"I haven't the first damned clue," I said.

"Please call me if you hear from him."

"Have a nice evening, Aaron." I clicked off the call and opened the door, my stomach flipping a slow somersault. With Richard Burke demanding a hanging and my detectives desperate to save their own asses, I was on my own here.

Wherever Parker was, he was in trouble. Maybe more than one kind. And if the cops were hunting a fugitive, they'd be looking for him in all the wrong places.

Which left finding him to me and Kyle.

* * *

Melanie had been locked up in meetings at City Hall all day and hadn't even talked to Parker since before work.

"He texted me that he wanted to let me sleep." She pulled her phone out and flipped it around. "He said he was going to get some coffee and go for a run because he got to ditch his sling today. His car was gone when I got up. That's all I know."

"Does Parker own a pocket knife, Mel?"

"There's one in his glovebox," she said.

Damn. I kept my face blank as I nodded.

"What the hell is going on here, Nicey? The police can't possibly really think he killed someone."

Sure they could. But that was way down my list of priorities at the moment.

"I don't think that. And I know you don't either."

Melanie shook her head. "I can't. I won't."

"Where would he have gone for a run?" I asked, waving the phone. "Is there a place he goes regularly?"

She shrugged. "Several. It depends on his mood. He didn't say specifically this morning, but he likes the river trails this time of year."

I opened my mouth to say something else and heard Kyle come in the front door before I got the words out.

"Hello, ladies." He kept an artificially light tone as he crossed the room to the chaise where I was perched, his eyes on Melanie.

She sniffled. "Hello. I'm sorry, I can't remember your name."

"This is my friend Kyle Miller," I said. "He's our resident SuperCop."

"Between the two of us, Nichelle and I do all right with the whole catching-the-bad-guys thing."

Melanie tried to smile, but more tears filled her eyes. "It's not like him to not answer my calls, Nicey. I'm scared."

"He's fine." I put a little too much weight in the words, but I needed to believe it as much as I needed her to. I tipped my head back to look up at Kyle. "What can we do?"

"Can I have a glass of water?" He widened his eyes slightly and flinched his head in the direction of the kitchen.

Subtle. Mel was upset, not stupid.

"Of course." I jumped to my feet and followed him.

"What?" I hissed as I grabbed a glass and filled it from the pitcher in my fridge.

"I still don't believe Parker did this, but Chris Landers called me right after you did. The evidence they have will probably convince a jury."

"He's not ignoring Mel because he's running, Kyle." I gave him the nutshell of my theory on the emails, the Facebook post, and Sammons. "Parker knows everyone who worked with Sammons and Burke. Could he have found something Sammons didn't want the cops to know?"

"Maybe. Have you talked to Parker today?"

"Nope." Dammit, why hadn't I remembered to call him last night?

Kyle sighed. "There will be cops all over his house, and I won't get in the door because I have no jurisdiction." He steepled his fingers together. "Where is his car?"

I shook my head. "Gone, Mel says."

"You happen to know the plate number?"

Of course I did. Was my brain-cluttering ability to remember useless information going to come in handy for the second time this week? I reeled it off.

Kyle nodded. "I need your laptop and a little luck."

I tipped my head to one side. "Because you have his plate number?"

"I can search the feed from every traffic camera in Virginia, DC, and Maryland. The recognition software isn't perfect, but we might very well get lucky, and with the timestamps and a couple of people who know him well, we can maybe figure out where he went."

Deep breath. "Gotta love technology. At least that'll give us a place to start." I sprinted to the car to get my laptop and set him up at the table. "I'll see if Mel remembers anything else."

* * *

If Melanie knew anything helpful, she couldn't make herself call it up. Jenna and I spent an hour trying to pull information out of her, and got a lot of tears and "I don't know"s punctuated by cursing herself for being busy.

I started back for the kitchen to see if Kyle was having better luck, and Mel's sniffling stopped me at the door. "It seems so stupid, how much anyone cares about this damned ballpark thing. Why did I stay down there listening to their bullshit all day? God, Nichelle, what if something happened to Grant and I was..."

I turned slowly, a puzzle piece floating neatly into place in my head. "The ballpark."

Jenna bounced to her feet. "What? Jesus, this is making me nervous. I only thought I had problems when I came over here."

I smiled at her. "Thank you for staying, doll."

"I'm happy to at least feel like I'm helping."

"You are."

Jenna's phone binged. She furrowed her brow and swiped the screen. "It's Chad. 'Tell Nicey the Virginia History League,' it says. What's that?"

"Oh my God." I lost the ability to focus on anything for a few seconds, then lasered on Mel.

"Who was in the meetings you were at today?"

"Dale Sammons, the planning and zoning director, the city manager, the mayor, the head of the Slip's historical committee, and a guy from the developer's office."

Bingo.

"BurCo, right?"

"No." Mel shook her head. "I was just telling Grant yesterday that it's weird to see Richard Burke all over the news this week, because I haven't seen him on an agenda or pushing a new project in forever. It's probably been nearly a year. This was a new company. I couldn't find much about them, except that they meet the state's small business contract requirement. Maribou, they're called. Who names a company after feathers?"

Parker's voice floated back to me. "Why not use someone with more of a reputation?" he'd asked Sammons. He wasn't talking about wine. Or baseball.

Not Maribou. MariBu.

The Virginia History League.

The perfect reason to jump into the stadium project.

That son of a...We'd been looking in all the wrong places.

I spun on one heel and sprinted to the kitchen, hollering for Kyle.

36

Kyle looked up from piecing together a map of where Parker's convertible had been when I fell into the chair opposite him.

"Richard Burke, Kyle. Does he own any other companies?"

"That kind of money? Probably. Why?" Kyle kept clicking. "The last time I can find Parker's car, he crossed the nickel bridge at six forty this morning."

"He likes to run by the river. But listen. Melanie says—" I paused. "Oh, shit."

He closed the computer and stared. "What?"

"Don't Richard and Annabeth Burke live down there somewhere?"

He nodded. "So?"

"I've been looking at this whole thing all wrong," I said. "I thought someone—Jinkerson, Rutledge, a jealous woman, Sammons, a gambling contact—killed Mitch for personal reasons. I thought the circumstantial crap was pointing to Parker in an unfortunate coincidence." I stood, pacing my tiny kitchen floor.

"You don't believe in coincidences." Kyle's eyes followed me for a minute. "You're making me dizzy."

"I think better when I move," I said. "And it looks like I'm right to not believe in them, because a string of them has made us walk through the exact doors this bastard wanted us to."

"What bastard?"

"Richard Burke. Mel says there's a new PC small-business developer on this ballpark thing. Company called MariBu. As in, Marilyn Burke? And Richard was out there playing polo with Sammons's BFFs last weekend. I think they're so chummy because Richard Burke is behind this ballpark push. There's a lot—a *lot* lot—of money riding on that."

"But he's a big history guy."

"That's exactly why he couldn't be publicly associated with it. Melanie just said she hasn't seen him pushing a new project at City Hall in a year. Why is that, I wonder? Saving up political capital for when he could find a way to come out on the side of the ballpark thing?" I paused. Andrews. Someone was offering him a pretty penny for our front page, and his notes said Sammons and Burke. I'd just assumed he meant Mitch. But what if he didn't?

"They have too much riding on this to lose it," I muttered. "Who owns the property Sammons wants to use down in the slip?"

Kyle's eyebrows went up. "Looks to me like your money's on Richard Burke. You really think he killed his own son over a business deal?"

"I really think he might've. But I'm still not sure. We have to find Parker and see what he knows."

"Why wouldn't he have already told us?"

"What if he can't?" My voice cracked. "He texted me last night and said we needed to talk. I tried him twice today and got nothing. What if ..." I couldn't finish. "We gotta go down to the river."

"What about them?" Kyle jerked his head toward the living room as he stood.

"Jenna will stay with Mel. She doesn't need to be alone right now."

"I'll drive." Kyle grabbed his keys.

* * *

I kept various appendages crossed and whispered prayers through three parking lots along the James.

When Kyle's headlights glinted off the back of Parker's silver BMW convertible in the fourth, I dropped my head into my hands.

"I didn't want to be right about this," I mumbled to the floor.

"Hang on now. No jumping to conclusions. There are only so many spots on this trail system you can get a car into, and this is a public place. The odds that anyone hauled a guy as big and strong as Parker out of here against his will in broad daylight are fairly slim."

I scrubbed my hands over my face and lifted my head. "True. But then where the hell has he been for the past..." I looked at my phone, "...fifteen hours?"

Before I dropped it back in my bag, it binged two rapid-fire text arrivals. I flipped it over, then let it fall to the floor of Kyle's car.

"What?"

"Charlie Lewis has a teaser for the eleven that Parker is a murder suspect and running from the law. My publisher sent me a screenshot. Right before he fired me."

37

Kyle stared, mouth gaping, for a full minute before he managed words. "Fired you?"

I shook my head, shoving aside the panicked tears that came on the heels of hearing Kyle say it aloud. I didn't have a word for how low Andrews could stoop. "Right now, I don't even care. All I want is to find my friend and set this tangled mess right. I can deal with Andrews," who still didn't know I knew about Shelby, or his deal with Sammons, "later."

The phone blared "Second Star to the Right."

Bob. Who'd no doubt been notified of my recent unemployment. What about him?

Kyle gestured to the floor, then poked me when I didn't lean to pick it up. "You going to get that?"

I shook my head. "I just flat lack the capacity to worry about one more thing. Does that make me a bad friend?"

Kyle patted my hand. "We all have our limits."

"Where is he, Kyle?"

He leaned to the glovebox and grabbed a flashlight, climbing out of his car and picking his way to Parker's, running the beam over the ground.

I gasped and tried to catch my balance as my heel slid. "I thought these were all paved," I said.

"They are, but look—the storm last night washed mud down the hill and over the asphalt. That's good for us, maybe..." He let the thought trail as he squatted next to Parker's car, then stood and went over his footprints in the mud back to his.

"Look, Nichelle," he said. "There are three sets of tire tracks here. Just three."

"Since the storm last night?" I scrambled back to where Kyle stood, my eyes following the flashlight's beam. Sure enough. "One is yours."

He nodded. "One is Parker's, and the other one..."

"A car came in and parked next to him," I said, bouncing slightly and grabbing his arm when my foot skidded again.

"So either he left with that person..." Kyle began.

Or he'd been dumped in the river. I didn't say it. I didn't want to think it. "Or he left with that person." I grabbed the light and shined it into the trees.

Kyle nodded. "That's the best lead we have, so let's see where it goes."

"How are we going to do that?"

"Richard Burke or Dale Sammons? What does your gut say?"

I closed my eyes and let my mind go quiet. I couldn't get this wrong. We didn't have time for error. Deep breath. "Burke."

Kyle nodded. "So where would a man like Richard Burke take someone he didn't want found?"

"Assuming he didn't..." I paused. "Yeah. Assumed. Like, if he wanted to know what Parker knew?"

"Or who he told?"

My eyes popped wide. "Kyle..."

He was already digging for his phone. I jerked the driver's door open and dove to the other side of the car for mine, punching the speed dial for Jenna's cell.

"Hey," she said. "Do I want—"

"Get out," I cut her off. "Get Mel and go to your car and get away from my house. Don't go home. Drive around, go to a mall—somewhere there are a lot of people. I'll call you in a bit."

"Okay," she said simply, and I loved her for just trusting me.

"Be safe, Jen."

"You too, sweetie." I heard her telling Mel they had to leave as she clicked off the call.

Kyle pocketed his phone as I wriggled back to my feet. "They okay?"

"I told them to leave."

"There will be two agents in an unmarked car outside your house in ten minutes. Maybe we'll get lucky and our guy will show up."

The more I thought about Richard, the surer I felt. "It's him, Kyle. Richard Burke couldn't be in on this ballpark thing publicly without good reason, and his son being dead has given him that." I slid into the passenger seat. "Melanie said she hasn't seen BurCo on a council agenda or advertising a new historical project in a long time. Let's go find out why."

* * *

Two blocks from the river, Kyle's phone blew up, binging and buzzing every iPhone sound at once. He pulled the car over and scooped it out of the cupholder.

"Miller," he said, putting it to his ear. I turned and watched, noting the tense flex of his jaw. "Put one on the runner and leave one onsite. I'll be there in ten." His voice had a commanding edge I wasn't used to hearing. He clicked off the call and put the car in gear. "Slight change of plans."

"Sounds like it," I said.

"I have to go help with...a thing." He shot me a sideways glance. "A couple of hours tops. Can I drop you at the newspaper office?"

Andrews could bite my ass. I'd have time to deal with him when I'd figured out what happened to Parker.

"Sure. I'll hunt up dirt on Burke."

"And I'll see why Bonnie just texted me that she found something interesting in that old file you gave me today. Just in case."

I nodded as he rolled to a stop in front of the *Telegraph* building, smiling when a shadow crossed his face as I opened the door.

"I'll be fine. There are still people here this time of night. Research isn't a dangerous pastime. Ask your favorite librarian."

He nodded. "I'll be back as soon as I can."

I got to my cube to find all my personal belongings packed into a cardboard box and set in the floor next to the recycle bin. "That jackass." My throat closed around the words, and I turned on my heel and went looking for a familiar face.

I found Troy at the sports desk, taking stats from high school games off email and typing them into a formatting sheet.

"You're here awfully late," I said.

"I'm in charge of getting these in by ten." He grinned.

I glanced at the clock. "You have one minute."

He punched two buttons on the laptop. "And that was the last one."

A grin spread across my face. "Perfect timing." For once this week. "Can I borrow that? I left mine at home and I need to look something up. Long story."

"Sure thing." He pushed it toward me, and I pulled a chair up next to his.

"Journalism in the Age of the Internet 101," I said with a wink. "The answer to almost anything can be found on the internet, as long as you know where to look. 102: Property tax records aren't sexy, but they come in mighty handy a lot of the time."

I punched up the city tax office's site and started hunting.

Ten minutes later I'd confirmed that the Burkes owned MariBu—but Mitch was listed as the principal on the business license.

What I needed was a peek behind the curtain. The kind my photographic recall of Kyle two-finger-pecking his password into my laptop earlier might get me.

I clicked to Lexis Nexis and punched in Kyle's credentials.

Welcome, Kyle Miller.

Parker didn't have time for me to worry about ethical implications. I searched BurCo. Loads of property listings, most of them sold or mortgaged to the hilt.

I scrolled back to the top and read slower.

For twenty years, they bought property, restored it, flipped it.

I scanned the list for Shockoe Slip addresses.

Twelve. Eight with older deed dates, four bought in the past five years. Way after Mitch started working for Sammons.

Leverage?

Or security?

A guy with a passion for history as big as Burke's, plus his deep pockets, could've easily gotten wind of Sammons's plans for the new stadium and simply purchased enough land to block it. Mel had mentioned imminent domain, but no way would the city of Richmond take land from Richard Burke.

So what flipped it?

I scrolled more.

About eighteen months back, the loans started.

Every property on their books had at least three mortgages and a line of credit. And there were a lot of them.

"Holy shit. They're broke," I mumbled.

Being poor is a rich man's worst nightmare. I'd even buy it as a reason for a guy like Richard to suddenly hop into bed with Sammons on this ballpark thing.

I went back to the top of the list, scanning addresses. None of them remote, or even what you'd call out of the way. We couldn't search all these places.

I tapped two fingers on the edge of the keyboard.

What next?

I ran Richard's name.

His personal home, plus two vacation houses. Each with two mortgages and a credit line.

Annabeth?

No property listings.

I tried Mitch.

Two hits.

A condo in an expensive high rise down at Rockett's Landing, and a single-family home built in 1874. On River Road. I clicked.

Tax records showed the house was previously owned by a bank, and Burke bought it twelve years ago for a quarter million dollars. Five thousand square feet, lovely part of town. Paid for. Free and clear.

What had a twenty-one-year-old pitcher with a weakness for women and booze wanted with a century-old mansion?

Time to go find out.

I copied the address and slapped the computer shut, looking around for the first time in an hour. Troy was watching me with a grin.

"I'm not sure what you just found, but I'm glad you're excited," he said.

I pulled out my phone and dialed Kyle, shooting Troy a grin. "I'm not sure what it is either, but I'd like to go have a look. Little bit of personal advice: Avoid snooping alone."

Voicemail. Damn.

I hung up and tried Aaron. Same result.

Landers. No dice.

Joey. Voicemail.

The third time I rang Kyle's phone, I got a text that said *Can't talk now, I'll call you later.*

"He's auto-messaging me? Now?" I dropped my phone on the desk and stared at the Generals poster on Parker's closed door.

Kyle knew I wanted something life and death, because I don't pester him unless that's the case. Which meant he had an equally important reason for ignoring me at the moment. I crossed every appendage I could manage without falling that his reason had to do with finding Parker.

But I had no time to wait around and hope I was right. My friend's life might very well depend on my next move, in fact.

"Anything I can help with?" Troy asked.

I tipped my head to one side. "As a matter of fact, yeah. Do you have a car I can borrow?"

"What happened to no snooping alone?" he asked.

I glanced at the address I'd scribbled, then copied it onto a Post-it, along with phone numbers for Kyle, Aaron, and Landers.

"I can't just sit here." I handed him the little yellow square. "Do me a favor: Keep calling these numbers, and when you get someone to pick up, tell them I went to this address and to come meet me."

"What is this place?"

"That's what I'm trying to find out." I stood and he tossed me a set of Prius keys that had seen better days.

"Be careful, Miss Clarke," he said.

"Thanks. I will. You get ahold of one of my cops and get them over there."

Probably overkill, because the odds were stacked in favor of an abandoned house no one could sell, a money pit, or a hundred other things. Just because it was close to where we'd found Parker's car didn't mean anything. Not by itself.

But my gut said it might. And maybe was better than the dead end I faced staying put.

38

Darkness seeped through the trees surrounding the old house, the headlights on Troy's battered Prius not making much headway as I shut off the engine a half-block away. I stood next to the car for a second and blinked, letting my eyes adjust to the inky black so I didn't have to use a flashlight. The less attention called to my presence, the better. Just in case my gut was right.

I tucked my phone and a mace canister into my pocket and picked my way along the side of the road. If I didn't know I was still in the city, I wouldn't have believed it—the quiet night almost pulsed with a life of its own, overgrown brush and trees reaching through it to pick at my sleeve and scratch my bare legs. Ahead, shades of indigo outlined hulking pieces of construction equipment at the end of the cul-de-sac.

Building something?

I missed the break in the bushes that marked the end of the driveway on the first pass, ducking and turning sideway to squeeze through them on the second. Just when I began to wish I'd brought a machete, I tugged free of the last prickly branch and found myself in a southern gothic secret garden.

Jasmine lay heavy on the air, my eyes barely making out the vines that grew wild up every standing surface around me. A stone fountain patchworked with dark splotches of moss stood in the center of the broken concrete circular driveway, filled to the brim from last night's storm. A few more steps and I made out the remnants of what was once a gazebo, surrounded by roses long since left to their own devices, their spindly arms lifting dark blooms to the sky.

Any other early summer evening, the dark beauty of the abandoned garden and the palpable pull of so much history would take my breath right away.

Tonight, I barely had time to notice as I faded into the shadows of the wall, tiptoeing around the perimeter in search of the house.

Probably a quarter mile up from the street, I found it.

Damn, some light would have been nice. I rolled my eyes up, not a star to be seen behind all the clouds.

Fine.

Be that way.

I kept moving through the shadows until I spotted a stairway at the back corner of the house. Probably to the old servant's quarters.

But it looked...

I crept closer.

It looked new. Because a lot of it was. While I felt some wood when I bent to touch it, what was left of the original material had been reinforced with metal. Metal that hadn't had time to rust, the smooth finish said.

My heart pumped double time.

Why was this the only property the Burke family wouldn't mortgage when they were in hock up to their aristocratic noses?

"One way to find out," I muttered, hoping like hell something—anything—in here might tell me where to look for Parker.

I took the steps two at a time, finding a builder-grade metal exterior door at the top.

I tried the knob.

Locked. Nothing is ever simple.

There was no glass to kick in, but there was a hundred-and-fifty-year-old wooden doorjamb holding the business end of the deadbolt.

I stepped back to the edge of the little stoop, turned to one side, and let an *ap'chagi* fly.

The impact rushed up my leg through my hip, making my eyes fill as I lowered my leg and surveyed the door. My heel left a divot in the center, and it seemed a touch looser in the frame.

I turned again, this time aiming for just above the knob. My foot connected hard enough to let me know I might be limping for a while, but the wood squealed as it splintered on the other side of the door.

I stepped forward and shoved, and the door swung wide.

Peeking into the room, I listened for footsteps.

None.

I put one foot across the threshold, then jumped around the edge of the door.

Nobody behind it.

I pulled out my phone and flipped on the flashlight.

To find a bedroom.

A young girl's dream bedroom.

Pink satin covered the walls, and a white FrenchProvencal four poster was half-buried under clouds of muslin canopy.

I spun in a slow circle.

Whatever I thought I'd find when I'd landed on the address, this was not even in the same zip code.

"What the hell?" I whispered.

Shelves full of stuffed animals and porcelain dolls. A vanity with a velvet-cushioned stool and a silver brush and comb set.

Why did Mitch Burke own a run-down mansion with a princess's bedroom in the servant's quarters?

I picked up the brush, tracing one finger over the monogram on the back.

His sister. My brain started down that road as my flashlight fell on a closet. I set the brush down and crossed to the carved door. The mural of cherubs and clouds swung out of sight when I pulled it open and shined the light inside.

Blood.

On the walls. On the dresses hanging in rows down both racks. On the floor.

And on Parker, still in his gym clothes, curled in the back corner like he was sleeping.

* * *

"Parker?" It was barely a whisper. I cleared my throat and tried again. "Parker!"

I rushed forward, slipped in something (I knew what. I just didn't want to think about it). And winced when I landed hard on my tailbone. Scrambling to my knees, I crawled to my friend, grabbing his shoulder and giving it a rough shake.

Please, God.

He didn't stir.

I called his name again, kneeling next to him and pressing my fingers to the side of his throat.

His pulse was thready, but it was there.

I ran the light over him and spotted a clump of yuck about halfway back in his hair and a deep gash on his left shin, still trickling blood around his calf and onto the floor. Jesus. I snatched a sweater from the rack over my head and tied one sleeve just below his knee, pulling it tight and knotting it.

Picking the phone up, I called 911.

"I have an unconscious man with a head injury and heavy blood loss." I glanced around, keeping my voice even. "We're in the back of—"

I stopped talking when I felt the blade against my cheek.

"Ma'am?" the dispatcher asked. "Are you still there?"

Fingernails dug into my hand, forcing me to let go of the phone. It disappeared, and the dispatcher's voice stopped.

I didn't move, the steel against my cheek keeping me stock-still. Had she had time to get location from my cell? Probably not more than the general area, and that's if I'd been on the nearest tower.

I tried to swallow the panic, praying Troy had gotten someone—anyone—on the phone.

The knife slid down my face to rest on my shoulder, point at my throat. I felt a trickle from my cheekbone to my jaw.

"Can I help you?" I asked, impressed at how blasé I sounded.

A throaty chuckle came from behind me. “Plucky little thing, aren’t you?”

Not a man’s voice.

The nails.

The room.

Parker.

Not Richard Burke.

“Annabeth.” I turned my head slowly toward the door, catching a glimpse of red as Mrs. Burke’s shiny patent Louboutin connected with the side of my head.

39

My head caught the side of a shoe rack and landed with a *thunk* on the wood floor when I fell back. I stayed still for a few seconds, the situation sinking in.

Had Annabeth Burke really killed her own son? Somehow, knowing Mitch Burke's mother was behind this was way worse than suspecting Richard. I blinked. And how had Parker ended up half-dead in a closet full of his long-dead girlfriend's clothes?

Nothing made sense, and not just because I was bleeding from my head in at least two places.

"Oh, come on, now," Annabeth called. "That didn't knock you out. Get up."

"So you can kick me again? I think I'll stay put."

She chuckled before landing a swift one to my ribcage.

I brought my knees to my chest, coughing.

I heard my phone land on a shelf, and the closet lit up, the flashlight still on.

"Get." She bent forward and grabbed a handful of my hair, dragging me to a sitting position. "Up."

I planted one hand on the floor and used it for balance, my eyes flicking to the knife in her hand. It was beautiful in a dark way, a pattern engraved into a blade that came to an even point. Less knife and more dagger. Long and narrow, with a silver handle, sharp on both sides.

Just exactly like Bonnie said.

She'd used it to kill Mitch too.

I glanced around, the blood in the closet making more sense, my eyes flicking over Parker. She'd used it to kill Mitch here. His severed artery had made these spatters. Parker might still have a chance. If I could get us out of here.

I turned back to Annabeth.

What kind of monster was this woman?

"Why?" I croaked.

"Oh, goody, is this the part where I'm supposed to pour my crazy little heart out to you so you can write it up for the whole city to read?" She clapped her hands together. "We'll just have a little girl-to-girl chat, is that it?" She sneered, stepping backward. "Let's not."

"Suit yourself."

A cold smile spread across her face, the chill leaching into my bones. "Sad, really. I've been reading your work for quite a while now—something about you reminds me of myself. Smart. Resourceful."

"Resourceful?" I blurted. "Lady, I'm thinking you killed your own son. And so far as I can tell, you've kidnapped a man and assaulted me. That's not resourceful. That's insanity."

A snarl flashed across her face in the weird half-bright, half-shadow, and she motioned for me to put my arms forward.

"Mitchell never learned." She grabbed a roll of duct tape off a shelf, and Kyle's agent commando voice floated through my thoughts. Deep breath. I leaned forward, laying my elbows against each other and facing my wrists in together. I winced as she wrapped the tape around and around, pulling it tighter as she started talking again.

"He just skated through life, screwing up and letting us bail him out. He was good at two things: charming women into bed and charming people out of their money. I wish I could say he got that from his father, but Richard's luck with money has never been great, and this stupid history obsession of his has finally bled us dry."

Journalism even before the age of the internet 101: No matter how much they try to pretend, most people really do like to talk. Knowing how to listen to the homicidal ones without dying is the tricky part.

She ripped the tape, sticking the end down, and stepped backward. I fought to breathe, every nerve ending aware of the creepy dagger she waved in big arcs as she spoke.

"All the money he's pissed away, and he wouldn't buy this house for my Mari. She walked by here almost every day. Fell in love with it. Begged Richard to buy it for years. But he refused, and then it was too late. When Mitchell turned twenty-one and got full access to his trust fund—he gave me the keys on Mari's birthday that year." She smiled. "It was perfect: Richard wanted Mari's things out of her room in my home, and I couldn't put my baby's things in storage. But Mitchell tired of indulging his mother when Sammons got him all gung ho about a new stadium. Richard spent the last dime we had to our name trying to keep them out of the slip, but then the economy went to hell, and he couldn't get a project off the ground to save his soul. Mitch started MariBu, and Richard eventually fell in behind his ballpark project. They stayed busy chasing politicians and contractors. And throwing away what money we could beg or borrow."

She straightened a stack of sweaters on a shelf. I shuffled puzzle pieces. Mitch wanted into the ballpark project. Sammons liked him and seemed to want his father's approval.

But his company had no reputation, like Parker said. He'd need respect.

And money.

"He was going to sell this place," I breathed.

"No." She shook her head. "He wanted to demolish it."

The construction equipment.

"Tear it all down and rebuild a restoration hardware faux mansion in its place for that little backwoods trollop he knocked up. I cried. Begged. Screamed."

She fingered the sleeve of a dress.

"But why kill him here? You kept your daughter's things so nice for so long..." I blurted.

Annabeth shook her head. "I picked up this ridiculous thing." She brandished the dagger. "Richard gave to Mari because it was his mother's. I swung it, and Mitchell leaned to grab my hand. It hit him. I didn't mean for him to get hurt. I really didn't." I didn't know who she was trying to convince, but it wasn't working on me.

I gave her a onceover, another piece clicking. She was five-foot nothing and probably not a hundred pounds soaking wet.

"You didn't put him in the barrel though. You couldn't. Not by yourself."

"You don't miss a detail, do you?" The baritone came from behind the closet door. "Bob Jeffers always did know a good reporter at thirty paces." Richard Burke stepped into the light, nodding my way. "I helped Bob with some history for a piece he did on the Klan many years ago. And then he refused to hire my son." He shook his head. "Not that anyone could really blame him. Like I said: He knew a good reporter when he saw one. It'll hurt old Bob to lose you." He turned to his wife. "I told you to hurry."

"I didn't expect her to be here. I was just seeing if he was dead yet."

Richard sighed like he was the only smart person he knew. "Why does that matter?"

Annabeth's jaw dropped into a horrified gape. "Richard! We can't bury him alive. It's barbaric."

I couldn't help the eye roll.

Neither could Richard. "So complicated. And now I have to find a place to put them both."

"Just dig a bigger hole, for Heaven's sake," she snapped. "We're not doing formal services."

"I'm aware of how to handle this," Richard said. "All I do lately is clean up your messes. I had this under control until you saw Grant down on the trail this morning, didn't I? For that matter, haven't I handled that too?" He got louder with every question, and her face was the same scarlet as her nails.

"I was upset! I just lost my only son!" she shrieked.

Ladies and gentlemen, the Manson family's answer to Fred and Ethel Mertz.

Come on, Troy.

Come on, guys. Someone answer your phone.

"You seem to forget that was rather your own fault, darling. Now everyone will believe Mr. Parker has run from the law, and he will finally be as hated he deserved when Mari died." Richard waved a hand my way. "The maid of honor eloping with the groom is cliché, but I'll risk it."

My eyes widened with every word until they wouldn't go any wider, my head tossing back and forth between them.

They had it all figured out. And Maisy would be front and center to tell everyone she knew it all along. I swallowed hard. Panic wouldn't get us out of here.

My eyes flicked to Parker. Was he even breathing?

The mace. I couldn't reach it with my hands bound, but maybe...

They were still bickering. Could I?

If I sprayed her and she dropped the dagger, he might beat me to it. Shit.

I raised both arms slowly over my head.

Richard flapped his hands. "Do what you want. If you get caught, I wasn't here." I noticed his black leather gloves for the first time as he stepped out of the closet.

One on one, I could take her. I thought. What did I have to lose?

I threw my elbows down and back like I was trying to hurt someone on the other side of the wall, just like Kyle taught me. The tape gave and my hand found the canister in my pocket as Annabeth spun back to me. She raised the dagger and I brought my arm up and sprayed her full in the face. Screaming, then coughing, she doubled over, the force of her arm sending the blade through her own leg. She hit the floor and I froze as Burke thumped the door open. "I know there are trees, but we do still have neighbors. Shut her up." When his eyes fell on his wife's bleeding leg and swollen face, he whirled for me.

I stumbled backward, tripping over Parker's legs and dropping the mace canister as Burke pulled an ornate revolver from his jacket. "They say this once belonged to Stonewall Jackson." He leveled it at me. "Just like this stadium business. If I want something done, I might as well do it myself."

The grim set of his mouth and flat cold gray of his eyes were the last thing I saw as mine fell shut.

* * *

The gun fired, and a thousand pounds of bricks hit me square in the chest.

Being shot felt a lot heavier than it had last time.

Burke roared and I opened my eyes.

Parker.

Parker was laying on me. Why was Parker laying on me?

Why was Parker bleeding from the corner of his mouth?

No.

Oh, Jesus, please no.

My eyes pricked with new tears.

I tried to scream, but I couldn't get any air.

"Parker, please be okay," I whispered. "You have to be okay."

I felt his chest try to pull in a breath. "Run...Sleeping...Screaming." Parker was trying to talk, but I couldn't hear him over all the shouting.

Something heavy crashed into my shin, and Annabeth Burke wailed, "Where are you going, you son of a bitch? Don't you leave me!"

So much shouting.

Coming closer. Getting louder.

Overpowering Richard and Annabeth's sniping.

"Parker, hang in there." I don't know if I managed to get the words out, but I wanted to.

Male voices—more than one of them.

"Back here! I see a light!"

Was that Aaron?

"Up here!" I tried to call. Still no air.

"Freeze, Mr. Burke."

Kyle.

"Nichelle?"

Aaron.

The tears spilled over.

Shoving with everything in me, I righted myself and landed Parker in my lap. Warmth flooded over my thigh, and I watched Parker's eyes flutter closed.

I wiped the corner of his mouth with my finger.

"No. Parker, stay with me." It was still a scratchy whisper.

I stroked the hair off Parker's forehead as his eyelids twitched, then opened. I found some air, and my voice. "Aaron! Kyle! Help us!"

I cradled Parker's head, the footsteps not coming fast enough. "Please, God. Please. No." I sobbed, trying not to think about how much blood there was.

I felt someone lean over me, heard Kyle curse, and then he and Aaron lifted Parker off my lap, barking orders at windbreaker-sporting ATF agents and uniformed Richmond officers.

I stayed frozen for half a minute before I jumped to my feet and hobbled after them, my hip screaming with every step. I didn't have to go far. Kyle was using linen from the canopy to pack Parker's wound, Aaron yanking the comforter off the bed to use for a stretcher.

"Don't let him..." I couldn't say it, the energy leaving me as I dropped onto the vanity stool.

"Jesus, what a night." Kyle shook his head. "I turned my phone on to call Bonnie—your cold case suicide was likely not, says the weird racehorse hormone in the tox report and the teeny nick in the vic's skull on the x-rays. Bonnie wants the remains exhumed, and I have some work to do before Sammons will answer for it, but your gut was right. I gathered that much before a call from the newspaper beeped in. That intern y'all have deserves a raise."

I nodded, my eyes not leaving Parker as the uniforms led Richard and Annabeth Burke from the room in handcuffs. Sammons wouldn't get away with killing his sister. But right then nothing mattered except that my friend was bleeding and there wasn't a damn thing I could do.

"Troy? He's a good kid. Bring him to the wedding," Parker's voice rasped.

"Parker!" I shot to my feet.

"Hey there, Superman. Keep talking," Kyle said, pressing harder on the wound.

"Whatever you're doing hurts like a bitch, Miller."

"I'd apologize, but it's probably saving your life, man."

They rolled him onto the comforter and lifted him, and I followed them outside. The back of the house was lit like a runway, an ambulance backing down the drive to meet us.

"I'm going with him," I said, and Kyle lifted me into the back of the bus.

I grabbed his hand and squeezed. "Get my phone from that closet and call Mel."

He nodded and slammed the doors, rapping on the back as the driver rolled forward.

"Clarke."

I leaned over Parker, tears streaming from my cheeks onto the blanket over his chest. "You scared the shit out of me," I sobbed.

"Three more times and we're even." He tried to smile. "I can't believe I was dumb enough to go with her. She was there when I came back up from my run this morning. She said she wanted to apologize, that she knew I didn't have anything to do with Mitch's death and they were having a press conference at nine to let everyone know that. Told me she missed Mitch and Mari, and wanted me to have something of Mari's as a wedding gift." He paused, wincing. "Hurts to breathe."

"Try to be still, sir," the paramedic, who was attempting to set an IV needle, said.

I squeezed Parker's free hand. "It's not stupid to want to see the best in others. Even when you get burned."

"I'd rather stay clear of this particular heat source." Parker rolled his eyes. "Melanie?"

"Safe." I squeezed. "You guys need another couple weeks of honeymoon."

"Secrets, murder...how hard can married life be after all this?"

I laughed and wiped at my eyes. "For you two? Piece of cake."

40

Fairy dust? Check. Heart-shaped bubbles? All over it.

We even had an early nightingale serenade blending with the harpist's music into soaring notes that were nothing short of magical.

Since everyone had read the entire ridiculous saga of the past week in the morning paper and Parker sported a very suave sling our crafty features editor had fashioned from a cut-up tuxedo vest, there wasn't a dry eye in a five-mile radius by the time he and Mel finished the "I do"s.

Bubbles flew, cameras flashed, and Tony Okerson boomed an enthusiastic introduction to Mr. and Mrs. Grant Parker.

The bar was stocked far beyond what had been paid for, a gift from Hulk, who was running the Calais show now that Sammons was sitting in jail awaiting a trial almost a decade overdue. No statute of limitations in Virginia for murder charges meant Jolene's death wouldn't go unpunished, after all.

Bonnie's cold case Nancy Drew work and Kyle's SuperCop smarts had the case pretty neatly sewn up: Tests on the exhumed remains confirmed that Jolene had been stabbed with a dirty needle and injected with the oxycodone—a refill of a prescription her father had for his favorite mare, which Dale signed for at the pharmacy the morning of Jolene's death.

In the middle of the revelations about her mother and her uncle, Celia broke down and confessed to blackmailing Alexei with her Google evidence that he'd been in trouble for poisoning someone back home. She wanted some kind of quasi-Montezuma's revenge on Mitch, so she told Alexei to spike his favorite dessert with pokeweed berries when he came to meet Sammons for lunch the day before he died. Alexei didn't do it, but Celia didn't know that until Richard Burke was arrested, because Alexei was afraid she'd rat out his youthful indiscretions. Celia told the sheriff she took the siphon from the barn to throw it out because it had Chateau de Burke run through it and she was afraid the men would all forget.

Jinkerson saw the news coverage of Richard and Annabeth's arrests and came back. He'd tried to fink to me on Sammons and thought better of it, then taken off when he got the idea that Mitch Burke's death was related to the Cacciones (who he owed a small fortune to that he'd borrowed from loanshark dot com at forty percent on Friday morning) and wondered if he'd be next.

Hulk made national wine headlines Friday when he bowed out of the Governor's Cup—Sammons had an employee who was dating Fulton's granddaughter wheedle her out of his magic seeds, which produced the plants Kyle had noticed on Tuesday. And the amazing Riesling. As soon as Hulk was in charge, he set about making it right.

The same judge Kyle had badgered his warrant out of Wednesday no-bonded Richard and Annabeth both on account of flight risk, and Bob had refused to run the exclusive I wrote while Parker was having a three-hour surgery to remove a minnie ball from his left lung and sew up his back until Andrews not only offered me my job back, but gave me a raise and apologized.

I caught Shelby's eye on the other side of the dance floor and forced myself to return her smile. I wasn't quite sure what to do with her little secret.

I was, however, certain it would come in handy someday.

A glass of wine appeared in my face, and I turned to find Kyle, looking positively dashing in his last-minute honorary groomsman tux, smiling at Parker and Mel, who waltzed with dreamy grins that belied the half-dozen stitches up the left side of his spine. "They look happy."

"To be fair, the kazillion milligrams of Demerol are probably helping on his part." I smiled.

Larry circled the dance floor, snapping photos, until Mel waved for everyone to join them for the last notes of *Save The Best For Last.*

"Though I suppose when the 'till death do us part' nearly beats the 'I do's, you're happy just to be here," I added.

Kyle nodded. "Observant as always."

Maisy, who'd told Sheriff Rutledge she was after emails and texts to prove I was messing around with Parker when she tried to hack into my laptop, glared at me from the bar. I raised my glass in her direction and flashed a fake smile. My eyes lit on Troy, who had Bob and Tony Okerson laughing at something he was saying.

Parker's cousins were either standing around drinking or hitting on single women. They'd taken it easy with the antics in light of their cousin's brush with mortality, thankfully. A plastic skeleton in Parker's shower to start the day was it so far—and even I giggled when Mel told me that story.

I blew out a slow breath. "Everything as it should be."

"Down to the last detail." Kyle took my glass and nodded in the direction of the doors to the deck.

I furrowed a brow as I spun to face them.

And forgot to breathe.

Joey raised his chin, stepping around the curtains. I let out a little squeal and met him in the middle of the dance floor.

"May I, beautiful?"

I nodded, stepping into his arms as the band struck up "You Look Wonderful Tonight."

"What happened to being afraid of questions?" It came out in a hoarse half-whisper.

"When the woman I love nearly gets herself filleted trying to help out a friend, I figure a room full of cops and reporters isn't the scariest thing I can think of."

The woman he loved. Me. And having him there murmuring in my ear in front of all my friends wasn't even a blip on my scary radar anymore.

I tipped my head back and caught his eye. "It's nice to have you here."

His shoulders rose under my hands with a deep breath. "It's nice to be here." He kissed the tip of my nose. "It's nice to be wherever you are. Every second that I can. So nice that I might've looked at an apartment on the river this morning."

Um. My lips wouldn't work. "Joey—I—what exactly are you saying?"

"Princess, I'm saying simply that I've lost the ability to contemplate living without you. All the air goes out of the room when I think about it." He tightened his arms around me and rested his chin on my hair before he moved his hands to my shoulders, barely swaying to the music as his eyes met mine. "I'm not sure what comes next, but I'm damned sure I want you to be part of it."

My knees went all watery.

"Tell me what you're thinking," he whispered, resting his forehead against mine.

My friends chattered and laughed around us. Parker was fine. Bob and I were fine. And Joey was here, swaying to the song with me, just like I'd daydreamed.

My eyes filled—with tears and love both—as I smiled.

I adored my life. Murderers, craziness, and all.

"I'm thinking that I'm well and truly in love with you, Mr. D'Amore." I moved my cheek to his shoulder, putting my lips close to his ear. "And I can't wait to see what's next for us."

DEADLY POLITICS: Nichelle Clarke #7

When a call girl is found dead in a popular governor's office, investigative reporter Nichelle Clarke must risk everything to uncover the dangerous truth behind the murder.

Reporter Nichelle Clarke's dream of covering a presidential speech is dashed when she finds herself intertwined in a high-profile murder investigation. While Nichelle is no stranger to facing dangerous situations in pursuit of the truth, the stakes in this story are higher than ever before.

Unsure of who she can trust , Nichelle must unravel a web of secrets behind an elaborate murder plot and dodge legal traps set by corrupt politicians. For if Nichelle can't uncover the conspiracy in time, an unthinkable disaster will strike the nation.

ACKNOWLEDGMENTS

This book was, without a doubt, the most fun to research yet, and I had more fun writing it than I have in a long time.

There are always many people to thank, and this time I'd like to start with the book advocates I'm lucky to call my friends: Dru Ann Love, Kristopher Zgorski, Lori Caswell, Lisa Kelley, and Shelley Giusti. Thank y'all for the hours you spend helping readers discover books and authors. Your efforts are appreciated more than any of us could tell you.

Thanks to the wonderful ladies who helped inspire settings and events in this book: Rebecca Cooper, Alison Rucker, and Jody Hynds Klann (my favorite scientist, who always looks up the answers to my gross questions).

Massive thanks to my writer friends, who inspire me, challenge me, and prop me up when bad days come: Wendy Tyson, Art Taylor, Mollie Cox Bryan, Gretchen Archer, Larissa Reinhart, and Ellery Adams.

Many thanks to Mignon C. Fogarty (y'all might also know her as Grammar Girl), for helping me out personally with a sticky punctuation issue in this book, and for the thousands of other writing questions I've found answers to on her website over the years.

Andrew Watts and the team at Severn River Publishing, thank you so much for your hard work, your vision for these books, and being such a pleasure to work with.

There aren't enough thanks to offer Julie Hallberg for reading and re-reading drafts, offering advice, watching my little ones so I can work, and just generally being a fabulous friend, but I'm going to try anyway: thank you, doll. You thought there was something here before anyone else.

Big hugs of thanks to my littles for understanding when mommy had to write instead of play. Y'all are without a doubt the best things I've ever done.

Thank you to my other half, my partner in adventure and (fictional) crime, my very best friend: Justin, thanks for being there for me, for an endless supply of hugs, and for always knowing how to make me laugh. I love you always.

And thank you, wonderful readers, for being the best thing about this fabulous job.

Any mistakes y'all find are mine, as always.

ABOUT THE AUTHOR

LynDee Walker is the national bestselling author of two crime fiction series featuring strong heroines and "twisty, absorbing" mysteries. Her first Nichelle Clarke crime thriller, FRONT PAGE FATALITY, was nominated for the Agatha Award for best first novel and is an Amazon Charts Best-seller. In 2018, she introduced readers to Texas Ranger Faith McClellan in FEAR NO TRUTH. Reviews have praised her work as "well-crafted, compelling, and fast-paced," and "an edge-of-your-seat ride" with "a spider web of twists and turns that will keep you reading until the end."

Before she started writing fiction, LynDee was an award-winning journalist who covered everything from ribbon cuttings to high level police corruption, and worked closely with the various law enforcement agencies that she reported on. Her work has appeared in newspapers and magazines across the U.S.

Aside from books, LynDee loves her family, her readers, travel, and coffee. She lives in Richmond, Virginia, where she is working on her next novel when she's not juggling laundry and children's sports schedules.

Sign up for LynDee Walker's reader list at
severnriverbooks.com/authors/lyndee-walker
lyndee@severnriverbooks.com

Printed in the United States
by Baker & Taylor Publisher Services